WHEN THE LIGHTS WENT OUT

Aaron S. Harp

Copyright © 2022 Aaron S. Harp

All rights reserved

The characters and events portrayed in this book are fictitious. Any similarity to real persons, living or dead, is coincidental and not intended by the author.

No part of this book may be reproduced, or stored in a retrieval system, or transmitted in any form or by any means, electronic, mechanical, photocopying, recording, or otherwise, without express written permission of the publisher.

ISBN: 9798818208985

Cover design by: Aaron Harp
Library of Congress Control Number: 2018675309
Printed in the United States of America

Dedicated to:

My Brother:
Without the feedback you provided along the way, this book would never have happened.

My Parents:
Without your constant support, I never would have had the confidence to finally publish a book.

Sean Heevy:
You were my best friend, and I have never forgotten those stories we wrote as children. Those were my first foray into writing. Without those, none of this would have been possible. Thank you, old friend. RIP.

Ed Vela:
For always being the loveable shithead that you are and for never letting me get off easy with being whiny when I was a kid. Most importantly, though, for always inspiring me to never give up.

CONTENTS

Title Page
Copyright
Dedication

1	1
2	13
3	29
4	57
5	64
6	73
7	89
8	120
9	144
10	176
11	201
12	215
13	235
14	252

15	272
16	285
17	300

1

Thursday, August 7th, 2036

My head slammed back against my seat as the plane dropped and came to a sudden stop. My stomach lurched as the plane hit a second pocket of turbulence, falling what felt like a hundred feet. It was a hell of a way to wake up.

Looking around, my eyesight shaky from the rude awakening, I made out the shape of a stewardess as she stumbled up the aisle to the cockpit door. Just as she got there, she was slammed viciously against the cabin's main exit door, the plane violently jolting to the left. My neighbor's head cracked the plastic wall paneling with a great thud, and he let out a terrible howl. A baby a few rows behind me had begun wailing as the adults' cries and prayers were beginning to echo out from all around.

From my first-row perspective, I watched with clearing vision as the stewardess climbed to her feet. She punched in a series of numbers on a keypad and flung open the cockpit door. I really wished she hadn't.

The cockpit was just as chaotic as the rest of the plane. A loud alarm was going off, and the movements of the two pilots seemed sporadic and scared. An air traffic controller coming through the radio in a garbled mess sounded frightened.

"NASA... Earth... Land... Wherever...!"

"Bill, what the hell is going on!" the stewardess yelled. "Are we going down?"

"Get back to your chair, Janet!" the co-pilot screamed back, flipping a few switches. He called off something technical to the pilot as Janet turned.

The plane dropped again, and Janet was lifted off the ground and smashed into the ceiling, headfirst and with a snap I could hear even through the chaos. No one else seemed to have heard the snap, their own terror taking precedent, but as the plane evened out and her broken body crumpled to the ground, they noticed, their screams growing louder.

"Attention all planes!"

This time, the radio was loud and clear, and, somehow, it managed to cut through the noise and reach me. I focused all I had on hearing what was coming through.

"Land immediately! Wherever you are, descend immediately! Repeat! All planes must land now! Per NASA warning, a CME is about to hit Earth. Attention all planes! Land immediately! Wherever you--"

A fierce roar of interference began to take over the radio again, while the air traffic controller repeated himself.

From every inch of space around me, the brutal caterwauling's intensity swelled, and it was being matched to a painstaking degree by the whine of the engines, their sound's viscosity growing in the air around. Thick and heavy, the clangor was consuming everything in its path.

The rattling of the plastic walls and windows was shaking my confidence that the plane would even hold together. That confidence was not helped as several overhead compartments busted open, and the plane abruptly fell another hundred feet before hitting a wall of stability.

Oxygen masks around the cabin simultaneously dropped from the holders above, sending another wave of cries through the passengers. The panic was growing, and I felt it just as strongly as everyone else.

My chest was tight, constricting more with each breath. The adrenaline coursing through my veins was causing muscles all over my body to twitch. I was going to die, and there wasn't anything I could do about it. I didn't want to die. Not like that.

Suddenly, everything seemed to shut off. All the air vents went quiet at once, and every cabin light went dark. The pilots' dash, just moments before having been a panel of dancing lights, had lost power. The engines, too, seemed to have turned off, their vibrations lessening, their high-pitched whine fading out as the turbines came to a halt. I wasn't the only one that was beginning to notice.

Passengers were growing quiet, their silhouettes looking around with confusion spreading, but as the plane slowly dipped its nose, the cries began again. At first, they were soft, muffled from the paralyzing realization of the circumstances, but they grew quickly as the prayers were ending. They didn't quite reach the same levels as before, many of the passengers inevitably coming to terms.

The pilots exchanged looks, the switches they were flipping no longer sending signals, but they continued their futile measures as gravity's hold grew stronger.

A strange, sickening sensation of weightlessness floated its way into my gut, nauseousness being the cherry-on-top to the night's events and emotions. The speed at which my feelings of terror were increasing matched the increasing speed of our descent. I had no real idea what was happening, but I knew what would happen.

I clenched my eyes, trying to take myself away from that moment, away from that place.

Green. I tried to imagine the green of our grass after a cool summer rain. It was a good color, one of my favorites. It always brought with it…

The sound of my girls laughing broke through the screams of the other passengers, flowing through my mind just like they were carried there on the summer wind. It was my favorite sound. Nothing filled me with more wondrous emotions. My daughters were my world; they were the best thing about me.

I could picture Hannah's smile. She was missing one of her front teeth. It had fallen out two days before we'd all left, and she was so excited it had happened before the big trip. We'd been planning a family trip to Hawaii for a number of years, and Hannah was so worried that the Tooth Fairy wouldn't find her if she lost the tooth while on vacation. We had assured her the Tooth Fairy would find her, but she had still been scared. She was six.

Behind her, I could see my ten-year-old, Lily. She was so smart. I could see her sitting on the sofa next to me. Her nose would be in some sort of book. Never a fictional book, though. She couldn't have cared less about teen vampires or the latest iteration of Katniss Everdeen. Instead, Lily had a fascination with learning all she could about the planet. I'd never met someone her age so utterly fascinated with geology and biology. If you asked her how many termites it'd take to eat a two-story house, she'd be able to rattle off some statistics and give you an answer almost instantly. She could even tell you what almost any kind of rock was if you were to point one out at random. Her mom and I had no idea where she got it from, but I was certain that girl was going to cure cancer.

Over Lily's shoulder, I could see my sweet Clementine. She was our firstborn and, what you may call, an accident. We'd had her when we were really still kids ourselves, having just graduated high school, but, somehow, she turned out better than normal.

Clem was seventeen, and, even at that age, she was already a better writer than most so-called 'modern novelists.' Like with Lily's intelligence, we had no idea where Clem got her talent for wordsmithing, but she could wind tales that rivaled even Tolkien. Sure, I may be a bit biased, but my little girl had the power to stir emotions with her words. She could take you to worlds you never imagined, and with the plane gliding toward an inevitable doom, I wished she were there to take me off to one of her fanciful worlds.

As I looked onto the memories of my daughters, my wife, Ellie, came into my mind; she was all I could see then. Her midnight-black hair danced as if underwater, and her blue eyes stared into mine, saying everything I wanted to hear, that I needed to hear. Those eyes looked at me through the space in my mind, and I felt her love reaching out and touching me. I could feel the warmth of her breath against my ear, her voice softly whispering.

"I love you."

"Hold on!" the pilot screamed out of the still-flapping cockpit door, bringing me back to my reality that didn't seem real.

Just beyond the pilots, the moonlight appeared to be lighting up a flat expanse of desert. It wasn't far away, maybe a thousand feet.

"This is it," I thought. A tsunami of fear and helplessness covered me like a shroud, my stomach twisting into knots, my nerves frying, causing me to shake uncontrollably. I wanted to scream out, but I couldn't. I needed to scream out, to join the other cries of dread. Nothing came out.

"HOLD ON!" the pilot yelled again.

I dared a glance to my right. The man next to me was crouched with his bloodied head between his legs, whispering a prayer in soft Italian. Out of the window, the ground was a mere two dozen feet away and getting closer. Cacti, lit by the full moon, sped by in a blur. Boulders that looked the size of Volkswagens dotted the landscape, little stone balls of death just waiting to tear through the fuselage.

There was a loud slam, and the back of the plane bounced up into the air, the nose slamming hard into the ground. The crushing impact decimated the nose structure, flattening the cockpit and the pilots inside.

The passengers and I were thrown forward in

our seats. The force was so strong that I thought the seatbelt would cut me in half. The incredibly unnatural feeling of the brain hitting the skull wall pierced through me like a thousand sharpened daggers.

A drink cart, airborne by the angle of the tail, came careening by. The cart slammed into the wall directly in front of me, spraying food and drink. It was followed closely by an elderly woman whom I'd seen getting on the plane with her wheelchair-bound husband. They'd seemed sweet. I'm pretty certain she was already dead by the time her fall was stopped by the wall.

With one more sudden jolt, the plane's left wing impacted the ground. It dug deep into the sandy surface and embedded itself. With full momentum, the plane twisted in the air.

As I mercifully began to pass out from the extreme shift in g-forces, the plane spinning out of control, I felt a pair of hands gently coming to rest on my shoulders, but looking down, there were no hands. In that last, split-second between consciousness and unconsciousness, the feeling of those invisible hands eased my nerves and unknotted my stomach, replacing my fear and dread with an overwhelming sense of well-being before ushering me into the darkness.

· · ·

The pain calling out from every molecule

of my body brought my mind back to reality. Though my thoughts were foggy, and a vibration punching at my brain was sending shock waves down my spine, the sensation of my muscles shredding themselves from one another was not diluted in the slightest.

Before my eyes even opened, the scream that had been building up finally broke its restraints. I let loose with everything I had, the pain, fear, helplessness, and every other overwhelming emotion and sensation all fighting for release.

When my voice could handle no more, I went silent, catching my breath and trying to put at least some of the pain out of my mind. It wasn't working.

Finally, I slowly opened my eyes.

There is nothing that anyone could ever do to be prepared for the sight I saw. The gentleman that had been sitting beside me was missing from his seat. Well, he was kind of missing, as the lower portion of his body was still strapped in. However, his upper half, along with the upper half of the chair, seemed to have been relocated.

I looked to my left, and what had previously been a row for three was now just half a seat. The remaining half was resting on the ground, the sliding friction of the crash having scraped away everything else. The young woman that had been in that seat had suffered a grisly, friction-induced death, only half of her remaining. I wished more than anything to forget that sight, those smells, those partial faces.

Taking in the complete destruction around me, I had no idea how I had survived. Was it that I was just extraordinarily lucky, or was there some truth behind the hands I wasn't entirely sure I'd felt? But that was a question for another time.

A tiny flame in the stewardess area had begun growing, just inches from where the remains of shattered alcohol bottles still littered the tattered carpet, caught in the threads, with the liquid dripping and puddling on the dirt ground. Even in my presumably concussed state, it was clear to me that flame was ready to take what was left of this plane. Once the alcohol caught, or if it caught just a bit of gas, there'd be no stopping it.

I watched the flame nervously as I fumbled with my seatbelt. My fingers could barely work, and the metal of the clasp had been bent during the crash. The flame caught a bit of alcohol and spread out instantly, tripling in size in a split second. With the last bit of myself I felt I had to give, I yanked hard on the clasp of the buckle, bending it just enough for it to slip free.

I collapsed to the ground, just in front of the young woman's remains. I made sure not to look at her, positive I would be unable to handle a close-up view of her atrocious end.

Warily, I pushed myself to my feet, creaking as I finally stood up straight. The flame was growing fast behind me, having already eaten away at half of the stewardess area. There wasn't time to wallow in the circumstances. I had to get out of there.

I walked toward the back of the plane as the cockpit was just a condensed tangle of metal, wiring, and pilots. With each step I took, I had to step over the remaining half-seats. Too many of these still held tight to the remaining halves of their occupants, motionless body after motionless body. I tried not to look, to keep my focus straight ahead.

Reaching the opening at the back, I exited my portion of the fuselage and wandered several dozen feet into the desert before stopping, turning back around, and crumpling onto the dirt and sand.

I had just survived a fucking plane crash. I had just survived a PLANE CRASH!

The thought rushed through my head as I watched the fuselage in front of me light up from the inside, the flame finally having fully caught, spreading faster and faster through the destroyed innards.

Off in the distance, to my right about four-hundred yards, the tail-end sat upside down, nestled against the foot of a mountain that extended high up into the sky. Following that mountain upwards, my eyes finally registered the greens, reds, and purples that were dancing across the landscape. However, the colors dancing on the mountainside were nothing compared to their counterparts that danced across the heavens directly above me.

I had always wanted to see the aurora, and its beauty was so grand that it was able to completely, yet momentarily, distract me. The colors and movements were elegant. They moved in a melodic motion that needed no instruments in order for their music to be heard. It was a magnificent sight.

I was torn away from the sight above, though, as every nerve in my body seemed to come alive at the same time. My adrenaline was finally calming, leaving a vacuum the other sensations were eager to fill. Muscles tearing, bones rattling and splintering, my skin being picked apart cell by cell; I could feel it all, but I couldn't handle that sudden blast of agony and collapsed to my back.

Staring up at the sky, eyesight growing blurry again and breaths heavy, tears caused by a clusterfuck of emotion and pain, the one thought kept running through my head: I had just survived a fucking plane crash.

2
Friday, August 8th

"Is he alive?" I heard a feminine voice say somewhere in the distant fogginess of my mind.

"Looks like he's breathing," responded a male voice.

The touch of two cold and grimy fingers on my neck brought me back to the world of the living. My eyes shot open and were instantly blinded by the bright sunlight of late afternoon, the night having come and gone. The person whose fingers had been checking for a pulse startled back, accidentally kicking me hard in the shin. Wincing in pain, I sat upright, holding a hand up to block out the sun.

"I'm alive," I spoke. Even I wasn't sure if it was a question or a statement. My voice was raspier than I'd ever heard it, and that rasp hurt, too.

Blinking adjustment into my eyes, I looked around. There were three people standing around me, each looking how I felt.

To my right, resting on her knees, was a woman that appeared in her mid-sixties. Her greying hair was matted with dried blood, and she had a nasty cut just above her left eye. The blood around the cut had dried and clotted already, but it was absolutely going to get infected soon if it wasn't looked at.

In the middle of the three was a girl in her late teen years. She looked remarkably like Clementine. They had similar face shapes, and they seemed to have near-identical eyes. Looking at this young woman, I could almost see my daughter looking back at me.

Unlike Clementine, though, this young woman looked like she had been blonde. Her hair was charred and burnt, flames having singed most of it away with no more than a few inches left at any given spot, but little specs of gold were still coming through. Her clothes were torn in several places, and they, too, looked as if they had been very close to a flame. The clothes were mostly singed on one side, so I guessed a fire had erupted right next to where she had been sitting.

On my left, there was a man in his early forties. He looked exactly like you would picture a white, middle-aged suburban dad. He was slightly overweight, showcasing a picture-perfect 'dad-bod.' He wore the stereotypical New Balance shoes, though the seams were ripped, and the material was flaking away. His polo, torn and tattered like the others' clothing, was still partially tucked into a pair of jeans that would have made any Wrangler fan happy. However, on his left thigh, there was a very large bloodstain that still seemed to be a bit moist.

"Water," I coughed through the rasp. "Do you have water?"

"Yeah," the young girl said, turning and running a short distance. She stopped and knelt beside a flipped-over food cart. It was a quick reach in before she stood again and ran back toward us.

I could not contain myself when she handed me the bottle of water. I twisted into it faster than a kid ripping through the wrapping on their most desired birthday present. The moment the first drop hit my tongue was nearly orgasmic. I just wanted more and more.

Gulping the water down, I pulled away and gasped for air.

"Easy," the older woman said. "Don't drink too fast. You could get sick."

She was right. Just as I finished the first bottle and was about to ask for a second, all the water came rushing back up.

After another two bottles, I was finally rehydrated. Sitting there, I looked from one worn and torn face to the next.

"What now?" I asked.

"There should be a rescue party coming soon," the man said. "It's been hours since we crashed. There has to be someone coming out this way. FAA, police, fire. Hell, even the news should be coming soon."

"I don't think so," said the older woman.

"Why? Why wouldn't they come for us?" asked the younger female, a tinge of fear creeping up.

"Before I retired, I used to work for JPL as an astrophysicist. Based on the power—"

"JPL?" the man interjected.

"Jet Propulsion Laboratory. Based on the power going out the way it did," the woman continued, "I don't think that anyone is coming. Look up."

We did. It was a beautiful sight. Even in the daylight, the aurora swayed through the cloudless blue above.

"First, based on flight time and looking around, I would say we're in Arizona or New Mexico. Auroras do not appear this far south, and if they do, something catastrophic has happened. Second, seeing auroras this far south and during the day?" She shook her head ominously. "Combine those with the fact that the power on everything went out, and I am willing to bet that we were hit by one of two things. Either a nuclear weapon was set off in the atmosphere, which would cause an EMP to impact pretty much the entire country, or we were hit by something called a coronal mass ejection."

"What the hell is a coronal mass ejection?" The man didn't seem to be buying what the woman was selling.

"Short version: The sun shoots off electromagnetic energy sometimes. Most of the time, it provides a really great light show, but a big enough storm hitting Earth could knock us back centuries. No gas pumps, no refrigeration, no water. It is essentially a sun-created EMP. Our society would crumble." Seeing the look of genuine disbelief on the face of the man, she added, "Don't believe me? Look at your watch. I bet it's broken."

"It is. It's broken because it just went through a plane crash," the man responded sardonically.

"That is a good point. But," she continued undeterred, "there are still many indicators pointing to one of those events having occurred. Maybe it's the astrophysicist in me, but I don't think it was a nuclear explosion. I think it was the sun."

"You know," I said, thinking back to just before the crash, "I was in the front row. Just before the power went out, a stewardess had gone to the cockpit, and I swear I heard something on the radio. It said something about NASA telling them to land all the planes because of a CME. CME? Is that that 'coronal mass whatever'?"

The woman's expression said it all. Her skin seemed to sag immediately, all color flooding from her face. She lost so much color, in fact, that even the massive cut above her eye seemed to dull.

No one said a word for a long while. The man and young girl, having no better answer and seeming to lose all will and/or strength to stand, defeatedly collapsed to the ground.

It felt like a movie. It was just a really shitty Sci-Fi channel movie. That's all it was. It was the B-side to a double feature; it was that god-awful trash that gets paired up with the newest animal/weather disaster crossover because this movie is so bad, it makes everything else look Oscar-caliber, even Crocodile Twister 24.

This shit doesn't happen in real life. The sun doesn't just come around and bitch slap us. Real-life is taking my daughters to school and arguing with them over a raise in their allowance; real life is arguing with Clem about her being too good for her boyfriend; real life is me taking a new work position because the last person to head this region's office was accused of sexual assault and jumped out of the board room window when confronted! Real-life is certainly not having a future comparable to the era of the Black Plague.

Finally, the young woman spoke up.

"That puts us back to square one, right? If so, like he said, what do we do now? If you're right, and the power is out everywhere, we can't stay here. We're in the desert, and all we have are a few food-cart snacks."

She was right. We all knew it. If we were to stay there, and the older woman's theory was correct, we'd soon run out of food and water. We'd die right there. We couldn't even wait long before leaving, otherwise, we would run through too many supplies, and we wouldn't have enough left to get us anywhere.

"Well," I responded, "I say we use the last bit of light to fill a few suitcases with supplies, sleep here tonight, then start heading west at sunup. Go to Phoenix and plan the next steps there, but at least we could hopefully get some supplies there."

"I like the Phoenix idea, but it's too hot to travel through the day," the man responded. "You were passed out most of today, but it was like a damn oven. No way we'd survive."

"You are right," the older woman replied. "We need to do as much traveling at night as possible. It may be a bit harder to see the stars through the auroras, but I think I can still use them to guide us."

With all of us in agreement, we had a plan. It may not have been the best, but it was a plan; it was something to hold onto.

We spent the next couple of hours scrounging around the wreckage. For the most part, we didn't do a lot of talking; we were all trying to wrap our heads around the plane crash and what may have caused it. Our silence was encouraged, too, by having to put a focus on not seeing the bodies around us. It was inevitable that we noticed them as we moved around, but none of us wanted to actually *see* them.

In our search of the debris, we found a half-filled bottle of Advil, a high-quality, six-person tent, and a suitcase that had two guns and some ammo packed away. They were only handguns, so they wouldn't be any help in hunting, but they were better than nothing. After all, only part of a gun's use is for hunting.

After not long at all, we had managed to salvage enough supplies from the wreckage that to take any more would just slow us down. We each grabbed one extra leftover dinner meal from the remains of a charred-out stewardess cart and ate in a little circle, finalizing our mental preparations.

"Where are you all from?" the young girl asked as we all finished eating.

"I'm from Nashville," the man said. "Name's Charlie Hansen."

"Los Angeles," the woman said. "Just coming back from a cruise in Mexico. You can call me Kim."

Sensing it was my turn, I said, "Well, I'm Sean. Sean Heevy. Orlando. How about you?"

"I'm from Utah, but I go to school at Georgetown. I'm Annie."

They were awkward introductions, forced and robotic. We all seemed to feel it as we fell back into silence.

"It was my fourth week in a row on the road," Charlie said finally, staring off into the sun. Shining through the vibrant aurora, our star was beginning to turn a vivid orange just above the horizon. He rubbed at his leg, just above the bloodstain that seemed to have finally dried. He was hurt, but at least it wasn't his artery.

"I told my wife that this was the last one. The last stop," he continued. "I'd already been to five different cities in the past month. Was passing through Atlanta from Buffalo. This time, I'd be in L.A. for two days, then I'd finally be home. She didn't believe me.

"My layover had been short, but I had enough time to call her before we boarded. When I did, I asked her if I could say goodnight to the kids. Bonnie, she's thirteen, and George, a hormone-filled sixteen. She said they were doing homework, but I could hear George in the background saying he didn't *want* to talk to me. I hope they're okay."

"When we get to a town, we'll find out that it was just an issue with the plane. You'll call your family, and everything will be okay!" Annie tried to console Charlie, but Charlie's mind was far off. "At least your family knows where you are."

"What do you mean?" Kim asked.

"My parents think I'm still at school. I dropped out and didn't tell anyone. I was going to wait until I made it to L.A. and got in my new apartment."

"Why didn't you tell anyone?" Charlie had come back to us.

"I didn't want them to laugh at me or talk me out of it."

"Why would they laugh at you?"

"Well," she started. She seemed a bit embarrassed as she finished, "I was coming out to be an actress."

"Good for you," Kim said enthusiastically. "If it is something you love, go for it!"

"I don't think it matters much now. I just wish they knew where I was."

"Where are they? Back in Utah?" Kim asked.

"Yeah. They're probably at home outside of Salt Lake."

"Are you going to try to get back to them?" I asked.

"I'll try," Annie said half-heartedly. "Figure I'll go with you all to Phoenix. Head north from there. My dad's a bit of a survivalist, so I'm sure he'll keep them safe. I just really wish I'd listened to him more when I was younger."

"You can't think like that. You can't think about 'what-ifs.' I may not be a survivalist, but I know that much. You've got the base of a good plan. You'll see your family again. What about you?" Kim asked, turning to me. "Do you have any family somewhere?"

My mind flashed back to the memories of my daughters' faces again.

"Yeah. I've got three girls and a wife. I was actually supposed to have been in Hawaii with them right now. We'd planned out a two-week trip, been planning for years. Then, last week, the director of our L.A. office jumps out of the board room window. Thirteen stories up. So, I was on my way to L.A. to begin my transition to that role before heading off to Hawaii for the last week of the trip. Who knows if they know what happened or not."

"Are they in Hawaii now?" Kim asked.

"Yeah. I got a text from my wife just after my plane landed in Atlanta. She'd said they'd landed and were at the rental car place."

"Then you know they're safe. That's good!" Annie exclaimed

"Hopefully. Their car could be stopped in the middle of nowhere."

"True," Annie conceded, "but having the car stall is a much better thought than their plane crashing into the Pacific Ocean, right? Yeah, we survived here, but imagine we were in the middle of the world's largest ocean instead of dry land."

"Good point." It really was a good point. There's no doubt it was better to have them stall on a freeway or get stuck on a back road than it would be to have their plane fall into the sea.

Annie turned to Kim and asked, "How about you? Any family that might be wondering where you are?"

"Me? I had put all my focus into work, so no family. Never married, no kids, and my parents are long dead. Just a cat named Dog."

"You named your cat Dog?" Charlie asked.

"Yeah," Kim responded, chuckling. "When I was a kid, I had heard this song by... I think her name was Norma Tanega. It was called 'Walkin' my cat named Dog.' It was one of the weirdest songs, but it stuck with me. Always thought it was funny. So, when I got my cat, I could not think of a better name!"

Somehow, we all laughed. Despite the situation surrounding us, we couldn't fight the ironic humor of a cat named Dog. It was simple; it was stupid; we laughed.

Once the laughter calmed down, we all sat there and watched as the sun faded below the distant horizon. The way the colors of the setting day rolled through the clouds above, going from yellow to orange to a dark purple, would have been amazing all its own. However, throwing in the ballet of colors from the auroras that still performed above, the sight was almost spiritual.

I had grown up religious, going to church every Sunday with an occasional Wednesday night service, but I hadn't thought about God in years, if not decades. As a kid, I'd enjoyed church and religion, but as I got older, it got harder for me to wrap my head around a lot of what was taught and told through church and the Bible.

Then, around the age of seventeen, I had a school project that required me to watch the original Cosmos television series with Carl Sagan. In one episode, Sagan talked about the vastness of the universe. He talked about how it was an infinite space, a black void that was everything.

The possibility of the universe being infinite and what that could mean was the nail in the coffin for my religious beliefs.

Sitting there, watching the sunset, surrounded by the still-smoldering debris from a plane crash which I miraculously walked away from uninjured, I couldn't help but think that there was no way luck played a part. How could anyone have walked away from a wreck like that unless there was a God or angels or something watching over and protecting them? I remembered the hands I still wasn't sure I had ever felt. I closed my eyes, and, for the first time since I was a teenager, I prayed.

. . .

Our pace through the desert was slow. Many things were in place to work against us in a fairly efficient manner. First, we hadn't planned on the suitcases being such a pain in the ass. Of course, they were incredibly convenient and allowed us to carry a large number of supplies; however, the desert wasn't smooth. With nearly every single step, the suitcases would get snagged on a bush or plant, tip on a rock, or gather up enough rocks in front of them that we'd have to stop and lift them. Lifting a fifty-pound suitcase is hard, but doable. By the fifteenth time, though, it gets to be a bit more cumbersome.

Secondly, even with the added light of the auroras, it was still slower to travel by night as we needed to take our time to see what was in front of us. In the first hour alone, we almost walked off two little cliffs that hadn't been visible until we were right on them. Also, there were plenty of creepy crawlies all around us that were capable of killing us with one little bite. Many of these were *tiny* creatures, too, so our attention to every step was necessary.

Thirdly, Charlie's leg. It hadn't been bleeding for a while, but the pain it was causing him meant that we were forced to take several breaks. We all understood, but it was a bit frustrating that it seemed every fifteen minutes he was needing to stop. We kept those breaks short, but every five minutes spent standing around was five extra minutes between me and my girls. I felt guilty for it, but the thought that we should just leave him crossed my mind several times.

With those main roadblocks to our progress, it didn't take long for doubt to creep up in me, and once that took hold, it was tough to get out of my mind.

I kept thinking to myself, "Who were we to believe we'd be able to cross a desert that was so obscenely foreign to each of us? Who were we to think we'd be able to survive in one of the most inhospitable environments in the world?"

Those thoughts were toxic, and I knew it, so I concentrated hard on thinking glass-half-full thoughts, the kind of positive thoughts that cause an uncontrollable release of serotonin. I thought so hard on thinking those thoughts that the only thing that came to mind was Peter Pan—Hannah had watched the movie the night before our trips.

"Think of a wonderful thought..." rang through my head. It did the job.

I could see Hannah laying on her stomach, coloring in a coloring book while singing along to the song on the TV.

"I'm sorry," Charlie called, tearing me away from my wonderful thought.

I swear, if he tore me away from my living room and daughter to ask for another break...

"I have got to stop again. My leg... It's hurting bad."

We all stopped and looked at one another, each trying to hide the frustration. We all knew Charlie couldn't help it, and we weren't frustrated with him, just the situation.

"Well," Kim said, "should we take a bit of a break and have a snack?"

"That sounds good," Annie replied. "I could use a little recharge."

I agreed, and we dropped our suitcases at the base of a nearby rock the size of a two-story house.

It was a pleasant spot. There was a gorgeous view of at least thirty miles of desert valley surrounded by steep mountains. The light from the sky shone down on the ground, at times giving it the shimmering appearance of light reflecting through water. We all devoured our food and sat in silence for a good while, watching with awe and exhaustion.

3

Saturday, August 9th

A massive roll of thunder shook the ground underneath us, startling me. I had no idea when it had happened, but, evidently, I'd fallen asleep. The thunder faded quickly, but it was followed by an even more horrifying sound.

Charlie's voice broke through the night with a guttural scream of terror. As I turned to look at him, I caught just the last bit of leg before it disappeared behind an unseen ravine wall, screams becoming even more horrible.

There was a loud thud as we all hurried over to the edge, cautious of not seeing it and meeting the same fate as Charlie. We looked over the slope. The screaming had stopped, but we could still hear a faint moaning from somewhere down below. Even with the dancing lights above, though, we couldn't see where it was coming from.

Thunder rolled out again.

"Charlie!" I yelled. "Charlie, are you okay?"

We waited for a response. Nothing.

"Charlie?" Annie followed.

"I'm here," Charlie called back, weak. "I'm alive, but my leg… My leg is pretty dead."

"I'm coming down, Charlie!" I said automatically.

Even though I'd contemplated leaving him in the desert many times, when push came to shove, I would never have actually done that. I was not the kind of person to leave someone. I knew that I owed Charlie nothing. I knew that going down to help him, or at least attempting to, could end very badly for me. I knew I had to try.

Slowly, I lowered one foot down onto the decline, gingerly putting more weight on it. As my confidence in my footing grew, I tried to take a step down, but the dirt slid underneath me. My foot lost all hold on the ledge.

I fell what felt like fifty feet down that side, tumbling and rolling. I felt the impacts with at least three different cacti on the way down and one branch of something that found a very unpleasant place to poke. Luckily, when I stopped at the bottom of the ravine, other than a few cactus quills and some bruises, I wasn't hurt.

"Sean!" Charlie called out, no more than five feet from where I landed. "Sean, are you okay?"

"Yeah, I'm good," I responded, getting to my feet, and pulling a few quills out of my arm.

Lightning snapped not far ahead of us, its

thunder shaking the ground again.

"How's the leg, Charlie?" I asked as I came to him. I didn't need an answer; he was right to have said the leg was dead.

Even in the pale light, I could easily see the bone rupturing through his tattered Wranglers. Not just in one spot, either: He had three spots on the one leg where bone had broken through. I had no idea how his leg was still attached. Moving him was going to be impossible.

A few more raindrops began to partner with the thunder.

"It's bad, Sean. I don't know if I'm going to be able to walk."

He wasn't going to be able to. It didn't take a doctor to see it.

"We won't know until you try," I replied, not wanting to admit the obvious.

I moved behind him and grabbed under his arms, gripping as tightly as I could.

"This is going to hurt, Charlie," I said, no sugar-coating to my tone.

"I know," he responded through gritted teeth. "Let's just get it over with."

With a heave, I lifted. Charlie tried to use his arms and his good leg to help with the weight, but the pain was draining him of everything he had. As we moved our first few inches, the leg rolled, barely attached by a few remaining sinews. There were nerves still attached, and Charlie felt every bit of it, screaming bloody murder.

"Stop! Wait a sec!" he screamed.

I put him down heavily, barely able to hold his sagging weight. In just that short time, I was already out of breath. I wasn't going to be able to drag him like that up the ravine. There wasn't a chance in hell.

"What if you carry me on your back?" Charlie asked, desperation creeping into his voice.

I looked at him and knew I couldn't carry him. He was too heavy for me. A life of typing on computers while sitting on a cushy chair behind a crappy desk in an overly cold office had made me weak. I hadn't visited the gym since high school, and now it was coming back to bite me in the ass. Staring down at him, I tried to think of any way I may be able to carry him.

A soft, yet growing, roar in the distance was beginning to draw my attention away. I couldn't help but feel it was coming to claim us.

"What is it?" Charlie asked.

"I don't know."

"Sean!" Charlie and I looked up to see Annie yelling from the top of the ravine.

"Look! Flash flood!" Kim yelled, pointing off in the distance towards the growing roar.

Even from my perspective, through dull lighting and jagged rocks jutting out, the debris flow heading our way was unmistakable. What looked like dozens of logs and trees spread from one side of the ravine to the other, and the torrent was traveling with such speed that there wasn't much time left to get out.

"Let's go!" Charlie yelled, urging me to get him.

The situation hadn't changed, though. I still couldn't carry him. It just wasn't possible. The only thing different now was that I didn't have time to think of a way to get him out.

"Sean," Charlie urged, a realization coming over him as the tears began to well up in my eyes. "Sean, get me out of here! My kids, Sean! Think of my kids!"

"Get out of there, you guys!" came Annie's voice above, the water so close now that the roar almost covered her words completely.

"I'm sorry, Charlie," I said with a painful croak.

"Sean! Don't you fucking leave me!"

Without another look at him, I turned my back to him and began scurrying up the ravine wall.

Charlie screamed and yelled behind me, and I knew he was crawling, scraping, anything, trying to get out. It was evident in his petrified tone.

"Sean, you mother---" His words were cut short as the water crashed through the ravine, mere inches below my own feet.

I crawl-ran up the side, digging my fingers and the toes of my shoes into the sand as much as I could. For every step up I took, I slid half a step back. Panic was spreading as the roar was now almost right on me. I found a foothold—really a plant that was just well-embedded—and used it to launch myself up several feet, but I wasn't out of danger.

As soon as I landed, the plant I'd just jumped from was overcome by the flow. Moment by moment, inch by inch, the water was growing closer. It was just a foot or two below, its growing rapids spraying my legs with a fine, dirty mist. It weakened the ground I was trying to climb on, so the continuation of my step-and-slide process was a practice in near-complete futility, but I had to keep trying.

I dug my fingers deep into the now-muddy ground. It oozed between my fingers and was just as difficult to climb as the gravelly surface it had been just moments before. I could feel my shoes gaining weight with each step upwards, the mud caking to the leathery soles, but I kept moving, step after step, slide after slide. By the time I reached the top of the ravine, the cascading water below was still rushing violently, but it had stopped its growth upwards.

Kim and Annie each grabbed underneath one of my shoulders and helped pull me the last bit of the climb. I collapsed onto my back, breathing heavily.

"Are you okay?" Annie asked with complete concern, her resemblance to Clementine in full effect.

"Yeah," I said in between pants. "I'm okay."

"Charlie?" Kim asked. It was evident by her tone that the question was merely a formality.

"I... I..." I couldn't tell them I left him, that I was too weak to carry him, and now he's dead. I couldn't tell them that he'd begged for me to save him, but I just left him. "I couldn't carry him."

Kim said nothing, but she placed a caring hand on my shoulder.

"I saw him get up," Annie said. "It was just a few seconds before he fell. He seemed shaky. It looked like he tried to take a step, and his injured leg gave out. That's when he screamed and fell."

"Why was he trying to walk?" I asked.

"Bathroom maybe?"

I didn't really know Charlie, but I broke down in tears. Charlie had a family; he had kids. Because I wasn't strong enough, because I wasn't capable enough, those kids would never have a chance to see their father again. I couldn't lift him, and so his kids would grow up without him.

He had begged for me to save him, but I turned my back on him. I left him. The memory caused my stomach to well with guilt, but a more painful thought took its place.

It could have easily been me with a broken leg after my fall; it could have easily been my daughters left without a father; it could have been my wife that was made a widow. I couldn't control my tears as I imagined how my family would react if they were to find out I died.

"It's okay," Annie said, putting her hand on my shoulder comfortingly. "You did all you could."

I didn't respond to her. How could I when I knew I'd never be sure I really had done all I could? I was grateful for her words and care, though. Whether she was proving her acting skills or if she was genuine in her sympathy, I didn't know and didn't care. Annie *seemed* to truly care about us, and that was all that mattered in that moment. I stood and hugged her tightly.

"Maybe we should just stay here and rest until tomorrow night," Kim said as another lightning bolt hit nearby, and its thunder crashed all around us.

"We need to keep moving," I said, pulling away from Annie and wiping away my tears. "We've only just started. We've got to keep going."

"Look," Kim said. "I would love to keep going, too, but that storm is still coming toward us. All that water down there came from somewhere, and that somewhere is coming here. The thunder and lightning are getting closer. We should just set up camp now and be ready."

She was right. That storm was ominously close, with raindrops starting and stopping every couple of minutes. It was only a matter of time before it was an absolute downpour. Also, I was most certainly not in a mental state to do anything, so I agreed, and we hurriedly began putting together the six-person tent.

By the time we were throwing in the suitcases, the sky opened, and the heavens showered down on us. The wind blew fiercely across the flat valley and pummeled the tent. I was the last to enter, throwing the last of the suitcases in before me. I zipped the flap closed, and we hunkered in for another wild night.

. . .

The wind beat at the tent, its canvas walls shuttering hard. The raindrops were so heavy and constant that they sounded like electrical interference. The barrage was nerve-rattling.

"Thank God for whoever packed this tent," Kim said. "I hope they are welcomed to heaven with open arms."

"If there's a heaven, they better be," I responded.

"If?" Kim asked. "You don't believe in God?"

"A few days ago? No. Today? I honestly don't know anymore." I responded. "You do?"

"It has always surprised me that any scientist can think otherwise," Kim said.

"What? Really?" My surprise pulled my focus away from the pounding storm.

"Absolutely! The universe is filled with

innumerable statistical improbabilities and anomalies. It is hard to comprehend that number of events just kind of happened at random. A handful of anomalies and unexpected discoveries would be one thing, but it seems like every time we turn around, there is something else we find that has a probability of occurrence near-zero."

"But just because there are so many unusual and unexpected things," I responded, "doesn't mean that there's some sort of all-knowing omnipotence that's responsible for anything and everything."

"I would disagree," Kim said. "At a certain point, there are too many for them to just be coincidence or random occurrences."

"So, then, that would mean that every single event, the wild and mundane alike, occur because this God has dictated them to occur. Correct? Essentially connecting everything into God's plan?" Though religion was never my choice for a topic of conversation, it was a relief to have something to talk about other than the current situation. It made ignoring the growing pit of guilt in my chest a lot easier.

"That is where I absolutely separate from organized religion," Kim said. "I do not think there is a plan for everything or everyone. I think, most of the time, we all make our own choices, and the consequences of those are just the natural order of cause and effect.

"However, I would say that there may be interference run at times due to specific people having a specific purpose at a specific time."

"But you just said you didn't think there was a plan. Wouldn't running interference at certain times only be necessary if there was a particular reason to do so?"

"Correct, but I see it differently than the 'God's Plan' of organized religion," she said. "I don't think there is an overall plan that impacts us *all* at *all* times. I do think, however, that at *certain* times, *certain* events may occur to *certain* people for some *uncertain* reason. Just look at our predicament. Why were we the ones to survive? Why did Charlie survive a plane crash only to be killed the next day by a flood?"

I had just begun to get my mind completely away from Charlie, so Kim bringing him into the conversation wasn't particularly appreciated. I didn't want to think about him at all. I was about to respond, shifting in my corner of the tent, when Annie spoke.

"Chaos," Annie said distantly. Kim and I both looked at her.

"Chaos?" I asked.

"Yeah, chaos. Basically, the way I understand it, from what my professor said, is this: Chaos Theory is, like, if you do something ten times, and each time you take the exact same actions, you'll still end up with ten different results. If we were to go back to being on the plane, next time, it would most likely not be us to survive.

"Think about the Butterfly Effect. With that, a butterfly flaps its wings in Tokyo, which, through a series of events, leads to an earthquake in Los Angeles. Because someone missed their tea in London, or because someone's Aunt Marge ran over a bird, we all found ourselves on that plane. If the events all occurred again, though, we could end up with different outcomes. That was my understanding, at least."

"I know a little about Chaos Theory," Kim said. "Most people I knew who were proponents of it were a bit out-there."

"I think it's bullshit," Annie responded. "I agree with a lot of what you said, Kim. There are too many coincidences out there for there not to be some sort of control, but I don't think it's God. I think it's because we're actually in a simulation."

"You believe in Simulation Theory?" Kim asked, a tinge of disappointment in her voice.

"Absolutely," Annie replied. I had no idea what that was, but I didn't say so. I just listened as Annie continued. "Think about it. The dinos were on Earth for almost two hundred million years! We've been here, what, two-hundred-and-fifty thousand? Yet, in just fifty years, look where our technology has gone. In 1979, look at the games and technology: Pac Man, Donkey Kong, Pong. Flash forward to a few days ago. With the metaverse taking over, we were already seeing severe issues of reality confusion. People were already getting real-life mixed up with virtual worlds. Some people were living their entire lives online and have been for four decades!

"Now, even if the electrical grid is gone, it'll probably come back eventually. If we could get as far as we did over just fifty years, imagine the kind of tech we'll have in five hundred years. What about ten-THOUSAND years from now? As long as we don't go extinct, our technology that far out is inconceivable.

"So, say, ten thousand years from now, scientists, like today, can take advantage of the most cutting-edge technology. They take this incredible tech, and they do what scientists do: They run simulations. They run simulations on who knows what! DNA replication; faster-than-light travel effects; the impacts of folding space-time on itself; hell, maybe even simulations to figure out if the Grandfather Paradox is real or not. One thing they would most certainly do is look at the history of the species and our civilizations. Just like we look back on ancient Egyptians and Romans and Maya today. In ten thousand years, that list will include us.

"If we could do it today, don't you think scientists would create a code that could run a simulation to see exactly how ancient civilizations came about? Wouldn't you be curious to see what would happen if a so-called civilization code was inputted, and it recreated past events in chronological order based on historical findings, while incorporating real AI that could learn and grow and have feelings and emotions just like people?"

Kim's face indicated she absolutely would want to see that. I would have loved to have seen it, too.

"Now, imagine you find evidence of a past civilization that had gone from a very harsh frontier life to visiting the moon in a matter of seventy years. You'd absolutely be curious as to how in the hell that happened.

"Looking at it like that, it seems inevitable that, eventually, we'll create an extremely lifelike simulation with legit AI that will show how our species evolved through time. With that in mind, and, taking into consideration all of the coincidences and setups that are so unlikely they're near miracles, to me, that points directly to the strong potential for us being in a simulation. And that's not even taking into consideration the gameplay side of things.

"We already have role-playing games that millions of people play. People create entire social circles and relationships with others that they never meet, with people who know their avatar name better than they know the player's real name. With games like The Sims, the entire purpose was to live a life online. Imagine what will happen to the psyche when you can play in first-person virtual reality with graphics indistinguishable from real life. People will never want to leave the game, and that was just a decade or so away before all of this!"

Kim and I sat there in stunned silence. Neither one of us had expected something like that to come from Annie. Granted, we didn't know each other well, and she had been going to Georgetown, but she had seemed so soft-spoken and shy. Talking about something she evidently believed fervently in, we got to see a whole other side to her. People can be surprising.

"Sorry," Annie said sheepishly, Clementine flashing again across her face.

"For what?" Kim said earnestly, wincing and rubbing at the cut on her forehead. "Never apologize for what you believe. Just never put someone down for what they believe." Annie nodded. "Your argument is very sound, and it is absolutely something I will think more about. But, if I may, if we are in a simulation, would there not have had to have been someone to create that simulation? Someone will have to have written that code, correct?"

"It could have been created or written by future AI, but yeah, someone, or something, most definitely has to write the code and implement it."

"Then, to me, that is God in the literal sense. The creator of the simulation would then be the creator of everything. He said, 'Let there be light' by putting it in code. The code was implemented, and the Big Bang occurred. Sounds like God to me."

"But then," I said, finally grasping what Simulation Theory was, "couldn't God just be some future thirteen-year-old in a basement somewhere that's curious, with the brains and tools to create a simulation?"

"Theoretically, yes," Annie said. "And, really, it could explain a lot. It would explain the times when it feels like we're just ants underneath the magnifying glass of some little kid."

We all fell silent once more, listening to the still-pounding rain with the image in our minds of some mad and torturous child holding a magnifying glass over the earth, a beam of light focused on the lonely planet.

"I *hope* there is a God," I said. "I hope there is a *true* God, I mean, not some maniacal teenaged shit with a magnifying glass. I hope there is a reason all of this is happening. I hope there's a reason I… we survived."

"As do I," Kim agreed.

"Me, too," Annie concurred.

We fell off to our thoughts, and then, to sleep.

.   .   .

All around me was a complete darkness that seemed utterly void of all matter. It was as if

I was swimming in the vastness of limbo, no weight or gravity pulling on me. I tried looking around, but it was impossible to determine if my head even moved.

A metal click came through the emptiness, and a spotlight beamed down onto Charlie and the ground he lay on. I could see him clearly, the fear spreading across his face.

"Save me, Sean," I heard him say. It wasn't Charlie's normal voice, though. It was airy and just a bit higher-pitched than before. The sound he made was also delayed from the movements of his lips, coming out a split second after the movement was made.

"Save me," he said again. "Don't let me die. My kids, Sean. Think of my kids."

The roar of the flash flood began to call out through the void, coming from the direction I felt was behind me. The panic spread on Charlie's face.

"I'm sorry, Charlie," I said.

"Don't leave me, Sean!"

Suddenly, I found myself where Charlie had been. I was staring up at him as he was then standing where I had stood, on the edge of the ravine, looking down at me with a pathetically helpless frown.

"Don't leave me, Charlie," my voice called out.

"I'm sorry." With a step, he dissolved into the blackness.

The roar of the coming flood didn't dissolve.

Instead, the sound grew louder, and I faced toward it. The leading edge was not far. The logs and trees were visible as the two-ton behemoths came crashing toward me.

There was nothing I could do except lie there helplessly, seeing my doom head right for me. I deserved this, though. I had earned such an end to my life by leaving Charlie. This was me getting my comeuppance.

I prepared myself for the horrific end. I tried to prepare myself for that split moment where I'd still be able to feel, when I'd be well aware of my body being crushed and ripped. I could nearly count the rings in the husk of a tree as it twisted directly into my face.

Luckily, I didn't feel the impact. Instead, I felt Annie's soft and gentle hands on my shoulders. I opened my eyes to see Annie and Kim both staring down on me with extreme looks of concern.

"It's okay," Annie said. "It was just a nightmare. You're safe." She pulled me in and gave me a comforting hug.

My mind raced back and forth, piecing together what had just happened. Charlie wasn't real; at least, the Charlie I saw wasn't real. I wasn't trapped on the floor of the ravine, about to die. There was nothing I could have done for Charlie. There was nothing I could have done. I *had* to leave him!

"Maybe we should stay here one more day,"

Annie said to Kim.

"No," I said, pulling away and collecting myself. "We've already lost enough time. We've got to start moving, or we're not going to have enough supplies to get anywhere."

"He's right," Kim agreed. "We can't lose another night."

We kept things generally quiet through our initial first few miles, and so my mind wandered. It wandered off to the comfort of my family's faces. Memories of those faces were the only things that abated my guilt.

I couldn't help but wonder about the kind of situation that they must have been in at that moment. Hawaii was an island landscape that none of them had any true idea about. Granted, even at ten, Lily may have something in her wealth of information, but I had no idea how useful that would be if the supplies ran out in the cities.

Hawaii had a massive population, and with it being an island, it had to import an incredible amount of goods. Without ships and planes bringing in products, the resources on the islands wouldn't be anywhere close to capable of handling the needs of the population. When people start to run out of food, when parents can't feed their children, things don't usually progress smoothly from there.

Since we'd saved for so long, we had been able to book our stay at a resort whose secluded setting was one of its biggest selling points. It was only a couple of years old, and it was built in a tiny inlet of Ahupua'a 'O Kahana State Park. They'd apparently spent decades trying to gain the ability to build there, and they finally were given the 'OK' a few years back. Because they were the only building allowed in the park, there were few people around.

With my family being thirty-or-so miles away from Honolulu while being nestled in the middle of a deep rainforest, they would at least be away from the main areas I suspected would erupt. The resort also had a relationship with a few nearby fishermen that still used traditional equipment, including motorless boats. Those fishermen were supposed to bring fresh catches by every few days, so as long as that relationship was upheld, they'd have food.

Despite everything else, those positives gave me a strong, gut suspicion that my family was okay; at least, okay for the time being. I had no idea if that would last, but the thought that my family was most likely in a best-case scenario rested my weary mind a bit. I could feel the tension in my muscles dissipate. I hadn't even realized how tense they were, but it was a major relief.

We broke for a midnight lunch not long after, talking about little luxuries we were going to miss.

Annie said she was going to miss air

conditioning. I had to agree. Not being able to go inside and feel that immediate cold blast of air on a day reaching near-triple digits was going to take some adjusting to. Not just for comfort, either.

We'd become so accustomed to being able to cool off that we had no idea how to exist without it. It had taken less than a century, and already, people were dying in droves during basic summer hot flashes. That was with air conditioning; it was hard to imagine the impacts with A/C gone completely.

Kim had chosen indoor plumbing. Another good choice. She chose it, not because of its convenience, but for its health and sanitary benefits. Without proper plumbing, she had explained, disease would run more rampant due to a general lack of hygiene. It would help bring about some of the costliest results of life without power: plague and death.

For me, it had to be grocery stores. The ability to just walk into a store and find any kind of food one could imagine was a luxury that can't be overstated. We'd taken for granted the ability to walk into a store and order enough meat to last for a week. Throughout history, we'd either have to hunt for that meat, or we'd have to farm it and kill it ourselves. We'd become spoiled with our recent eating habits.

The ability to purchase food anywhere in the country had allowed so many other things to be accomplished. When you don't have to put energy and focus into growing or killing your food, you can develop things like A/C or indoor plumbing. When food isn't a worry, you're free to think about the wonders of the universe. The ease of access to food had allowed our civilization to reach astounding heights; the lack of access to food would be a force for destruction.

It was a nostalgic conversation, morbidly nostalgic. We were all still adjusting to what we thought was going to be the new way of life. We still didn't know for sure if the world really had been knocked back several centuries, or if we were just the recipients of some of the worst luck imaginable, but thinking about the luxuries we had taken for granted was strangely therapeutic.

After our midnight lunch, we continued in the direction that Kim said the stars indicated was west. I walked with my head down, not really thinking about anything at all. I was falling into the rhythm of our steps, listening to the crunch of the sand beneath our feet. I stepped over rocks and bushes, but my feet were keeping an instinctual beat.

Even looking straight down at the ground, my vacant mind only barely registered a strangely shaped rock I was just about to step over. Something about that shape made me stop. Rocks aren't naturally rectangles.

I wasn't sure if my mind was playing tricks on me or what, but I found it hard to comprehend that I was staring down at a copy of the Bible. We were in the middle of the desert, who knows how far from the nearest town or person, and we come across a bible. What in the hell were the chances?

"What is it?" Kim asked as she came up alongside me, rubbing her head and wincing.

"You won't believe this," I said, crouching down and picking up the book.

Her eyes widened in surprise as she read the cover. She glanced at me with an 'Are you kidding me?' look.

"What'd you find?" Annie asked, joining us.

"A bible," I said.

"What is the likelihood that we'd come across a bible out here?" Kim asked rhetorically.

"Especially you, Sean," Annie added.

"Why's that?" I asked.

"Because you're the one who's on the fence about religion. I'm pretty solid in my belief, and so is Kim. You were the one unsure, and now you're the one to find the book."

"You found an eight-inch book in the middle of the night," Kim said, "in the middle of the desert! There is no way I would classify that as just a coincidence, Sean. Not based on the last few days and our conversation last night. Not a chance."

It was truly baffling, but I didn't feel as immediately as they did regarding why I found the book. For me, it was damned odd, but that didn't mean that the book was placed there by God for me to find. It just meant that life is strange.

I slid the bible into my suitcase, and we began walking once again. This time, the conversation was full. Annie and Kim would not stop talking about where the limit was between a coincidence and a sign. It was interesting at first, but by the time we were setting up camp for the day, I was beginning to wish they would stop.

They continued through dinner, and only when we were cozying up to sleep did their conversation wain.

"Sean?" Annie asked. "Can you read something from it?"

I debated pretending to be asleep. I really wanted to be asleep; I didn't want to read or focus on anything, but I obliged.

Pulling the book out of my suitcase, I opened it.

"There's a little dedication in here. 'May this book help you find your way like it did for me. - Mom.'"

"That's sweet," Annie said.

I flipped through the pages, stopping on a random one, and, in the slowly brightening light of early dawn, I read.

"Matthew 13:1. That same day Jesus went out of the house and sat by the lake," I started.

"Why does it sound normal?" Annie asked. "I thought the Bible was supposed to read like: 'Ye, go forth to thou home to find thee thou-est.' This sounds like some regular book."

"Must be the version," Kim said, again rubbing at her head, a painful expression across her face. "A lot of bibles had been printed since the '70s and '80s that were adapted to a more modern flow."

"Are you okay?" Annie asked with concern, ignoring Kim's answer.

"Yeah," Kim responded, faintly smiling at Annie. "Just a bit of a headache. I'll take an Advil if it keeps it up."

Looking at her, I wasn't sure if an Advil would do anything. Her cut was beginning to look discolored. There was also a faint smell that was coming from it, barely lingering in the air.

"Keep going, Sean," Kim urged.

"Such large crowds were gathered around him," I continued, "that he got into a boat and sat in it, while all the people stood on the shore. Then he told them many things in parables, saying:

"A farmer went out to sow his seeds. As he was scattering the seed, some fell along the path, and the birds came and ate it up. Some fell on rocky places, where it did not have much soil. It sprang up quickly, because the soil was shallow. But when the sun came up, the plants were scorched, and they withered because they had no root. Other seed fell among the thorns, which grew up and choked the plants. Still other seed fell on good soil, where it produced a crop—a hundred, sixty or thirty times what was sown. He who has ears, let him hear.'"

"You reap what you sow," Kim said. The tent fell to silence.

Finally, Annie said, "Thanks, Sean."

Soon after, I could tell both Kim and Annie were sound asleep. Their breaths had become consistent and slowed, an occasional snore coming out. I couldn't sleep, though. I kept thinking about that damn verse.

I could see how Kim thought it was saying you reap what you sow, but I didn't think that's what it was saying. I looked it at as if it was sending a message to spread your seeds. Not your literal seeds as in to have as many children as possible, but your seeds of experience and choices.

I thought about those words, and I saw a message of drive. It was telling us to try many things, to experience and learn all that we can. Some things in life, you'd fail at immediately. Others may seem great at first, but they live fast and die fast; enjoyment for them could be there today, but tomorrow? Who knows? Still, other things that you may try will be picked and torn at by those around you, suffocating any chance at success. And still, other choices and paths you take in life will grow and thrive in ways that you could never have imagined.

Does the farmer fail to plant the other seeds,

the ones that fall to the rocks or get choked by the thorns? No. The farmer still scatters those seeds.

The words, for me, spoke of a life of taking chances and living it without fear of failure or a fear of what others will say or how they'll react. It spoke of a life in which difficulties and failures would occur, but the recognition of that doesn't mean that life is better spent without trying.

I looked at my own life. My family was everything to me, and I had always tried to make the choices I felt were right for them; I'd do it all again. I'd do it all again, but I would make a few changes.

Right then and there, I made a vow to myself that, if life ever returned to normal, we wouldn't return to our lives as they were before. I vowed to make my children's childhoods the most interesting, educational, and impactful as I could. They would never step foot in a school again. Instead, we would just travel. We'd go from place to place, and my daughters could learn from real-world experiences, rather than from what some pompous intellectual put in a textbook. Clementine could use the experiences for stories and novels, maybe even changing literature forever; Lily was already smarter than most of her teachers, but getting her fingers dirty would send her knowledge to a realm my wife and I would never have fathomed, and Hannah could retain a bit of the purity that the world inevitably takes from every single one of us. But that's if the world returns to normal, a big 'if.'

4
Sunday, August 10th

The odor in the tent was rancid when I awoke the following dusk. It smelled like something had crawled into the tent and died while we were all asleep. It was stomach-churning, especially when that was the first thing any of the senses registered upon waking.

I looked over at Annie. She was still sleeping, though her eyes seemed to be fighting to stay closed. Her resemblance to my daughter was excruciating. The scene of her fighting to stay asleep was near-identical to the one I'd seen time and time again as I would peek my head into my daughters' rooms before heading off to work in the mornings. That image gave me a feeling of helplessness. It was as if my daughter was right in front of me, suffering through the worst of life with there being not a damn thing I could do about it. I swore to myself, at that moment, that I would do all I could to get Annie out alive.

I looked over to Kim. She was shivering a bit, and I could see the sweat rolling down her face.

She had sweated so much through the day that her clothes were soaked. The smell was most certainly coming from her.

"Kim?" I called, trying to wake her and shaking her softly. She didn't move. There wasn't even a flutter of the eyelashes.

The cut above her eye was not pretty. Through the day, it seemed to have taken a drastic turn for the worst. There were little black lines that were streaking away from the epicenter, which had swollen severely, breaking open a bit, with a nasty yellowish puss oozing out. My stomach couldn't handle seeing the source of the smell.

I unzipped the tent as fast as I could, trying to swallow back my stomach's inventory long enough to make it outside. I stumbled through the hole, and not a second too soon.

Annie had evidently heard me because she appeared just as I was wiping my mouth.

"What is that smell?" she asked.

"Kim," I replied, trying to assure myself that I was done.

"What do you mean?"

"Kim's cut. It's infected. Trust me, don't look at it if you can avoid it."

"We have to get her out of there, then! If it's infected, we have to help."

Just looking at Kim, it was clear she was not going to be able to move, and without any antibiotics, she wasn't going to get better. This was Charlie all over again, but at least Kim wasn't begging us to save her.

"Annie, she's-- I hate to say it, but there isn't anything we can do for her. It's past a point where we could help. We'd need antibiotics, penicillin, some sort of medicine, and all we have are a few Advil."

Annie looked over my face for a few seconds, studying my resolve, I assumed. Finally, she ducked into the tent, only to reemerge a few moments later, upchucking right next to where I had.

"I liked Kim. I *like* Kim," I corrected myself as I tried to rub Annie's heaving back reassuringly. "She's sweet and incredibly smart, but it's out of our hands now."

Annie didn't say anything; she just sat at the entrance to the tent, letting her stomach calm. Her eyes stared through the ground, darting back and forth from time to time as if watching a bug running by.

"Could we drag her?" Annie asked, looking over at me through eyes I was almost sure were Clementine's.

"Drag her?"

"Yeah. We've got to get her out of the tent either way, right? Would there be a way we could turn it into a makeshift gurney or something?"

It wasn't a bad plan, but, looking at the tent, I had no idea where to even begin. Then, I thought of the supplies.

"We can't," I said. "Well, I'm sure we could, but if we do that, we lose, not just her supplies, but one of our bags of supplies, too. We'd be adding extra risk for us when we have no idea how long she'll survive. We could do that and leave two bags here. Then, in just a few hours, she dies. At that point, we'll have accomplished nothing and be out several days' worth of supplies each."

"What a world we're walking into," Annie said, hanging her head defeatedly.

"I don't like it either, Annie," I said, trying to be as comforting to her as she was to me. I knew I was failing. Comforting was never my strong suit. "In this new world, though, you have to look out for yourself. We're being relegated back to natural Darwinism; even the smallest of cuts can be a death sentence."

It was absolutely one of the shittiest jobs I'd ever done in trying to console someone. Annie started to cry quietly.

"I fucking hate this," she said. "Why couldn't I have just died on the plane? Why did I have to survive? I don't want to live in a world like this!"

"Don't say that," I said, hugging her. "You're alive, and you know what that means?"

"I'm stuck in this hell?"

"No," I said. "Well, yes, but besides that! It means you still have infinite possibilities. Just because things are harder doesn't mean that you can't still find happiness."

"Happiness doesn't exist here," she said into my chest.

"You'll never know if you just give up," I replied.

Annie didn't respond, but she kept crying. I let her. Sometimes, you just have to cry. It can be an extremely cathartic experience for someone in a high-stress situation. You can't let it take over, but it's like screaming: Sometimes, you just have to let it out.

It took several minutes more, but Annie finally collected herself and pulled away.

"What do we do?" she asked.

"Our choices are limited," I responded, knowing that neither of our choices felt humane in the least. "We can leave her and the tent here, and we just sleep under the baking sun going forward. It won't do much for anyone, though, except maybe keep the animals away for a few days. Or we take the tent with us, and…" I trailed off.

"And what?"

"And… we speed up the process a little."

Annie looked confused for a second, then her eyes widened. She looked aghast.

"We can't do that!" she said.

"I think it's the only right choice, Annie."

I couldn't believe I was saying that. Never once in my life did I ever think I'd be arguing for someone's murder, especially now, with the guilt of Charlie so ripe. But it wasn't really murder, I told myself. Kim was already so far gone, and we had no hope of finding her medicine in time, her time, or the time it would take to get through the supplies. As harsh as it may have seemed, it was the right thing to do. It was like when you have a dog that's suffering a fatal illness: Sometimes, you have to put them down to help them avoid the pain that's coming. Sometimes, that act of killing is a true and complete mercy.

"Think of it like a dog--"

"Kim is not a dog!" Annie yelled through her sobs.

"I wasn't saying she is. I'm simply saying that when it's inevitable, speeding up the process for someone, or something, to save them from horrible and excruciating pain isn't wrong; it's good. It's merciful and right."

"Kim doesn't get a say?" Annie asked with snark, yet ignoring my point. "She doesn't get to determine how she dies?"

"Do we ever get that choice, Annie? Besides, do you think Kim would want to rot away from the inside? Alone in a tent with nothing but the pain to be there for her? We didn't know her well, but, from what we did know, I seriously doubt that would have been her choice! Annie, it fucking sucks, I know, but it is the right thing to do."

She never gave her full agreement, but Annie seemed to understand it needed to be done. She dropped her head and walked away. She made it a point to face away from me as I carefully moved Kim out of the tent, holding my breath so as to not vomit again. Kim never batted an eye. It seemed that, for all intents and purposes, she was already dead.

Once I packed up our stuff, I rolled Annie's suitcase to her and gave her what I hoped was a reassuring squeeze on the shoulder.

I found a nearby rock that was light enough for me to pick up but heavy enough to do the job in one go. This was a necessary evil, but I didn't want to do it. I certainly didn't want to have to do it multiple times, either, for my sake and Kim's.

Luckily, the rock did the job in one go. The sound it made was one I will never forget and one I will never describe.

5

Monday, August 11th -
Friday, August 15th

All night, as we continued walking through that seemingly never-ending wasteland, I couldn't fight back the shame. I had been so positive it was the right choice; so confident that it was the right thing to do, but I couldn't shake my mind from going to potential futures that Kim would never have. I took away any possibility she would ever have of seeing Dog again or of finding out if she was right about this being a worldwide catastrophe. She'd never see another sunset again, nor would she ever taste the refreshing coolness of a glass of cold water on a summer day. She'd never again know what it felt like to laugh so deeply that her insides hurt. She'd never see the stars again, and she'd never again feel the warmth of a loving hug. She'd never experience any of those ever again, and it was because of me.

I knew it wasn't really because of me, but my

mind still told me it was. Unlike with Charlie, *I* had struck the final blow, so, even though she was going to die sooner or later, and there was no disputing that fact, her last breath was had because of me.

To make matters worse, there was now a tension between myself and Annie. She had taken exception to how I had done it. She had thought I'd use a gun, that that was a much more humane way to have done it.

"I couldn't use the gun," I'd tried to rationalize with her. "Look, we don't have much ammo, and we may need every single bullet at some point. I knew a rock that size would do the job just as quickly. She didn't feel a thing. I promise."

"You smashed her head in with a goddamned rock, Sean," Annie said to me without turning around.

"Would you call yourself a fighter, Annie?" I asked, a bit of annoyance in my tone.

She just kept walking, not saying a word.

"Neither am I," I said, taking her silence as her answer. "If I fired that gun, the sound would have echoed all through this desert. However unlikely, if someone had heard it and decided to make our supplies theirs, we'd have no say so in the matter. We'd probably end up buzzard food by the end of it."

"Buzzard food?" Annie said. "You mean like Kim?"

I didn't respond. It wasn't worth adding to the tension by continuing to put forth an explanation. No matter what I said, it wouldn't change how Annie felt about the matter.

For the next several hours, we walked in silence. When we stopped for lunch, we kept conversation to a minimum, only talking when trying to figure out if we were still heading west or if we'd gotten lost. Once we picked back up again, we went back to marching in silence.

After two days, we each had one meal and one bottle of water left. That meal wasn't even close to what a meal should have been. It consisted of a travel-sized bag of pretzels each, the kind that was served for free on the plane, and a bag of carrots of the same size. Our situation was dire.

"We have to figure out a plan," I said. "We're pretty much out of supplies, and there's no way of knowing how much longer it'll take to get to more."

"There's nothing to plan," Annie said.

"We have to think of something."

"No, we don't, Sean. Two of us are already dead, and we've been walking for so long now that my blisters have blisters! I'm constantly hungry; I'm dehydrated, and we haven't seen the slightest hint of civilization since we started walking! I just want to lay down and die!"

"I won't let you, Annie," I said, still seeing flashes of Clementine on her face.

"What, you're going to take *my* choice away,

too?" Annie retorted with a sting.

"You aren't yourself," I argued.

"You don't even know me, Sean. You've known me for just a few days. Fuck you if you think you are going to take my choice away from me."

As much as I wanted to continue to argue, I couldn't. As awful as I felt about it, a part of me was jealous she had that choice. It would have been nice to just lie down and die; just stop fighting and move on to a more peaceful realm; just forget about the pain of starvation and dehydration. But I had no choice.

I had to keep fighting for my family's sake. Just because they were half the world away didn't make me any less responsible for them. I was going to get to them no matter what I had to go through.

"I can't just give up, Annie," I said to her. "I've got my family. I have to get back to them."

"That's fine," she replied, uncharacteristically cold. "But when I lay down, don't you even think about taking my choice from me. Just leave me. Don't even look back."

We finished our food in silence and began walking again.

Shortly before what felt like midnight on the fourth night, I noticed the sound of Annie's footsteps behind me had stopped. When I turned to look at her, I could see her silhouette sitting on the ground, legs folded Indian style.

I began walking to her when she called out, "Don't you fucking dare! Stop. Turn around and keep walking."

I stopped and just stared at her silhouette for a long while. She was right. It was her choice, and I had no right to force her to keep moving. She may have seemed like a kid, but she was an adult. She could make her own decisions.

But she was just a kid. She was just a year or two older than Clem. Yes, she was in college, but college students were really still kids, just barely getting a taste of what life offers. She was kind, warm, and wonderful. I felt I had a responsibility to care for her, to make sure she made it home. I'd sworn that to myself, and she deserved a chance, even if she didn't feel she could handle it.

I went to take another step, but I stopped, picturing my wife and daughters. I couldn't take responsibility for Annie, no matter how much I thought I should. Staying alive to find my family was the only responsibility I had anymore.

"Goodbye, Annie," I whispered under my breath, turning and continuing walking in our original direction, hating myself for making the decision. Just as with the others, I knew it was the right one, but I hated myself all the same.

I had not gone far, maybe another half-mile, when I came to the top of a hill with a magnificent view of another valley laying out in front of me. The expanse was covered with saguaro cacti that almost looked to be moving. It wasn't the serene setting that made my jaw drop, though; it was the small adobe home right smack dab in the middle of the valley. It even had bright lights illuminating its interior.

Immediately, I dropped the suitcase and began running back into the night. My legs sliced through the air faster than they ever had, overcoming their tiredness and weakness with a sudden shot of adrenaline. I hopped over little bushes and dodged knee-high cacti, hoping that I would soon see Annie's silhouette in the night.

As I continued to run, I never saw her. I looked all around, calling out her name as loudly as I dared. Eventually, I ran to a point which was way beyond where I should have found her. Fearing the worst, but hoping for the best, I chanced one very loud call for her.

I listened as my voice carried her name through the night, waiting and hoping for a response. The only answer I got was that of a coyote howl that was easily a mile off.

I couldn't just give up, though, so I went right to the spot where I was fairly certain I had left her. There I stood, waiting through the rest of the night, hoping that she would return, but as the morning began to break through, there had not been a single sign of Annie. I couldn't explain why, but I bowed my head and prayed for her.

· · ·

I approached the house, alone and exhausted. I didn't even bother trying to hide myself. If they didn't help me, I was screwed. Either the desert would kill me, or they would. If they were of the generous sort, I figured approaching from the open would seem less threatening and maybe convince them to help.

At about a hundred feet out, I saw my first sign of movement. It wasn't much, just a shape that moved past a window, but it caused another shot of adrenaline to release through me.

A short distance later, about fifty feet, I heard something I had not expected: a generator. The sound of the engine carried over that flat land right toward me; there was no mistaking it.

For the first time since before I boarded the plane, I felt a genuine excitement of the best kind. With a generator, a world of opportunities had just opened.

The sound of a shotgun pumping closed the door on those opportunities.

"You better have a good goddamned reason why yer on my land," came a man's gruff and aged voice behind me. I was caught so off guard that I couldn't respond through the shock.

"I ain't askin' again."

"I was in a plane crash!" I said finally.

There was a long silence during which I nearly pissed myself several times. Even I wouldn't have believed me.

Then, "Likely story."

"I swear!" I said, fearing what this man would do to me if he didn't believe me. "Almost ten days ago now! Delta Flight 4850 from Atlanta to Los Angeles! It was a 737! Only four of us survived the crash. We got some supplies from the debris and started walking. I have no idea where I am, and I ran out of food and water two days ago, and I am just trying to make it to my family!"

The man didn't respond to my panicked explanation, so I continued, trying to calm myself down.

"In my wallet, back right pocket, my ticket should be folded up in the billfold, and there's a picture of my family in the credit card pouch!"

I waited for him to grab my wallet. It felt like a lifespan. Finally, I felt him reach in and grab it. A moment later, the two barrels of the man's shotgun appeared on my shoulder, turning me around to face him.

He handed me my wallet and placed his gun on his own shoulder, barrels facing away. He was elderly with sun-worn, leathery skin. His white-haired beard would have made him a perfect candidate for a Civil War re-enactor. He had a look in his eyes that made it clear he was a friendly man, but that he wouldn't hesitate to pull that trigger if I gave him cause.

"Follow me," he said. "Yer lucky yer daughters remind me of my granddaughters."

I didn't dare say another word as I followed this stranger toward his house, hoping that he was about to be my savior. For a moment, however, I couldn't help but think that he was leading me toward a Texas-Chainsaw-Massacre-type death. I had no alternatives, though, so I followed him into his home.

6

Saturday, August 16th – Wednesday, August 20th

The home's interior was extremely quaint. It was the obvious residence of someone who was retired. Everything inside was entirely well kept but at least two-decades old. The wallpaper looked like it may have been installed just before the catastrophe struck, but the pattern on it gave it away as something that would have actually been installed when I was a child.

The furniture was very much like the wallpaper: it all looked new. There were no stains, no snags or tears in the material, and no squeaks or sags. The furniture's upholstery, however, was in a floral design that would have made my grandmother feel right at home.

The sound of Frank Sinatra froze me in the doorway. I knew that the generator I had heard meant they had power, but I was certainly not expecting to be greeted by 'Fly Me to the Moon' upon entering. What a nice surprise it was.

"Take a seat," the man said to me, motioning toward the sofa. It wasn't a request, but it wasn't quite a demand, either.

The sofa was comfortable to my backside. It was the first time in days that it was resting on something with padding, and only then did I realize how truly sore my ass actually was. Not just my ass, either, but as I leaned into the back cushions, a tension in my back immediately subsided. It was instant relief to a stress I had so quickly gotten used to.

"Jack, honey, it looks like a coyote got another one of them chickens somehow!" an elderly woman's voice came from around a corner. "You're gonna have to deal with'em sooner'r later!"

As she finished, the elderly woman walked into the living room and stopped in her tracks. She was a short woman, no taller than five feet. Her hair was completely white, and it was curled up, looking very much like it had been permed. She also had what I'd heard referred to as 'southern hips.'

She stared at me with a look of apprehension and a bit of fear.

"Gladys, this is Sean," Jack said. "Sean, this is my wife, Gladys."

"Nice to meet you," I said to Gladys. I tried to put on a warm and welcoming smile, but it didn't seem to translate to her.

She turned to Jack and said, "What'n the hell

do you think yer doing, Jack? I wanna speak with you in the kitchen. Right now."

Jack got up dutifully and followed Gladys into the kitchen. It didn't provide them much privacy, though, as the room had no doors.

"Why did you bring 'im here?" I heard Gladys ask.

"Sweetie, you have to trust me. Come back into the livin' room and listen to him."

"Jack, you know even better'n I do that invitin' someone into our home today is not like it used to be. You can't just be invitin' anyone in you feel like."

"Gladys, did you see 'im? That poor man out there has been through hell. He ain't no threat to us. Trust me. Or don't trust me, and, like I said, just come out and listen."

Jack appeared back from the kitchen and sat on a chair that was perpendicular to the sofa I sat on. He rested his shotgun on his leg, its barrels still pointed away from me.

After a moment, Gladys followed him and stood directly behind his chair, hands resting on Jack's shoulders.

"As you probably heard," Jack said, "my wife here ain't too keen on me bringin' you in our home."

"Honestly, I don't blame you," I said to Gladys. "I don't know for sure what's going on, but if what I think happened, really did happen, I'm surprised you didn't shoot me on sight. Thank you for that, by the way. Not shooting me, that is."

"The Lord works in his own way," Jack said. "Before we go any further, tell us what happened to ya. The whole thing, not some short version you spout out to avoid pissin' yerself."

Embarrassed that Jack seemed to know I had nearly peed my pants, I went over the whole story with them. I went over how my family and I had been planning a trip to Hawaii for years; how that trip had been thrown into question when the guy jumped out of the board room window; how my family and I had split, and that I would meet them later; I told them about the plane crash, or what I could remember of it, at least; and I told them about my companions and their fates. By the time I had finished, Jack had placed his shotgun against the fireplace mantle, and Gladys had taken a seat next to me.

"My word," Gladys said, taking my hand in hers.

"This may be a stupid question, but 're you hungry?"

I didn't say anything to him, but he immediately read the look in my eyes.

"Gladys, make this boy some eggs and bacon, if ya don't mind."

"Absolutely," she responded as she stood to make her way to the kitchen. She stopped and turned. "You want some, too?"

Jack nodded. "Thank ya, honey." Turning

back to me, he said, "There's a shower down the hall and through the bedroom on yer left. Don't take too long, but feel free to clean yerself up a bit."

I thanked him profusely as he just nodded and looked at me with a gaze that now had more sympathy in it than anything else.

Along the hallway's wall, there were several hanging portraits. They seemed to progress through time as I made my way down the hall. The first couple of photos were black-and-whites of much younger versions of Jack and Gladys. Next, a portrait of Jack and Gladys, young and full of a sparkle that only comes from two people deeply in love. They had their arms wrapped around one another. Gladys's wedding dress was frizzy, yet elegant, and Jack's tuxedo was extremely dapper.

After their wedding photo, there were a pair of family portraits. The first showed Jack and Gladys in what looked to be the late-70s to the early-80s. This time, they were joined by a third. The parents and their little girl were all dressed in matching outfits of a striped shirt and a pair of stylish bellbottoms. The second family portrait was nearly identical, other than the different outfits and the second child, a baby, that Gladys was holding.

The next few pictures focused on Jack and Gladys's daughter and son as they grew up. There were high school and college graduation pictures, which were followed by wedding pictures for each of the children. Finally, there was one large photo on the wall that faced down the hall toward the living room. This was my favorite.

This photo was the newest and had been western-themed. It showcased Jack and Gladys's whole family, and it had grown large. What had started as two people with two kids had ended with those two kids each having had four of their own. With the eight grandchildren, Jack and Gladys had also been able to greet what appeared to be at least four great-grandchildren.

Seeing them all in the one photo, decked out in cheesy, touristy cowboy outfits, filled me with a wave of brief peace. Everyone in that picture looked so incredibly happy and worry-free, and the goodness of the patriarch and matriarch had not seemed to disappear with the power. It was good to know that good people were remaining good.

"That was our fiftieth weddin' anniversary," Jack said from behind me, startling me. "Sorry," he said genuinely.

"It's alright. Fiftieth wedding anniversary? That's pretty impressive."

"It was a good fifty, too. I retired the week after this photo was taken. Sixteen years ago. My family had thrown me a little western-themed party knowin' we were 'bout to move out here."

"Looks like a great family!"

"They were," he responded solemnly. "Here," he said, handing me a towel. "You'll need that. Help yourself to any clean clothes in my closet that fit ya."

I thanked him, and he walked back to the living room. As I moved into the bedroom, it dawned on me that my case really wasn't that special. Sure, surviving a plane crash was a hell of a thing, but in tough or violent times, everyone has their own story of survival. And if they didn't have one at that point of the current cataclysm, they'd have one soon. That is, if they managed to survive the incident.

But everyone had a family or loved one that they cared for. Most people had loved ones scattered across the country, now nothing more than intangible memories. People like Jack and Gladys, they'd most likely never know what happened to their loved ones. They couldn't just get up and go. Not at their age, and if their kids and grandkids had young children or babies, the idea of them coming to Jack and Gladys was borderline preposterous. I felt for them.

The image staring back at me in the bathroom mirror shocked me away from my pity for Jack and Gladys. There was only one word to describe the figure I found myself staring at: gaunt.

My hair was disheveled and matted with a spat of blood that had also dotted my cheek. I assumed it was from either the guy next to me on the plane, or it was horrific splash-back. If it was splash-back, I could only imagine how awful it would have been for Annie to see me drop the rock down onto Kim. At that moment, I completely understood why Annie had felt the way she had.

My eyes were sunken, and their once vibrant blue was faded. The whites of the eyes were bloodshot, and the white that was still coming through was slightly yellow. The circles around my eyes were deep and looked like they would probably never fully go away. My cheekbones protruded, making my face look more shadowy, more desperate.

I knew I had already tightened my belt a couple of notches, but in my mind, that hadn't translated to the fact I was becoming a walking skeleton. I almost looked like someone had put clothes and a wig on one of those lifelike dummies from Halloween stores. I was certain that if my kids had seen me looking like that, I would have given them nightmares.

Pulling myself away from the depressing image of what I had become, I turned on the water. Nearly instantly, it was warmed. My body seemed to release the last bit of stress and tension it was holding as the cloud of steam washed over me and the first droplets of that soon-to-be-extinct luxury of hot water hit my skin. I felt my shoulders satisfyingly sink to a droopy position. My knees buckled slightly, so

I kneeled to the ground. The water rolling off my crouched back was thick with sand and dirt, grey and brown tinting the porcelain tub. I let myself sit there like that for just a minute before washing myself.

When I was dried off, I managed to find a shirt that fit and a pair of swim trunks that I was able to tighten enough that they wouldn't fall off. I felt a bit funny, though, as the swim trunks were extremely short, not even reaching halfway down my thigh. I knew that was the style in the seventies and eighties, but it was never something my generation ever got used to.

The smell of bacon wafted through the house, and my stomach rumbled audibly. I could even see my stomach quake a bit with each growl. Instantly, I felt slightly nauseous. Annie and I had been living off smaller and smaller rations of meals that, even when consumed in full, were already less than a few hundred calories, and those had been gone for days. My body needed sustenance, and it was telling me that it needed it immediately.

Jack and Gladys were already sitting at the dining room table when I entered. They had not waited for me, their plates already nearly half empty. I couldn't blame them.

I simply do not have words for the experience that followed. All I can say is that I had never tasted, and will never taste again, a better, or more satisfying, meal in my life. There is no way one can describe the sensation of that first full meal after days of starvation, especially when that meal consists of crispy, greasy bacon.

With our breakfast finished, Gladys showed me to a spare room which they said I could use. I thanked her profusely as she nodded and closed the door behind her, leaving me alone in the room.

I didn't bother getting under the covers or undressing. I just fell onto the bed, curled into a little ball, closed my eyes, and I was out.

. . .

I was awake for at least thirty minutes before I finally rolled out of the bed. From the light streaming into the room, it seemed to be around midday. As for which day, I had no idea, but I had a feeling it was not the same one I'd fallen asleep on.

When Gladys greeted me, she was wearing a different outfit. She informed me that I'd been asleep for two and a half days. They hadn't wanted to wake me, thinking that in my condition, as much comfortable sleep as possible was greatly needed.

Jack was just returning to the home, smiling to see me up and walking. He'd been out hunting the coyote, which had apparently gotten another chicken while I was asleep. With him was the trophy of his hunt: the coyote's carcass.

After he went through the process of cleaning and prepping the kill, Jack came back inside.

"Good to see you up and about," Jack said. "Truth be told, I wasn't exactly sure if you'd even wake up."

"Thankfully, I did," I responded with a chuckle.

Over the next couple of days, I continued to rest and recuperate. The meals, full of more calories than I needed, began to give me my strength, and the nights in the warm bed allowed me to feel rejuvenated and well-rested. My energy was returning, and the idea of getting back on the road again was one I was feeling ready for.

On the fifth night, we were sitting around the dinner table, our plates empty other than the crumbs of a dinner well-consumed.

"Since I've slept most of the time I've been here, I've forgotten to ask," I said. "How much do you know about what's going on?

The pair exchanged looks.

"Bits and pieces," Gladys said.

"We got a little bit of news comin' out, but it wasn't comin' through very clear. Had a CB radio that managed to keep kickin' and was pickin' up a bit'a news for about twenty minutes, but it fried after that. Things seemed pretty confused, but it was enough to know things aren't good." Jack said.

"What was it? What have you heard?"

"Well, we do know the power outage is all over. Seems like all the way down to at least Brazil and all the way to Alaska. We heard one or two mentions of Australia and India going dark, too. Not sure about anywhere else. And, again, we aren't even sure 'bout that."

"Well, remember that Kim woman I told you about?" I asked. "The older woman that was in the plane crash with me? Well, she apparently was an astrophysicist or something. She said she thought it was something called a coronal mass ejection."

I proceeded to explain what that was as best I could, which was so poorly I was sure Kim was rolling in her... well, she would have been rolling with embarrassment. Jack and Gladys seemed both horrified, yet unsurprised, as I told them the meaning that Kim had attached to the event.

"When I was in the Marines, we knew 'bout the capabilities of EMPs," Jack said. "This doesn't sound too entirely different."

"Kim did say it was a 'sun-created EMP," I responded. "But I honestly have no idea. I'm a marketer by trade. I know a little about science, but I couldn't tell you much more than the basics."

"Is it something reversible? This coronal mass ejection?" Gladys asked.

"I'm not sure," I said. "Kim made it sound like it was, at minimum, semi-permanent. Seemed like she thought a few years to get completely back to where we were wasn't out of the question."

"That sounds 'bout right," Jack said. "Besides the radio nearly catching fire, we had several cables actually catch fire. If wires were burstin' into flames, it's gonna take quite a while to get things rebuilt."

"What would that mean, Jack?" Gladys asked.

Jack looked at me for a moment before turning to his wife. "It means that the lives of most everyone out there are about to get harder than they could have ever imagined. It means generations of death, disease, and dread. It means, that even though we could get things rebuilt in five years, we'll have already fallen so far away from civilized behavior by that time that there will be, essentially, no way of comin' back"

Gladys took Jack's answer in. She looked like she wanted to ask him something, but she glanced at me instead, a cautiousness behind her eyes. Jack seemed to notice her caution, too.

"It's okay, Gladys," Jack said. "I'm gonna show him here in a little bit, anyway. And the answer to your question is 'no.' You and I shouldn't fall into that category. We're more prepared than most."

I looked at the pair quizzically. They were

being very coded, and it sparked my curiosity.

"Show me what?" I asked.

"Well, when we bought this land, there wasn't a house here. There was a buildin', but not the house. See, in my time as a Marine, I saw some pretty horrifyin' things. I know better'n most what people are capable of. And, even worse, I know better'n most what governments are capable of. I knew somethin' was going to happen to bring the absolute worst out of people. Sooner or later, it always happens.

"I tried tellin' people that they should be ready, and they all just laughed and called me a 'prepper.' It didn't bother me none. I just had cared about me and mine, and I figured that if things didn't go bad, at least we were well stocked." He laughed a bit at the last part.

"When this piece of paradise came available, I knew I had to have her. It was a perfect place to set up base."

"What made the place so special?" I asked, intrigued.

"Come with me," Jack said, standing up. He turned to Gladys and continued, "Might as well take him down now. You comin'?"

"I'm gonna stay up here. Gonna go ahead and knock out the dishes."

Jack kissed Gladys on the cheek and ushered me to a door that I had assumed was just their pantry. Instead, it housed a flight of stairs leading into what looked to be a dark and dingy basement.

Jack flipped on a light as he reached the landing, and the room was, indeed, a dark and dingy basement. It was pretty much empty, too. There were a few scattered tools, but otherwise, the room was barren.

I couldn't help but feel disappointed. From the build-up Jack had created, I was expecting boxes and boxes of MREs or canned beans or something. Instead, the room was empty.

Jack, seeing the disappointment and slight confusion on my face, chuckled.

"Looks pretty normal, huh?"

"Yeah," I responded. "What's going on, Jack? It's just a basement."

Jack smiled wryly. "Come on! You really think this is just a basement?"

I looked around, and, for the life of me, I couldn't see what Jack was obviously hinting at. Everything looked completely as it should.

"From the way you're acting, no, I don't think it's just a basement, but I have no idea what it actually is," I said.

"Good," Jack responded, his smile turning bright through his beard. He moved to the far wall of the basement and knelt right in the corner, pressing on the bottom brick at the end of the back wall.

A sudden hiss of air from my immediate left made me jump. It sounded like a pissed-off cat had just lunged right by me. However, it was quickly evident that the sound was not caused by an animal lurching; instead, it was caused by the *floor* lurching as a four-by-four square opened and began rising out of the ground. White, fluorescent light poured out into the darkened basement from the growing hole, and it was immediately clear the inside was immaculately clean.

The ground panel raised up to about eight feet and stopped. The hole in the ground was now filled again, and, at about three feet off the ground, there were little rails.

Jack walked through a gap in the rails and stood on the new floor.

"Come on," he said. "Never ridden an elevator before?"

"Never ridden a *hidden* elevator in a *basement* before," I quipped back as I stepped beside him.

Jack smiled and pushed a little button on the railing. With a clink, the elevator began moving down into the white room.

7

Wednesday, August 20th – Friday, August 22nd

The space Jack was leading me into could not, by any stretch of the imagination, be considered a room. It was more of a shaft that had seven doors lining its circular wall, stacked one on top of the other about twenty feet apart. The shaft reached nearly two hundred feet down.

As the elevator lowered us, I turned to see Jack was staring at me, a giddy smile on his face. He looked like he had waited ages to show this place off.

"What is this place?" I asked.

"It's an old missile silo that's been converted," he said proudly. "We've made a few changes, but it's as strong as ever. It's just a bit more versatile."

The elevator stopped at the top door, where a small glass window, roughly the size of a microwave, showcased a wondrous site beyond.

Jack opened the door, and an immediate blast of humidity slammed me as we walked inside.

The room was exploding with trees and bushes, flowers and berries, shrubs and weeds. It was as if Jack and Gladys had brought the outdoors in.

The ceiling was about twelve-feet high, and some of the trees were needing every inch of it. There was a wide variety, too, but they all seemed to be tropical species. There were a few nearby trees that seemed to have a brood of coconuts ready for picking. Several trees were bursting with bunches of bananas, each just about ripe. It was astonishing.

Jack saw the look on my face and laughed.

"Pretty amazin', innit?" Jack asked, sounding very pleased with his accomplishment.

"I don't think 'amazing' quite covers it!"

"This was one of the hardest floors to make," Jack told me as he led me down a little dirt path.

As he continued to talk, I began to take notice that it wasn't just plants that occupied the room, an insect swooping down and buzzing my ear made that clear. There seemed to be a panoply of species, ranging from the bee that buzzed me to spiders, weaving their webs and moving into the vegetation.

An entirely unexpected sound came from above me, indicating the ecosystem in that room was far more intricate than I would have ever thought possible. It took me a second to fully believe that there really was a seagull above me, but there was. It was perched on a set of metal crossbeams that were connecting several lights.

"We divided this floor into three sections," Jack said. "This one here is the tropical ecosystem. If we keep goin' this way down the path, we'll hit a door that leads to a deciduous or temperate ecosystem. From there, we'd come to the continental one.

"See the lights above us?" He indicated the lights hanging from the crossbeams. They looked like the stage lights you'd see at rock shows or in theater productions. Half of them were on, shining out bright, sun-impersonating light; the other half, however, were off, red filters still visible over their bulbs.

"They're all UV lights and special hydroponic lights," Jack continued. "We've got two sets. One for day, and one for night. They're designed specifically for indoor, industrial growth of outdoor plants. Each room is lit by lights designed specifically to emulate the given climates."

"Why these climates? Why any of this?" I asked, trying to wrap my head around the need for a massive space like this to have so many animals. "I mean, why have seagulls down here?"

"We wanted to make sure the ecosystems down here were as close to natural as we could make'em," Jack said. "We're usin' each of these rooms to help grow and harvest food. Best way to do that is to make this area as close as possible to where they come from. Once you start approachin' it that way, you need insects to pollinate. With the insects, you need some sort of predator to make sure the area doesn't get overrun by a single species.

"There are certain things Gladys and I have grown accustomed to. Things like bananas, strawberries, and grapes. Well, those 're luxuries we didn't want to go without. So, here we are." Jack smiled back at me.

"How big are each of these sections?" I asked. It felt like we had walked at least a quarter-mile already, and it still looked tropical as far as I could see.

"The diameter of the whole complex is 1200 feet. I don't remember the square footage down here."

"Basically, it's big!"

"Yes, sir," Jack chuckled. "The great thing 'bout this place is that it can create its own electricity. That generator upstairs is purely for the structure above ground. When we run out of gas, we'll make the move down here. We'll still use up there, of course, but we'll have full power down here. This will become our home.

"The system is completely hydroelectric, and it's completely self-sustainin'. At the bottom, we have four tanks, a thousand gallons each. They store and process the water. There is a constant flow in and out of these; it never stops. It sends some to our turbines for electricity, the other portion is used for personal use. Showers and such. Once the water is used, it's cycled back through the system. There are H20 nets throughout the rest of the complex, too. Helps us to not waste anythin'. No sweat drop, no tear go to waste."

"Wait, it's still electrical, though. Why didn't it get fried, too? And why not connect the power down here to the home upstairs, instead of using the noisy generator?"

"The systems down here were off and unplugged, and since it is a closed system here, it all still works. As for why we use the generator instead of connectin' the house to down here, we were afraid that, if we were able to keep livin' up there, we would."

"What's so bad about that?" I asked. "You have a pretty great spot."

"Up there, it's comfortable. It's a life of luxury. Sounds great. But bein' above ground at all times, livin' there, could be... Look here, my whole life, the world always has been dangerous, but now? It's beyond that. It's wild. Stayin' in that home keeps Gladys and me visible to anyone comin' in. It puts us in danger, and I certainly do not want to put Gladys in danger."

"So, you force yourself to make the move by taking away the ability to stay?"

"Exactly."

"Well, why are you still up there? Why not conserve the gas in case you need it and just move down now?"

"We have a specific store of gas reserves for

needs down here that we're not touchin'. And, yeah, my logical mind tells me we should've already been down here a week ago, but there's somethin' to be said for sleepin' above the ground. Seeing the sky is nicer than we give it credit for.

"Tell me," Jack continued, "how far out were you when you first saw lights or someone movin' here?"

"It was a ways. I was at the east end of the valley, at the top of the rim."

"That is why we will need to be below ground. We're old, and Darwin would argue we'd be some of the first to go in tough times. We've got a lot of things that people are goin' to want. And, yeah, I was a Marine, but at my age, there's only so much I'd be able to protect us from. A small, wanderin' group? Probably. A group of organized looters? That's just laughable. I got a helluvan arsenal down here—you'll see—but one well-armed eighty-five-year-old gettin' hit from all sides by a dozen crazed, yet organized, people won't last long. Only makin' a move down here would guarantee our safety."

I understood. He wanted to protect Gladys, and he knew that staying up there put her in a danger that he couldn't save her from. Moving below would be their only chance, and every day above ground was one more day where they were tempting fate.

After a few more minutes of walking, we

came around a corner and were greeted by the elevator door.

"Wait," I said, confused at how we ended up back where we started. "How are we back at the elevator?"

"I think you were too busy lookin' around to notice, but the path divided a while back. We took the path that led back to the start. Wanna move on to the next levels, and you can literally get lost in here."

Once on the elevator again, it lowered to the next floor. The floor was protected by the same door and window.

Jack opened the door, and we walked into what appeared to be a hotel lobby. Not just any hotel, either; this was not a Motel 6. The floor was a luxurious red carpet that just shouted class and wealth. The trim and floorboards were a magnificent gold that contrasted classically against the red. It was like stepping into a hotel during the heyday of 1920s art deco and extravagance.

"We may've overdone it on this one," Jack said.

"I think you did it just right," I responded, trying to pick my jaw up off the ground. "And you said living up *there* was living a life of luxury!"

"Like I said, there's something about sleepin' above ground. No matter how nice it is down here, we can't fake the sky. We can try to make up for it, though. It's kind of the goal of this place, and you ain't seen nothin' yet." he said as he smiled.

"Now, this is one of two floors designed just for livin'. Each of the two floors, this one and the one right below us, are split into two. Each section is essentially self-sufficient; basically, we have four seven-bedroom, five-bath houses across these two floors. There had to be room for our whole family, just in case they could be here."

The next level down was the second floor for living. We passed by it; Jack said it was identical to the one above except it had black carpet.

Jack opened the fourth floor's door, and I entered what appeared to be an industrial kitchen. It was massive, with stainless steel appliances for every position.

"As I had said, we had expected, or hoped, that our family would join us here," Jack explained. "With a family of near thirty people now, a big kitchen is necessary, but what I want to show you on this floor isn't the kitchen."

Jack walked through the kitchen, me a short distance behind him, admiring the accomplishment that was this complex. At the far end of the room, Jack dialed in a combination on a lock and opened the door it protected.

Beyond it was an extremely thorough arsenal. The room itself was easily fifteen-by-fifteen, shelves lining each wall from a foot off the ground to a foot from the ceiling. The shelves showcased a staggering selection, big and small.

Jack had everything from small, single-fire weapons meant more to scare someone than anything else, to what looked suspiciously like a bazooka.

"Just wait," Jack said, opening a little compartment just inside the door.

He pulled out a remote and pushed a button. In the center of the room, just as the elevator had done before, a panel opened and lifted. This time, however, there wasn't an elevator inside; instead, there was a shelving set up that looked like the interior of a candy store; a candy store for the NRA. Jack had several plastic containers, the same used for jelly beans and gummies, each filled with their own specific ammunition, reaching from just above my knees straight up to the ceiling.

Jack pushed another button on his remote, and the dispensary wall split down the middle. Behind it, Jack seemed to have stowed away what appeared to be a personal anti-aircraft setup.

"This one is of my own makin'," he said. "Put it together from several other guns. This baby'd take out a C-17 at cruisin' altitude if given the chance. Well, that's a bit hyperbolic, to be honest, but it'll make a bad day for someone."

"Jack," I said, looking around at the overwhelming weaponry, "I think you would be able to annihilate anyone that tries coming at your home. Why don't you have all this stationed upstairs?"

"Time. We didn't expect this to happen now, and we just weren't ready."

For the next thirty minutes, Jack bragged about nearly every weapon in his collection. I had no idea what he was talking about, really. I had never held a gun before we found the two in the luggage. I didn't know the difference between a 9mm and a .22, other than they were most likely different sizes. Jack and Gladys had been so amazing to me, though, so I had no problem letting Jack gush about his collection.

Finally, Jack concluded his bragging, and we moved back to the elevator and down to the next floor.

The fifth floor held a contingency of vehicles, a basketball court, a racquetball court, and a library. The cars that were lined up about a hundred feet out from the elevator were all classics, not a single one newer than 1984. There were several old Corvettes, each restored to pristine condition, sitting next to a beautiful old Chevy Bel-Air. Beside the Bel-Air sat what looked like an exact replica of Eleanor, the Mustang in *Gone in Sixty Seconds*. At the far end, there was an old motorcycle and sidecar that had been painted to look military issue.

"Next floor down, we have our water systems and a few more recreational things. Playground for the kids, a few bowlin' lanes, things like that," Jack was saying as he ushered me back onto the elevator.

"Jack," I said hesitantly, "if you don't mind me asking, how much did all of this cost? I don't mean to pry or anything, but I can imagine that just one of these floors was insanely expensive."

"You're not wrong," Jack said as the elevator began moving down once again. "All in, this whole complex, the land, and the cost of buildin' the home on the surface, I think we're in at close to twenty."

He didn't need to say the million for me to know that's the 'twenty' he meant.

"But you were a Marine. How did you afford this?"

"Luck," he said with a nearly imperceptible shrug. "When I was a kid in the fifties, I mowed lawns on the weekend for some spare cash. Did it for a number of years. In 1964, at the age of fourteen, I took what I'd managed to save to that point and decided I wasn't gonna do what other kids my age were doin'. I wasn't gonna go and buy a bunch of comics.

"Instead, I went downtown and put my $1,467.23 into some stocks for a new business because I liked its name. The years went by, and I completely forgot about 'em. A few months before I retired, we were cleanin' out our old place, gettin' ready to have a garage sale, when Gladys came across an old box. In that box, I found my stock certificates for Berkshire Hathaway. You may know 'em. It was Warren Buffet's business before he died. When we went to cash 'em in, we knew they'd be worth somethin', but we were shocked to find out that the stock was worth just under forty-million dollars. Crazy, huh? From fifteen hundred to forty million without havin' to do anythin' more than mow lawns for a few summers."

The white room interrupted Jack as it suddenly began flashing red, a siren wailing out. The wail was bouncing off the silo's walls, painfully deafening.

"What's going on?" I yelled.

"Somethin's wrong," Jack yelled back.

I fought the urge to reply sarcastically as Gladys's voice began echoing from speakers positioned all around.

"Jack," Gladys said, "you two need to get up here right away. We've got visitors!"

Jack pressed another button on the elevator's railing, and we began ascending rapidly. Within moments, we were rising into the basement, Gladys waiting for us expectantly.

"How many?" Jack asked immediately as he stepped out of the elevator.

"Not sure," Gladys responded, "but it was at least ten. Maybe fifteen."

Jack hurried out of the basement and to the front windows of the house. He pulled back the floral curtains just enough to peer outside. In the distance, there was a large gaggle of people walking directly toward the house. They weren't just meandering or struggling, either. They were walking with a walk that said, 'We're coming, and we'll take what we want.'

Jack turned to me and said, "Sean, I hate to ask ya this, but will ya come out with me?"

"You and Gladys saved my life, Jack. Anything you need from me, you just need to ask."

"Follow me," Jack said, nodding.

He led me into his and Gladys's room, flipping the mattress over to reveal another stash of weapons, though this stash was much smaller than the one downstairs. He grabbed an AR-15, made sure it was loaded, and handed it to me.

"Two things to remember," he told me. "One: do not put yer finger on the trigger until you are absolutely ready to fire. Two: Do not point it at anyone until you are ready to fire. Until then, keep it pointed down."

I nodded.

The gun felt strange in my grasp. I'd never held a rifle, and I had not expected it to be so heavy. I'm not sure why that surprised me; after all, it's a massive piece of metal.

Jack stood with his own rifle in hand and led me to the front door.

"You ready?" he asked, a bit of nervousness squeaking through in his usually stern and confident voice.

I just nodded, and Jack opened the door to the desert night and the mob of people beyond.

. . .

The desert evening was calm, and, under any other circumstances, it would have been an incredibly lovely evening. In reality, it was anything but lovely as Jack and I made our way closer and closer toward the group.

Even in the dimmed light, we could easily make out thirteen people. There seemed to be an array of young and old, but there didn't seem to be kids. I was incredibly grateful for that; if things got bad, I certainly didn't want to have the blood of any kids on my hands.

That's when it really sank in for me: I was walking toward what could possibly end in a shootout. I could soon be responsible for yet another person's death, or, even worse, I could be dead.

I was just some marketer that had a knack for convincing people to buy shit they didn't need, and, when they weren't buying, I could easily look at the analytics and find out why. I was not Clint Eastwood; I was not Wyatt Earp. I should not have found myself walking through the desert with an AR-15 in hand, approaching a group of, for all I knew, innocent civilians, ready to mow them down in a hail of bullets if need be. I shouldn't have been there, doing that, but I was.

As we got to within twenty-five feet of the group, nearly close enough to see the whites of their eyes, Jack stopped. I followed his lead.

"That's far enough," Jack said, loud enough for the entire approaching group to hear him. Luckily, the group stopped; however, two men at the front of the group raised their hands and took a few extra steps forward. The left hand of the man on my right held a shotgun.

"How ya doin'?" the man with the shotgun asked. He was a bearded, overweight man that was easily 6'3.

"What can we do fer ya?" Jack asked.

"We could use some shelter and some supplies," the other man said.

"We don't have enough supplies," Jack responded immediately. "You're more than welcomed to camp right here for the night if you need to."

The two men across from us glanced at one another.

"See," the man with the shotgun said, lowering his arms and gun to his sides, "Your running generator and electric lights are telling us a little different."

I could feel the tension growing, and my finger kept creeping closer and closer to the trigger of my gun.

"Yeah, we have a workin' generator," Jack confirmed. "However, we don't have any extra supplies. I'm sorry."

The man with the shotgun took another step forward. Jack lifted his gun and pointed it directly at the man's chest. The man stopped. He seemed to be weighing if that western-looking Santa Claus was capable of pulling the trigger on him.

"Look at us," the unarmed man said, pulling a handgun out of his waistband. "There are thirteen of us and just two of you. Let us by before something unnecessary happens."

"Only two of us came out," Jack said. "There may be more inside."

The man with the shotgun took another step toward Jack and me. Jack lifted his gun a bit more and pointed it right at the man's head.

"If you take one more step," Jack said, "there won't be no warnin' that's comin' after. Right now, you got three choices."

"Do we now?" the man with the handgun responded sarcastically. "What would those be exactly? Just so we're clear."

"You can kindly accept our offer of campin' here for the night; You can politely refuse that offer and be on yer way, or we see if this retired Marine is still as much of a crack shot as he used to be."

The pair of men across from us glanced at one another again. They didn't seem to have expected Jack would be military. They probably thought he was some crackpot old man with a gun, and me, his trusty, and much weaker, sidekick. However, Jack having a military background did seem to be giving them pause.

"We don't have all night," Jack said. "What'll it be?"

The man with the shotgun seemed to relax a bit as he put his right hand out.

"We'll kindly accept the offer to camp here," the man said.

Jack lowered his gun, and the man took a step forward. Before his second step, though, he quickly raised the shotgun.

Jack managed to get off a single shot, just as the invader's shotgun got level with his chest. Jack apparently was as good a shot as ever as the man's face was obliterated by the projectiles. It was one of the most atrocious things I'd witnessed. One second, the man's face was there; the next, it wasn't, the man collapsing to the ground. Thankfully, the spray of projectiles didn't hit the woman behind the asshole.

The man with the handgun threw his hands up and dropped his gun. He wanted no part in the escalation now.

"Don't shoot!" he said.

"I didn't want to," Jack responded, moving his gun to point at the remaining instigator's head. "You and yer group got ten minutes to make it outta sight."

"We're going," the man said, turning to leave.

However, Jack stopped him. Jack was a good man.

"Wait," Jack said. The man turned to him, wary of a potential trap. "You see that group of mountains over yonder? The group with the six peaks almost on top of one another?"

The man looked to where Jack was pointing and nodded.

"Head toward the peak on the far left. As you get closer, you'll come up on a trail. Take that trail. It has some rough spots, and it's long, but there're several good shelter points on it, and it'll take ya directly to Flagstaff, Arizona."

The man looked at Jack, dumbfounded.

"Thank you," he said finally.

"Best get movin'."

For the next ten minutes, we watched silently as the group slowly faded into the growing dark of the valley, the corpse sitting motionless next to us in the brightening moonlight.

When the group was out of sight, I crumpled to the ground. My knees were weak, the fear suddenly vacating my capacity. I couldn't keep down the dinner.

"You alright?" Jack asked.

"Depends on your definition of 'alright,' I guess," I responded, wiping my mouth.

"Let's get back to the house," Jack said, turning back to the building.

"What about him?" I asked, indicating the corpse.

"Leave 'im," Jack said. "If any more coyotes

come by, maybe they'll go after him, rather than the damn chickens."

As we entered the home, Gladys was coming up from the basement below.

"It had to be done," she said, coming and hugging Jack. "I saw it on the security cameras. You did what you had to do, honey." She kissed him. "Can I get you anythin'?"

"Get me my Johnnys," Jack said. "Please," he added.

Gladys smiled her reply and moved over to the radio on a bookshelf at the edge of the room. She pushed a few buttons on it, and the familiar twang of Johnny Cash's guitar broke the silence. It was a fitting song. She moved into the kitchen and returned a minute later carrying two glasses of whiskey.

"I fell into a burnin' ring of fire. I went down, down, down, and the flames went higher. And it burns, burns, burns, that ring of fire." Jack sang along absentmindedly as he sipped on the whiskey, his deep and craggy voice fitting in well with Cash's.

As we sat there listening to the song, my mind began to wander, taking me back to the tropical paradise that held my family captive. I tried to keep my mind away from them, but it wouldn't stay away.

It had been two weeks since the lights went out, and, even on a secluded resort that had deals with local fishermen, their supplies had to be running low. There was no telling how much water that resort had access to, and if things had gotten bad in Honolulu, there was no telling how many people had begun to migrate out of the city.

We were in the middle of the desert, with no cities for at least a hundred miles, yet we were still confronted by a group of people. What would the circumstance for my family and that resort be when they were just thirty miles outside of a city holding a million people? The terrain there was as equally unforgiving as here, granted for different reasons, but if people could find this place, they would certainly approach that resort sooner or later.

For the next hour, despite what I'd just been through, or maybe because of it, I could not think of anything else other than the numerous *horrible* possibilities my family may have been in. I was safe and comfortable under a roof with a full belly, or what was a full belly until I puked it up. They could be suffering in the elements and starving. It was a morbid line of thought that caused me to make my way quickly through several glasses of whiskey.

"Have you thought about yer next move, Sean?" Gladys asked me as she entered the room from the kitchen, carrying another glass of whiskey for myself and Jack.

"Get to my family," I said, taking the glass and thanking her.

"But how do you plan to get to'em?" Jack asked. "They're in Hawaii, right? With the boats and planes dead, how you thinkin' you'll get there?"

"I'm not sure," I said, swallowing down a gulp. It was a good whiskey, and I wasn't even really a drinker. "I honestly hadn't really gotten beyond: Get to the coast. I was planning to figure the rest out when I got there."

"I don't think that'll be likely," Jack said, taking a sip of his own glass.

"Why's that?"

"People," Jack responded. "We're gonna be at least three weeks in by the time you get to the coast."

I wasn't sure where he was getting that number. At the pace I'd been going, I didn't expect to get to the coast for at least another month.

"People are gonna be goin' crazy by then," Jack continued. "Water and food'll be runnin' out, and in the cities on the coast, there ain't readily accessible supplies beyond grocery stores. They can't just go pick some fruit or walk to the nearest stream. In some places, certainly. L.A.? San Diego? Long Beach? Not a chance.

"When you get there, I wouldn't expect that you'd have much time to rest, let alone come up with a plan to get to Hawaii. I don't mean to scare you, but I have a feelin' you'll be dodgin' bullets all the way to the coast."

He may not have meant to scare me, but fear definitely shot through me as he spoke. He wasn't telling me anything I hadn't suspected, really, but hearing it stated out loud was something completely different.

"I'm open to suggestions," I said.

Jack went silent. He seemed to go into deep thought, trying to help me formulate a plan.

"Jack, what about The Gabby?" Gladys asked.

"The Gabby?" Jack said, a moment of realization dawning on him. "That's right! I had completely forgotten about The Gabby."

"Who's Gabby?" I asked, intrigued.

"Not who," Gladys said.

"What," Jack finished.

"Okay, then, what is Gabby?"

"*The* Gabby is a boat. A sailboat, to be precise," Jack said. "It's a beautiful boat. Belonged to an old colleague of mine. He always said that he wanted to take me out on it. He has it docked in, uh, Marina Del Rey, I think. I doubt he'll be there. He lives in Texas."

"Have you ever sailed before?" Gladys asked me.

"I've never been on a boat before," I responded.

I had known that I'd probably have to take a boat of some sort to get to Hawaii, but a sailboat? By myself? As desperate as I was to get to my family, I wanted to get there alive, and I had serious doubts about my capabilities as a seaman.

"It'll be extremely hard, Sean," Jack said. "The boat ain't small. It's a thirty-two-footer. Usually, for takin' somethin' like that halfway across the Pacific, you'd probably want to have at least two or three people. You'll be by yerself. That'll make it that much tougher."

"Yeah," I said, fighting the urge to tell him how utterly thankful I was for him hammering down on how impossible it would be. "I don't think I'd be able to handle it."

"I think you could," Jack said. The confidence and steadiness in his voice surprised me. There wasn't an inkling of doubt or apprehension. He seemed to completely, and without reservations, believe what he had said. "Again, I don't think it'd be easy, but, so far, you've survived a plane crash, nearly a week and a half in the summer desert, and out of the four people to survive the crash, yer the only one left. You've been through hell, and if you made it through all of that, I've got faith in you."

"You barely know me, though," I said. "What makes you so certain?"

"When yer in the Marines as long as I was, you get a talent for learnin' who can survive when things get hard, and you can pick out the ones that'll cower with their tail between the legs. You can pick'em out a mile away because yer life depends on it. And you? You don't strike me as the kind to crumble in a crisis, even if you did almost piss yerself when I approached you."

"I appreciate the vote of confidence," I said, "but it may be misplaced."

"Sean, here's somethin' you should know 'bout my husband," Gladys said. "Jack is not one to mince words. I will never forget when Kevin, our son, was nine-years-old. He was workin' on his homework one night, and when Jack got home, he sat down at the table with Kevin. After about ten minutes, Jack comes to me in the kitchen, gives me a kiss on the cheek, and says, 'Gladys, sweetie, I know you and I aren't the sharpest tools in the shed, but how did we make a kid as dumb as him?'"

I looked at Jack, surprised that he would say something like that about his own kid, but Jack was smiling at the story.

"It sounds worse than it was," Jack said. "There's some things a parent can tell about their kids. Sometimes, you can tell yer kids are smart and have potential with education; other times, not so much. Kevin was one of those other times. Nothin' wrong with it, either! There's lots of trades that pay extremely well, and knowin' geometry or physics for'em ain't a requirement. Sayin' Kevin was dumb wasn't supposed to mean he'd never amount to anythin'. I was just sayin' it was clear books weren't his thing."

"See?" Gladys asked me rhetorically. "He has no problems sayin' when somethin' ain't a fit."

"If I see someone tryin' somethin'," Jack said,

"and it's clearly outta their league, I tell'em straight. If I thought you had no chance of makin' it, you bet yer ass I'd tell ya, and I certainly wouldn't suggest it as an option."

"I'm glad you think so," I said. "And I appreciate the candor, but I'm just a marketer."

"Yeah, you told us," Jack said in a slightly patronizing manner. "But that's what you were before. If you want to get to your family, you gotta decide what you *will* be going forward. You think the world needs marketers now? No. Stop livin' in the life that ain't comin' back."

He was right. I was thinking of myself in terms of the world with lights. I kept thinking of myself from last month, but last month was never going to repeat. The world of before was not coming back. I couldn't continue to think of myself as a marketer or a businessman; I could not continue to think of myself through the lens of a past reality. Reality had changed, and I had to change with it.

"From the story you told us, Sean," Jack said, "yer a survivor. I have no doubt that'll keep up."

I didn't respond as Johnny Cash wailed in the background, keeping the silence from being too awkward.

"Take the sailboat," Jack said. "I think it's really yer only chance."

I had a feeling he was right, so after a few more long moments of pondering and a big swallow of whiskey, I agreed.

"Good," Jack said. "The only questions left now are: Which route and which car you takin'?" This caught me off guard.

"What do you mean 'which car'?" I asked.

"I mean, which car're you takin'? All the cars in our garage are older and without computer garbage in 'em. They all still work."

I was dumbfounded. Jack and Gladys's generosity was unmatched. They could have easily turned me away like the others, but they brought me into their home; they cleaned and fed me, and now they were providing more help than I could have ever hoped for.

"Why are you doing this?" I asked them, tears of pure gratitude welling up.

"I'm gonna be honest with you, Sean," Jack said, sitting forward in his chair a bit. "When I came up to you in the desert, I didn't believe a single word you were sayin'."

I wasn't too surprised by this. He didn't really hide his disbelief that well originally.

"I was actually debatin' shootin' you right then and there. Who keeps a family picture in their credit card slip? Maybe I was bein' paranoid, but I really didn't think you were alone."

"Why didn't you shoot me then?"

"Gut feelin," Jack said, hesitating. "It was instinct, I guess. Yeah. It was instinct."

"Thank you," was all I could manage; I was at a loss of words, despite clearly recognizing that there was some other reason, something more, that he wasn't telling me.

Jack stood a moment later, saying, "Gladys, can you clear off the table? I'm gonna go to the library downstairs to grab my maps and see if we got any books on sailin'."

With a handful of maps but absent sailing books, Jack returned soon after, and over the next hour and a half, Jack, Gladys, and I all stood around their dining room table, studying several U.S. road maps that were laid out before us. Jack was going over the two best routes to get to Marina Del Ray. One was safer; one was faster. The safer route added at least an extra couple of days, but it avoided any potential big cities. The faster route took me through Phoenix and Los Angeles. Cities were bound to be dangerous, so going through two of the country's largest may save some time, but that's if I would be able to make it through them alive.

"You sleep on yer choices tonight," Jack said after a while. "Personally, I think yer best bet is to play it safe. It may take a little longer, but it's better than what the cities may hold."

I thanked them, and after saying our goodnights, we retreated to our rooms.

Laying back on that comfortable bed, I grew excited about the prospect of motorized transport. I was thoroughly looking forward to being able to sleep at night and travel during the day, and having the car's air conditioner would be like heaven, even at high noon.

As my mind grew weary of thinking, I reached into my bag and pulled out the Bible. I opened it to the very first page of Genesis. I figured, if I was going to read it, I was going to start from the beginning.

. . .

When the morning came, I surprisingly didn't have a hangover. Instead, I felt a mixture of dread and excitement, sadness and giddiness. I had grown to like Jack and Gladys, and I was sad to part ways with them. They had shown me a kindness that the world needed. However, the idea that I was, once again, able to press on with my journey, and I was going to do so in a vehicle, had me feeling like a kid on Christmas.

In the kitchen, Jack and Gladys had already made up a bag of supplies. They had loaded me down with enough water and food to get me to the coast and then some, even including some of their precious eggs and an entire bunch of bananas from below.

Gladys and I said our goodbyes in the basement, the elevator rising out of the floor.

"I'll be prayin' for you," Gladys said. "I know yer gonna make it to yer family, but a little help from the big man couldn't hurt."

"Thank you, Gladys," I said. "I can't thank you enough."

She kissed me on the cheek and looked up at me with a smile only a grandmother possesses.

"Come on, Sean," Jack said caringly, urging me onto the elevator.

A few moments later, we were walking into the garage.

"I think you should take the motorcycle," Jack said. "It won't have the air conditionin' like the others will, and if you get caught in some rain, yer gonna get wet. But I'm sure the roads are gonna be plugged with stopped cars. The bike will make it easier for you to get through some squeezin' if need be."

I really wanted the air conditioning. I had so looked forward to sitting inside a covered cab, cold air on full blast. I was not really looking forward to still having the hot sun baking down on me, but I could easily see that the benefits of the bike outweighed me not having A/C.

"Yeah," I said reluctantly. "I guess you're right."

"Don't worry," Jack said, "it may not have A/C, but when yer drivin' at speed, the wind can still be refreshin', even if it is a bit toasty. Do you know how to ride one?"

"I actually do," I said. "It's been a really long time, but, when I was a kid, I used to ride motocross."

"That'll make it easier, then!"

We moved to the motorcycle, and Jack had already placed two AR-15s and two handguns in the sidecar. He saw me looking them over.

"Ammo for the guns is in the bike's two saddlebags. Should be enough for any trouble you may come across."

"Hopefully, I won't have to use them."

"Better to have'em and not need'em, than to need'em and not have'em."

We threw my bags of supplies into the sidecar next to the guns, and I turned to Jack. He handed me the folded-up maps with the two paths highlighted; the faster option in yellow, and the safer option in green.

"Which path you takin'?" Jack asked.

"I'm going to go with the safer route," I said, a look of relief crossing Jack's expression. "Figure that if the highways in the cities are blocked with traffic, getting through those will probably take just as long. And I'd be under potential threat the whole time. Just not worth the extra two or three days it may save me."

Jack nodded, agreeing with my reasoning. Then, "Listen," Jack said, clearing his throat. "Gladys and I, um, talked about it last night. When you find yer family, we'd love it if you found yer way back here. If yer able to. We have everythin' that any of us would ever need, and we have more than enough of it. It's pretty clear that our family ain't gonna be able to get here, but I think you could. We could use you, and once you have yer family, I'm sure y'all could use this place. We'd love to have you back, Sean."

I was taken completely by surprise. Never in a million years would I have expected the couple to extend this offer. They were continuing to astonish.

"Thank you, Jack," I responded earnestly. "If I find my family—"

"When," Jack interrupted me. "When you find yer family."

"When I find my family, I'll take you up on that offer. Sincerely."

"We look forward to that day, Sean," Jack said. "And, if you can, try to bring the bike back to me." He winked.

"No promises," I smiled.

"Goodbye, Sean. Take care of yerself."

"You, too, Jack."

A few moments later, a large slab of the concrete wall at the far end of the garage lifted, revealing a long hill leading up to the surface. I watched in the side-view mirror as Jack waved me off, the slab of wall closing behind me as I passed under it and out onto the driveway. Just moments later, the orange sky of morning became visible. I hit the throttle, and the bike whizzed out of the opening onto a dirt road.

8

Friday, August 22nd –
Saturday, August 23rd

Riding through the barren desert, I was surrounded by incredible beauty, the likes of which I had never seen before. When driving through the landscape of what Jack had told me beforehand was called the Petrified Forest National Park, it felt like I was being enveloped by nature herself.

There were colors painted in the desert sands that should have been painting the Martian landscape, rather than Earth's. There were cliff sides and rock formations that stood in such precarious ways that they almost had to have been specifically, and purposefully, placed at very precise points. Even fossilized tree trunks dating back a hundred million years were periodically dotting the sands.

It was a breathtaking landscape that filled me with wonder, while at the same time exasperating the overwhelming crunch of loneliness that had slowly begun to wrap its fingers around me. Even though the landscape was wide open, its emptiness was claustrophobic, nothing around to squeeze in on me but nothingness itself. I would have given anything at that point for a landscape with a few more standing trees.

It was the first time I'd truly been alone since before the plane, and that wasteland made it evident that there was no one around to help me if something were to go wrong. If I were to crash the motorcycle and break my leg, there would be no one I could count on to either help me or put me out of my misery. Whatever happened, I was completely dependent on myself alone.

Before, even though I knew that Annie and Kim weren't going to be much help in a fight, they were better than nothing. Walking through the desert, we had each other. When I was coming back up the ravine from trying to get Charlie, they were there to pull me up. They helped carry me to safety, but that was completely gone. Any failure would be squarely on my shoulders, and on my shoulders alone.

At least I had weapons, food, water, and transportation, though. I couldn't help but wonder about poor Annie. It had been several days since we split up, and six days since she ran out of supplies. If she were still alive, her situation would be grim.

My stomach pretzeled with guilt as I went

up a small ravine, crossed over the park's main road, and continued on into the desert. I had an uprising of will to turn around and try to find her. If any of us deserved a desert death least, it was Annie. She didn't deserve to die of starvation or dehydration while being baked in the blazing sun. Annie, most of all of us from the plane, deserved to live, but nature was cruel.

I knew that, just like with Kim and Charlie before, there was nothing I could do. Even if I had started looking for her right after leaving Jack and Gladys's. I had no idea which way she'd gone, and she'd had such a head start, I'd never have found her. Her fate was out of my hands, so I did the only thing for her I felt was worth trying: I prayed for her.

For the next few hours, the drive was long and windy. It was a lot of slow-moving, making sure to not pop a tire on the uneven roads I'd occasionally be on or to not hit small cacti. There were ravines and washes that I had to maneuver around, and a number of surprisingly muddy areas where the bike nearly got stuck.

As the sun began to practically blind me on the horizon, I started keeping my eye out for a good place to camp. I was hoping to find either some outcropping of vegetation or a rock formation; something that could be used to hide from travelers, should any come by. All around, though, the wasteland of nothing but cactus, small vegetation, and dirt was holding strong.

After a short time, I descended into shadow as I rounded a corner into a canyon. The walls reached high into the sky, blocking the sun and dropping the temperature instantly. Not far into the canyon, an area of the incline on my right caught my eye. It was better than any outcropping of vegetation or rocks. It was a cave.

The incline to the cave's entrance was too steep for me to take the bike, so I'd have to leave it below. It was risky, but I stopped to check it out anyway. The wall wasn't too steep to climb, and the ground under feet was steady and firm.

The darkness of the cave in front of me seemed tangible. I could reach out and touch it, making it swim through the air like smoke on the breeze. It felt as if it were reaching out to touch me, chills going down my spine. It felt evil.

I shook off my paranoia and stepped into the cave. There was a lingering smell of firewood that seemed fresh, just a day or two old, and there was smoke still lingering in the air.

"Explains the tangible shadow," I told myself, still trying to hold back the thought that I'd walked into an evil place.

Walking another several paces into the cave, the objects in front of me were completely invisible until I made painful contact with them. When my head hit rock for the third time, I decided that it wasn't worth going in any further.

After retrieving my supplies from the bike,

I returned to the cave, making a fire just a few paces from the entrance. As it flicked and popped, I watched it create dancing shadows on the ceiling, letting myself fall into a trance. My mind completely shut off. It was a pleasant way to spend the hour before I fell off to sleep.

The sun woke me the next morning as it crested the far canyon wall and blared its warm, orange rays directly into the cave. I stood and stretched over my burnt-out fireplace, my back cracking slightly. Considering I had slept in a cave with tiny rocks poking into my back all night long, it was a surprisingly good night's sleep.

I turned toward the back of the cave, curious to see if the light streaming in would show just how deep it was, which wasn't nearly as deep as I had thought it would be. It looked like I had almost reached the back of it the night before.

Just in front of the back wall, which was lit with the golden orange of the morning, there was a small campfire that looked to be just a couple of days old. It must have been the source of the smoke I'd seen and smelled. Between me and the campfire, there was a boulder that was jutting into the flooring of the cave. There was something stretching out from the far side.

I took a step closer, adjusting my angle. A pair of shoes came into view. Then, legs. As I rounded the side of the boulder cautiously, I was greeted by a horrible sight.

Annie. It was Annie.

Her once youthful skin was beginning to rot away, and bugs had already begun to stake their claims to certain areas. Her eyes were open, but they were decaying fast. That smart, sweet young woman that once reminded me of my Clem now sat in front of me, imprinting a visual into my psyche that I would never forget.

It had taken me a day on a motorcycle to get to that cave, so it must have taken her two to three days at least. She'd somehow survived another three days on her own with no supplies. She must have crawled into that cave when she had lost all strength, knowing she'd never leave it. Based on her condition, I guessed she had been dead for several days.

"I'm sorry, Annie," I said.

I gave her a not-so-good requiem before turning and walking back to the front of the cave. Gathering my items together, I couldn't help but feel a bit dirty. Though I slept a good distance from her, the idea that I'd slept so close to a corpse was a bit unsettling. I tried to shake it off by remembering the music of Jack and Gladys's house, singing a bit of Johnny Cash quietly to myself.

Once riding again, the morning was unexciting, but I was getting the occasional image of Annie's rotted face along with a pang of guilt. I'd promised myself I'd do all I could to get her out, but I couldn't keep that promise. I broke that promise to myself, and the young woman that reminded me so much of my own daughter had died because of it.

Like with Kim and Charlie, I knew Annie hadn't really died because of me, because I broke that promise to myself. I knew that she had given up hope. I knew I couldn't burden myself with survivor's guilt. But somehow, Annie continued on for several more days after our split. Maybe her hope wasn't as diminished as I'd thought.

"Fly me to the moon!" I sang loudly, trying to excommunicate the survivor's guilt from my mind by switching to Frank Sinatra. "Let me play among the stars!" It worked.

By what felt like ten in the morning, the terrain began to change. Soon after, I was in what the map said was the Coconino National Forest. It was mountainous and full of trees and underbrush-I wanted trees, but trees I could still ride through.

Not far into the forest, I found myself riding on a tiny, one-lane road that looked out over a several-hundred feet drop straight to a rocky death on one side and a steep, mountainous incline on the other. The road, if it could even be called that, was more like a wide hiking trail, just barely large enough for both the bike and sidecar. Its surface was rocky and uneven, potholes everywhere and not a hint that it had ever been paved.

It wound around the mountain for a couple

of miles when it had another sharp turn. As I made the turn, my heart sank. Just after the corner, my tiny path had been blocked by a stalled side-by-side.

I rolled to a stop, in utter disbelief at my bad luck. Of all the places to come across a stalled vehicle, that was one of the only places on the whole trip that had to be clear, and this side-by-side vehicle was almost as wide as the entire path. There was no way my bike was getting passed it.

I checked for a set of keys and found them in the ignition. I tried turning the engine, but it wouldn't start. It was apparently another of the sun's victims, so I stepped back from it, trying to formulate a plan.

I decided to just try pushing it, so I gripped its steering wheel with one hand, steering the wheels toward the edge of the road, and firmly gripping the frame with the other. Then, with my feet dug into the dirt, I pushed with everything I had. It didn't budge an inch. It was completely locked.

I stepped back to catch my breath and regroup. After a few minutes, I decided to try rocking it off the edge. I walked up to it once again and propped my feet against the mountainous incline and gripped the top of the buggy's large frame. I pushed it rhythmically, trying to use the vehicle's inertia against it. It gave a bit, but as I put more of my weight into it, I could just not get the vehicle to a point of tipping. Finally, I gave up, sinking to the ground, breathing heavily.

Staring into the blue above, I lifted my hand and flipped off the sky.

There really was no way around that vehicle. I had to make a choice. Either I turned around and went through the cities, or I'd have to leave the bike behind with a good portion of supplies, and then hike this path all the way to the coast. That wasn't even a choice. Hiking could take months, and, even though the cities would probably be dangerous, I didn't have months.

I was able to get the bike turned around surprisingly easily, and after a short time, I found that trail-road widening. Once it hit the width of two full-sized trucks, it smoothed over to pavement. I followed it for several miles before it came to a four-lane highway. After checking the map, I turned right onto the entirely vacant road, coming to the top of a hill a moment later. From there, it was clear why the road had no stalled-out vehicles.

When the cars shorted out, they coasted. Apparently, the brakes shorted out, too, or something. Whatever it was, there was a pile of wrecked and charred vehicles at the bottom of the hill. There were dozens of vehicles. Trucks, big rigs, electric cars. It wasn't pretty.

As I passed it, I tried to keep my eyes straight ahead. With vehicles so torn, I had absolutely no desire to see what the effects on the occupants were. I'd already seen enough dead bodies for one lifetime.

Not long after, the scent of the air began to turn from fresh pine to a burnt ash. When the mountains faded away, it was obvious where the smell was coming from. The city of Phoenix sat in the valley below, a once strong testament to man's ability to appropriate even the harshest of environments.

That testament was on fire.

. . .

I was coming into the burning metropolis on the 87, heading straight for the heart of the city. The plan was to take the 87 to the 202, which would take me right through downtown. It'd connect to the 10 soon after, and it'd be a straight shot to Los Angeles from there.

I knew that it wasn't going to be nearly that simple. Just looking at the cityscape, I felt more like I was about to ride through an active war zone, rather than one of the biggest cities in the country; in a world with no lights, though, those were not diametrically opposed.

Cars were stalled all along the road, but they remained far enough apart that driving around them was easy. Most of the cars were empty, but one or two still had solitary occupants that had been dead so long they'd begun to lose any semblance of being human.

While still a few miles outside of Phoenix proper, the sprawling landscape of a twenty-first-century façade was already surrounding me. A set of McDonald's Golden Arches stretched high into the sky, a giant tease to all those around, a brutal reminder to the aching bellies looking upon it of a time that had now become history. Gas stations lay vacant; schools sat quiet; offices sat still. The city seemed dead. It was then that the first volley of gunshots rang out and carried their way over my engine's roar.

The pops of the weaponry were echoing from the underpass below me, flashes of light exploding out with each fire. They stopped as suddenly as they started, but they were just a sign of things to come.

Just a couple of miles from my turn-off onto the 202, there was another series of rapid rifle fire. It was quickly joined by the sound of a different make and caliber firing toward the original shots. More weapons joined in until it sounded like armies were battling one another. I passed as quickly as I could, and just when the gunshots seemed a safe distance away, a massive explosion ripped through the streets.

Turning my head to look back, the intersection where the battle had been occurring was just a rising ball of flame. Something had gone off in one of the corner buildings.

The 202 remained much of the same. The road was dotted with a few more vehicles, but it was still passable. Gunshots rang out all around, but no more explosions went off. There were screams, though, that were as equally terrifying to me as any blast.

As I rounded a corner that faced me directly towards the burning skyline of downtown Phoenix, the road was blocked. It wasn't blocked by vehicles that had gotten stuck or by some accident. There was a line of vehicles stretching from the median to the outer wall. It was a legitimate roadblock that had to have been set up by people.

I slowed the bike to a stop while still a great distance from the cars. The freeway around me was blocked in by walls, and I was in between exits. I looked behind me to gauge how far back the previous exit was, but as I did, a 1950s Chevy truck pulled up and parked itself in the middle of the previous ramp. I was blocked. My only hope was to go forward and hope that these people were here to protect a neighborhood. That was a completely naïve hope, I knew, but it was *something* to hope for. In great tragedies, locals have been known to take up weapons to protect their neighborhoods from looters, but that block wasn't in a neighborhood; it was on a freeway.

I made sure that I was prepared in case the people ahead of me weren't of Jack and Gladys's make. I emptied the entire first aid and medicine kit into my backpack. Several canisters of food and water followed, and one of Jack's handguns on top of those. I had the other handgun holstered, but a backup would have been nice to have. Finally, I squeezed one of the ARs into the backpack, butt down the side. With the zipper closed, the rifle's muzzle stuck out over my shoulder, but it fit.

I got back onto the bike and began slowly moving toward the roadblock ahead. One by one, several men opened the doors of their respective vehicles and walked toward me. They each carried weapons; shotguns, rifles, and handguns. Someone even had a bow and arrow. They were a band of Mad-Max cronies that looked more caricature than real.

I slowed the bike to another stop as one of the men took a few steps toward me. It was feeling eerily similar to the confrontation in the desert.

"Get off the bike," he yelled. "Turn around and walk away. That's all you need to do. Do it and live."

I turned the bike off and stood next to it. I was absolutely petrified, but I wasn't going to show them. I knew that weakness was not a trait that would help someone survive.

"Sounds good," I said. "But I'm not leaving my bike."

The man in front of me seemed a bit surprised by my defiance and my apparent lack of fear. I actually surprised myself, as well, at how confident and brave I'd sounded.

"See," the man said, "I'm being nice. My boys here weren't even fans of giving you a choice. So, I'm not going to offer this again."

I could remain defiant, I knew, and die right there. I could tell them to go fuck themselves, but I'd only end up dead. What good would that do? None. I'd be worthless to my family if I were dead. My bike was crucial, but not having it was not an immediate death sentence. Live today to experience tomorrow.

"Okay," I said, starting to walk away.

"Don't you take another fucking step!" another man yelled at me as he stepped forward from the backline. "Leave the backpack!"

I hesitated. I was already leaving a good number of supplies; to leave my backpack, too, would mean I would most likely be dead in a few days. I caught eyes with the man in front just as I felt a resolve pass through me. I reached for the gun in my waist and pulled it out. Every man but the two who had done the talking lifted their weapons directly at me.

I could feel my adrenaline red-lining, my hands shaking and my stomach turning into knots. What the fuck was I doing? Was I really about to fucking play chicken with these people? How dumb can you be? The response from the apparent leader was one I hadn't expected.

"Put your guns down," the man in front said.

"Take your backpack and go."

"Ben," the second man said, "Why are you letting him take supplies?"

The first man, Ben, turned toward the second and said, "Frank, I'm not killing anyone I don't have to."

"Good for you," Frank said, stepping a half step to the side and lifting his gun.

"Let me rephrase," Ben said, "*we* are not killing anyone we don't have to. We have enough supplies. We'll have what's valuable. Let him go, and let his death be on someone else. My conscious is heavy enough."

I slowly walked backward, keeping a watch on the growing confrontation in front of me. My hands were shaking more violently than ever, and I had to be careful not to pull the trigger by accident. The stare-down the pair was engaging in was far more than a game played in a cafeteria between school kids; this was Russian-fucking-roullette. The stare-down broke.

"No," Frank said, lifting his gun quickly.

Hell broke out in such a flash that Ben was dead on the ground with a hole in his head, and Frank had turned to me and fired before I even realized the first shot had gone off. I ducked the moment I knew what the hell had happened, unfortunately dropping my gun in the process. The men who had been united against me just moments before were now being forced to choose sides within their own banded militia.

My dad had told me a couple of times what it was like when he was in battle. He served in Afghanistan, and I never truly grasped the absolute terror. With the bullets audibly slicing through the air inches from my head, I understood.

I thought my heart was going to seize, its beats heavier and more forceful than ever. As the bullets splattered into the freeway and my bike, shrapnel flew in every direction. Pieces of metal and pavement cut through the air and embedded into my skin, creating tiny, painful lacerations. With every pop, the fear increased. Every single shatter of my surroundings could be my head next. Crouching behind my bike, I screamed, but the thunder of gunfire around me was so powerful that even I couldn't hear me.

My chest was continuing to grow heavier, and the adrenaline was beginning to cause chest pains to spread through me. I was trying to catch my breath, but it was impossible. Breathing in and out, my lungs begged for what could be their last taste of air. They were pleading with me, but I couldn't give them enough.

When the glass of the motorcycle's windshield shattered, showering me with tiny shards of glass and adding to my tiny cuts, I knew I couldn't stay there. I had to get off the freeway if I was going to survive. My fear, though, wouldn't allow my legs to get me anywhere. Instincts had kicked in, and with the bullets still flying, my instincts chose neither flight nor fight; they chose cower and hide.

I tried to psyche myself up, to make my move. The other side of the freeway had an exit I thought I may have been able to make a sprint for, but it was a long way, and all I could see was myself falling face-first onto the pavement with a hole in my back. Another bullet slammed into the concrete next to me.

I took in several gulps of air, repeating to myself to just run. Just run. I tried to think of my dad and how he must have been in situations somewhat similar. How would he have dealt with it? How would he feel to see his son cowering, afraid to take action?

Afraid or not, I couldn't wait any longer. I shook the shakiness out of my hands and jumped to my feet, beginning my sprint forward in the same motion.

As I reached the divider, at least one of the men noticed my movement. Bullets began to pop by, exploding into the concrete barrier in front of me, my fear almost winning out and dropping me to the ground.

"Oh, fuck! Oh, fuck! Oh, fuck!" I yelled as I reached the concrete divider and hurled myself over it.

I took a minute to try to collect and gain some semblance of control over myself. With the gunfire still erupting behind me, that wasn't going to happen. A break in the bullets hitting the divider gave me the window of opportunity I needed. I stood and ran faster than I'd ever run before, even having to slide across the hood of a car in the process, but the firing in my direction had stopped. Finally, I made it onto the exit and was blocked from the battle above.

Even though I was away from the gunfire, I was on the verge of a panic attack, and I still wasn't safe. Everywhere around me was a perfect vantage point for another ambush. Buildings, all several stories tall, lined the street for a few miles. Several buildings had flames breaking through what had once been windows, lapping high and trying to catch the floor above. Non-burning windows were broken out sporadically, any one of them making for a literal killer shot, but I had to get away from the freeway. I knelt and pulled the backpack around, my knees threatening to completely give out and my fingers shaking so violently it was hard to grasp anything. Making sure it was loaded, I pulled out the AR-15 and zipped the bag back up.

Backpack back on and weapon in my vibrating hand, I moved to the side of the street, keeping as close to the buildings as I could. My eyes kept watch on the windows across the street, my ears listening for the slightest hint of a threat. Besides the battle raging on the freeway behind me, all was silent.

Two blocks into the city, I began to more diligently look for a place that would be a good shelter for the night. There were only a few hours of daylight left, and it'd take at least a full day for me to get out of the city.

I crossed a vacant intersection, checking both directions for people. There was no one around, and the building on the corner, a bank, had a great view of the freeway and the city streets.

The lobby of the bank was a mess, and, seeing as how all of its ground-floor windows were smashed out, I wasn't surprised. There was glass, bullet casings, money, and blood everywhere. This building had seen something very tragic. No one was there, though, not even their corpses.

I made my way to the back of the bank, where a stairwell led up to the second- and third-floor offices. The second floor's hallway was as equally destroyed as the lobby. I hadn't planned to look for shelter on that floor, so it wasn't of any concern.

The third floor was likewise destroyed, with the doors to every office wide open. I stood at the top of the stairs, listening for the hint of a sound, rifle at the ready. After several moments, though, it became clear that I was alone in the building.

Taking a few minutes, I walked down the hall, closing a few of the doors at random intervals. I wanted the door to my office closed and locked, and if anyone came up there during the night and saw just one door closed, they may think there was a reason for it and get curious. Walking back to the very front of the hall, I entered the first office.

With the door closed behind me, I closed the blinds and lowered my backpack to the ground, the AR resting against the bag's side. I dropped my head as I let the stress fall away. I had the tiniest modicum of safety.

"Oi," a voice with an Australian accent said from a darkened corner of the room. "You staying here? Really? All these rooms, and you choose mine?"

I startled around, reaching for the AR. I found myself looking at a young aboriginal man with long hair pulled back into a bun. He didn't appear older than his early twenties, but the dirt and grime were adding at least half a decade to him. Underneath the dirt, it looked like his nose had stopped someone's fist. He had his hands up, feet pulled up to his chest, a sleeping bag wrapped around them.

"You don't need that, do you, mate?" the man said as he unrolled out of his sleeping bag. "Not going to hurt you, just wondering why the bloody hell you had to choose my room?"

"Room closest to the stairs seemed the least likely to be checked."

"My thoughts exactly," the Aussie responded.

"I guess that means that the thinking's flawed," I said, turning around to leave the room.

"Wait," the man urged, taking a few steps toward me. There was no hint of malice in his voice, only a desperate pleading. "Going to a different room, are you? Alright if I join, you reckon?"

I looked him over. He seemed unassuming, and he didn't seem to have any weapons. I nodded.

"Oi, thanks, mate!" he said excitedly. He grabbed his sleeping bag and rolled it up. He picked up a camera and camera bag and threw those around his neck, moving toward me.

"Where's the rest of your stuff?" I asked.

"This is it," he responded.

We headed to the far end of the hallway and entered the last office. It was facing the street I'd come in on, and I could see the remains of the roadblock on the freeway a couple of blocks away.

We locked the door behind us and closed the blinds again. He unraveled his sleeping bag and lay against the wall on the far side of the room. I pulled mine out and lay it on the far side of the desk so as to be blocked by the door.

Opening the Ziplock that contained my pepperoni-sandwich dinner, courtesy of Gladys, I heard the man's stomach growl from the other side of the room.

"Here," I said, tossing him the sandwich. I pulled out another and took a bite.

"Good on ya, mate!" the man said as he bit into it. "Oi, that's good!"

We ate quietly over the next few minutes, but he seemed in a talking mood, and I had some questions of my own.

"What's your name?" he asked.

"I'm Sean," I replied politely. "What about you?"

"Call me Ed."

"Nice to meet you, Ed," I said. "Where you from?"

"Brisbane. It's a city in Australia. I know you Yanks aren't good with geography." He broke out into a grin. "I'm just joshin' you, brew. I *am* from Brisbane, though. Wasn't joking about that. I worked for the BBC out of London. Was a photographer. Where you from?"

"Orlando. Is that why you're here in the U.S.? For the BBC?"

"Orlando? Mickey Mouse, yeah? Love that little bugger! But, yeah," he replied, turning to stare out the window into the darkening city. "I was in L.A. for the DNC. Was covering the President's nomination acceptance speech."

"Were you there when it happened?"

"Five meters from the President, brew. He was mid-speech." He trailed off a bit, and I wasn't sure if I should push for more, but the need to know how cities broke was strong. I had to push.

"What happened?"

"What do you mean?" he replied.

"Like what happened to L.A.? To Phoenix? Anywhere, for that matter. I was on a plane when everything went down. After the plane crashed, I was in the desert until today. I don't really know much."

"You were in a plane crash *and* you've been in the dezzy for two weeks, brew? How're you livin'?"

"I'll tell you mine if you tell me yours," I responded.

The man's eyes searched the ceiling with a vision unseeing of the popcorn. He searched his memory, playing the events over in his head, seeming to be unsure if he had the strength to relive them.

"It's a long story," he said.

"I've got time," I replied. I reached in my backpack and pulled out a pack of Reese's Peanut Butter Cups. I opened them, taking one for myself and tossing the other to Ed.

"Thanks," Ed said, a smile spreading across his face as he bit into the chocolate. "Never thought I'd have another one of these again."

"Hold on," I said. Moving to the desk, I opened a few of the drawers, but they were all empty. Holding up my index finger, I opened the door and hopped to the office across the hall. It had belonged to exactly the kind of person I'd hoped it would have. In one of the desk drawers was a half-filled bottle of vodka and two glasses.

"Never was much a fan of vodka," Ed said as I handed him a glass, "but this should be damn delightful. Good on ya."

"I don't really drink at all," I said, pouring myself a glass. "But, as Tom Cruise said in

Risky Business, 'Sometimes, you just have to say, "What the fuck?"'"

With our glasses filled, I pressed again.

"What happened, Ed?"

9

Thursday, August 7th – Saturday, August 23rd

The air of the Staples Center was charged. There were tens of thousands of people yelling and screaming, signs waving in the air. They each fed off one another, absorbing in the exaltations of joy and hope and giving them back in as equal a way as possible. They were each sharing the happiness and anticipation of the future.

Thousands of phones were lifted high, recording the scene, their tiny screens shining onto the faces of those oblivious to the coming catastrophe. They smiled as they live-streamed to their social media followers, still covering themselves with a filter, despite each having spent hours to look their best for the event. Above, the massive screens that the Lakers and Clippers used during their games were shining bright with catchphrases and images of the dancing crowd, casting an ever-changing rainbow of light onto the throng below.

Many in the crowd were also sporting cameras strapped to them. Broadcasting live and in real-time, these cameras were strapped to their chests and their heads. The cameras on the head were raised six inches to give a clearer picture of the stage. This setup allowed people from all over the world to experience the floor-level excitement through virtual reality, the feeds being broadcast through the ever-expanding metaverse. This meant that anyone, anywhere, was able to sign in and get a taste of what it actually felt like to be a part of the horde.

As the first speaker of the day came to the front of the stage, the room was afire with the passionate cries of "Four more years!" The speaker fed off it, giving and taking with the crowd in a duet that claimed they were going to bring about a brighter future.

The music that filled the surroundings as the first man left the stage reverberated through each person. It was the final chemical to the mixture, turning the scene into a full-on state of drunken political delirium. The chants of "Four more years" took over again, growing with the beat of the music. It was a return to nature, a hedonistic battle cry that had been adapted for the twenty-first century.

At the front of this mass of people, there was a small break before the front of the stage. Holding the crowd back was a small metal rail that had security placed behind it every few feet. Secret Service patrolled as the main source of security, though there were a few stadium security sticking out from time to time, their bright yellow jackets easy to spot. The Secret Service agents were keeping their eyes out on the crowd, scanning the entire arena for anything that would have struck them as unusual. They were the only ones in the building that seemed completely unaffected by the intoxicating atmosphere.

Nestled safely in the calm between crowd and stage, Ed held his camera to his eye, snapping a shot of the nearest Secret Service agent as he pressed his hand against the radio in his ear, sight penetrating the second floor of the stadium. Ed reached into his camera bag hung over his shoulder and swapped to a telephoto lens. He snapped a few shots in the direction the agent was looking, just in case something was there. Swapping back to his smaller lens, Ed turned to the crowd.

A dozen feet or so from the railing was a young boy that caught Ed's eye. The boy couldn't have been older than seven. He was sitting on his father's shoulders, smiling broadly and brightly, a balloon in the shape of the President's head tied around his wrist. After snapping a photo of the boy, Ed wiped away something that had landed on the lens.

"35mm film, Ed? What are you, still looking

for that Kodak moment?" a female photographer mocked as she passed by. She was snapping away on a digital camera and lens that Ed knew cost more than his car.

"Yeah, nah. 35mm's brilliant," Ed responded, pulling out a new 35mm film roll from his bag. "Oi, Lisa," he called after the female photographer. She turned as he continued, "How many awards have your photographs won, again?"

She raised her lip at him, flipping him off in the most aggressive of ways. Ed laughed at her as he pocketed the first roll and continued snapping.

Over the next several hours, speaker after speaker took the stage. Some fed deeper into that energy of animalistic passion, while others merely managed to survive it. All the while, the crowd never lost the taste of that stimulating air.

When the President was introduced, Ed thought the building may collapse. The roars and screams vibrated through the concrete and into his feet, causing Ed's toes to go numb. He tried to ignore it as best he could as he snapped away at his camera. The crowd went quiet, all focus being put onto the President as he began to speak. Ed turned and focused on him, hoping he could get just the right moment captured.

As the President reached the five-minute mark, the lights of the stadium flickered. The President had a moment of confusion pass over his face before his hand reached up to his chest. Just as his knees looked to be giving out, the entire stadium echoed with an excruciating reverberation in the speakers. The metallic click that followed shut everything off. It all happened in half a second, but it all played out in slow motion for Ed.

Though he couldn't see an inch in front of him, the sounds of growing confusion in the crowd told Ed they'd seen the President grab for his chest, too. It sounded like they were all trying to convince each other everything was okay, that soon the emergency lights would kick in, and they'd see the President standing on the stage, laughing it off.

Ed's gut was telling him that the emergency lights weren't coming on. He couldn't explain it, but it was just an overwhelming sensation, a force screaming at him to get out of there.

He closed his eyes and put every ounce of concentration toward remembering the layout of his surroundings. His concentration lapsed, though, as he couldn't help but chuckle at himself.

Why the hell did I close my eyes? It isn't like it really made any difference.

With a deep breath, he refocused his mind. What was around him? What was to his left? A trash can. It should be several steps—

"There it is," Ed whispered painfully as his shin slammed into the invisible trash can.

Limping ahead through the darkness, Ed made progress, and, eventually, he found himself creeping through the backstage area, but he was having a hard go of it. He hadn't stepped foot back there before, so he had no idea where anything was. He took one hit on his head that he was sure would cause blood to roll down his face at any minute.

Even in the dark of the backstage area, the growing tensions from the audience were palpable. Ed could feel it getting to him, too. His muscles were straining, and his stomach was starting to flip as his doubt grew. Panic was just in front of him, begging to be let in. It wanted to take full control, and the unknowns of the whole situation told him he should let it.

What the hell was happening? Was it some sort of basic power outage or was it something more? The President had looked to be collapsing to the ground. Was it an assassination attempt?

There were so many questions tossing around in Ed's mind that it was just as difficult to keep the panic at bay as it was to navigate the black.

Rounding a corner, he saw a woman holding up a lighter. It wasn't much, but it lit a three-feet radius in which he could see she was dressed professionally, high heels and notepad. There was a single Secret Service agent blocking the doors to the back hall and subsequent exit. The agent and woman were mid-argument.

"I'm from the New York Times, damn it!" she was yelling at the agent as Ed approached.

"I don't care where you work, ma'am, no one is getting through." Ed could see the Secret Service agent was young, not much older than 30. He was clean cut with a square jaw, muscles tense throughout.

"You can't do this!" she yelled back. "Freedom of the Press, you bug!"

"Do you think that name-calling will help your cause?" the Secret Service agent responded.

The female journalist seemed to be entirely done talking, though. She tried to force her way by the agent, elbowing his nose in the process. That did it for him. He threw her to the ground and began to put her in a zip tie. As she struggled, the lighter fell out of her hand, and the room went black again.

Ed acted on instinct. The Secret Service agent was preoccupied, so, if he was going to try, there was no better time. He felt around the ground for the lighter, taking only a moment before he had found it. He slammed through the doors the Secret Service agent had been protecting and into the hallway beyond, holding his camera close to his chest. The Secret Service agent didn't seem to notice or care, being too preoccupied with the hostile woman.

With the clanking of the closing doors, Ed flicked on the lighter and began running through the halls, following the periodic signs pointing toward the player and guest exits. Even with the lighter, though, it was a painstaking and time-consuming activity. There was not a hint of other light in those halls.

With the darkness all around and such a minimal window to the world of light, the feeling of claustrophobia began to grip at Ed's chest. He couldn't see the walls, but he could feel them. With every step that produced no way out, it felt like the space was growing smaller, tighter. His heart began to beat faster, thudding against his chest, screaming for Ed to get the hell out of there. As his pace was picking up, he felt the walls around him break. He was at an intersection.

Looking left, then right, Ed had no idea what he was looking at. Either direction was the same blackness as the other. There was no discernable difference.

He was going to go right. He didn't know why, but it felt like the right choice. As he took his first step, the blackness to his left lit up with a strange greenish light shining through an opening door. Much of the light was blocked by frantic silhouettes streaming through to the other side, but it was enough.

As the last person exited, the door shut behind them, and the hall went dark again. Ed wasn't far away and made it to the door with relative ease. No one was left guarding it, and, shockingly, it was left unlocked.

The garage Ed entered was lit by that same strange green light, which seemed to be streaming through the exit at the far end. It was off-putting, unnatural, adding to the chaos of the surrounding scene. There were people running back and forth, yelling and screaming at one another, each giving their own directions. There were several cars parked along a driveway, the solid black shapes of the Presidential motorcade, American flags flying from either side of the hoods.

Ed lifted his camera and snapped a few photos of the scene. He'd photographed some atrocious things, but the scene in front of him was one of the most terrifying for him. He was surrounded by the people who were supposed to be in charge. Each face belonged to someone with power, even the baby-faced interns that also seemed to be present. However, not a single one of them seemed to have the slightest clue as to what the hell was going on. They looked as confused and worried as everyone else.

"No press!" came a nearby voice.

Ed turned to see who had yelled at him, coming face to face with a brawny Secret Service agent whose expression bore no signs of levity.

"But this should—" Ed couldn't stop himself.

"What part of no fucking press did you not understand?"

"Wait, your camera works?" a female who had been walking by said as she stopped and turned to the two.

"I reckon it does," Ed said, confused by her sudden interest.

"The President is secured! Go!" Ed heard a voice yell. It was quickly followed by the screech of tires as the first car in the motorcade sped off.

"He's with me," the woman said to the agent after studying Ed for a moment. "Come on. Hurry up!"

She didn't wait for Ed, turning and hurriedly walking toward the line of vehicles. Ed ignored the nasty glare given to him by the agent as he jogged to catch up to the woman. He was just reaching her as she got into the last vehicle of the motorcade, and he followed her in. The door closed immediately after him, and the vehicle began moving. He felt a flash of shame as he realized he had just taken the last seat.

Pulling out of the garage and into the city, there was an audible gasp from the car's occupants. Every single light was off, but the city danced in color, reflections off the buildings onto one another filling Ed with a strange, underwater swimming sensation. The sky, what was visible through the darkened façade of downtown Los Angeles, was ablaze with the aurora borealis, the source of the strange green. No one had expected it. It was beautiful, but it just added to Ed's skepticism and worry.

The streets were dotted with cars, stalled and unable to restart. The vehicles' occupants had already begun leaving the roadways, but when they saw the motorcade drive by, there were calls and shouts. The freeway was no better.

The heavy traffic of early evening blocked much of the roadway, but most of the occupants had already begun making their way down the nearest exit ramps. Again, though, there were the occasional shouts coming from the crowds as the motorcade sped down the inner shoulder.

As they drove closer toward the airport, it had become obvious that the outage was at least city-wide. The only light was coming from the aurora above, which stretched across the sky in every direction, and not even their cellphones would turn on.

Deciding that the woman who invited him to come may have some answers, Ed pulled his attention away from the scenes outside and turned to her. She was in her mid-fifties, and Ed recognized her from somewhere. He couldn't place her, but he knew that she was someone important in the President's administration.

"I'm Ed," he said, holding his hand out to her.

"I know who you are," she said, shaking his hand. "The work you did during the Indonesian Uprising was quite impressive. Very moving. You're with the BBC now, if I'm not mistaken."

"Yes, ma'am," Ed replied.

"Impressive for someone so young. I'm Corinne May, Chief of Staff to the President."

"I knew I recognized you. It's a pleasure."

"Likewise."

"If you don't mind me asking, ma'am, what the hell is going on?"

She studied him in the light of the aurora before finally saying, "I don't know."

Well, that wasn't reassuring.

"What about the President? What happened? You reckon he's alright?" Again, she studied him for a moment before replying.

"I don't know, but we all will soon. He should be on the plane when we get there."

"Why me, ma'am? Why'd you bring me along?"

"You're a good photographer, and the President's official photographer no longer had any working cameras. You came in at the right place, right time. Congratulations."

Corinne turned her head to look out the opposite window, and Ed knew better than to ask any other questions. Instead, he turned to stare out his own window, letting his mind fill with questions and possibilities.

Why had the President collapsed just as the lights went out? Why in the hell was there an aurora in Los Angeles? Why were the motorcade vehicles working, but no other vehicles were? What the every-loving-fuck was going on?

The movement of the light outside, the roar of the car's tires on the shoulder's rumble strip, and the motion of the vehicle put a spell over Ed. He fell into a daze, shock of the growingly traumatic incident taking hold. His mind couldn't process any more thoughts. His limbs wouldn't move. He was just a corporeal form taking up the seat, his mind giving a big 'Fuck that' to the circumstance and shutting off. Before he knew it, the car was slowing, and his trance broke, revealing that they had made their way onto the runway of LAX.

There were several darkened shapes of planes that sat scattered around the airport, baggage carts and other employee transportation vehicles joining them. But amongst the shapes lit only from the glowing particles above, one stood out from the rest. It wasn't dark. Instead, each of the windows along the fuselage was lit from within. Even from a distance, Ed could see the shapes of people darting about inside.

Soon, he found himself one of those shapes, foggily being pushed into a seat and told to buckle in. The sounds around him were far off, dulled and muted. The colors around him had faded, while his eyes were realizing for the first time just how bright artificial light really was. As the people running past him each found their seats, the plane left the darkened airport behind.

Within moments of reaching cruising altitude, Corinne appeared at Ed's side.

"Come with me," she said.

She led Ed to a conference room where there were already a handful of other people. Unlike Ed, though, who was dressed in a 'The Ramones' shirt and jeans, these people were all officially dressed. Ed suspected that, like Corinne, each of these people held rather powerful positions.

The clothing couldn't hide their worry and fear. What looked to be a General, or some sort of high-ranking military official, sat at the conference table with his head in his hands. A woman on the far side of the room sat with a gaze a thousand-yards vacant. Her eyes were bloodshot and tears had streaked her mascara.

"Take a seat, Ed," Corinne said, indicating one of the chairs.

Looking up at the sound of Corinne's voice, the General said, "Who the hell is he? Why is he here?"

"His name is Ed, and he is here for documentation," Corinne said in a voice indicating her decision was final. She moved to the front of the room and turned to address the occupants. "I'm sure you're all wondering what is going on. I wish I had good news to tell you. I've just been informed by... well..."

She paused, having trouble finding the words. Pulling up a chair, she sat and rested her head back, a sense of pure exasperation.

"Get the fuck on with it," the General said, voice shaky and tense.

"The President is dead. The doctors just told me something... something happened with his pacemaker, and he had a heart attack. He was dead before he even got on the plane."

You could have cut the air in the room with a knife. The woman whose gaze had been distant broke out into tears, further dispersing her mascara across her cheeks. They had all feared the worst, and the worst had just been confirmed.

"We were able to get into contact with NORAD. The Vice President, as I'm sure you all know, is on one of the Navy ships in the Pacific. There has been no contact with them as of now. We'll keep you updated if that changes, but, for the time being, the Speaker of the House will be assuming the position. Madame Speaker?" Corinne said, turning to face an elderly woman with too-tight skin and beady eyes. She'd been so sunken into the back corner of the room that Ed hadn't even noticed her before.

The Speaker of the House stood up on weakened knees, and, over the next several minutes, she was sworn in as the acting President of the United States, Ed being tasked with photographing the process. When they were finished, Corinne took her spot at the front of the conference table again.

"Now, Madame President, I'm sure you are wondering what the hell is going on. Well, most of our satellites are offline and unreachable. However, we do have a weak signal coming in now from the White House." As Corinne continued speaking, the wooden wall behind her opened to reveal a screen. "I'm sure you all have met Dr. Steve Szalinski. He is joining us to tell us what he has already told those at NORAD."

The screen behind her lit up. It was broadcasting mostly static, but the image breaking through was of an equally shock-stricken man.

"Thank you, Corinne," Dr. Szalinsky said, his voice managing to come through much clearer than the picture. "I'm not sure how long the signal will make it through, so I will try to get you everything you need to know as quickly as possible. Two days ago, scientists at NASA had registered a massive solar eruption. This eruption, known as a Coronal Mass Ejection, more colloquially known as a solar flare, was massive. One of the biggest that we think the sun has ever produced. It was pointed directly at Earth. This has happened before, though at a fraction of the scale. There was an event in the 1850s called the Carrington Event. It was strong enough that it lit telegram wires on fire. That was nothing compared to this event.

"'So, what does that mean for us? What does that mean for today' you may be asking yourself. Well, simply, it means exactly what you have already begun to surmise from the things you have seen and experienced in the last two hours. A storm the size of the one we witnessed was powerful enough that it obliterated any satellites exposed to it. The sun's electrified particles were so incredibly charged and abundant that, upon hitting the atmosphere, they essentially created a worldwide EMP.

"I could get more in-depth about the scientific terms, but we'll save that for another time. What you need to know for now is that the United States is not alone. This seems to be global. A few of our satellites that were in such positions behind the Earth as to avoid fatal damage have allowed us to communicate with a number of other nations. No matter where, though, the news has not been good.

"So far, we've found through connections in Brazil and Chile that the entirety of South America is dark. Japan has reported that Asia has been very hard hit. We don't have confirmation on China, but, based on the situations in the areas around it, we suspect China to be down.

"The U.S. Ambassador in Moscow managed to get through to his counterpart in Japan. Russia seems to have been ground zero. There were reports coming to the Ambassador that thousands of square miles of land in Siberia were burning. Just spontaneously combusted. Those are just hearsay reports, though, relayed to us through many connections. We aren't sure how reliable those are, but, based on some initial data, it does look that Russia is taking the brunt of it. It's... It's not good. Plain and simple, we in the U.S. got very lucky."

"It doesn't sound too goddamned lucky," the woman with bleeding mascara said.

"If we had taken the same hit Russia did, the entire middle of the country would be on fire. From northern Texas to the southern tips of the Great Lakes; from the Smokies to the Rockies. It would all be on fire. Tens of millions of people would have died in an instant. As it stands, we think it hit a relatively unpopulated portion of Siberia. So, yes, *Press Secretary*, we got very lucky." He put a patronizing emphasis on her title.

"If that's what Russia is seeing, based on your data and projections, what should we expect?" the General asked.

"Well, we believe that the force has fried pretty much the entire electrical grid. We should expect that the power is out across the entire planet."

"How long will that take to get back up?" the new President asked. She was doing surprisingly well at trying to hide her terror, Ed thought, but he could still see it behind the beady eyes.

"Well, there is no way to know for sure—"

"Give us a timeframe, an estimate," the General interrupted.

"Well, based on the supplies and parts that would be needed, the process of making those supplies and parts, the process of transporting those supplies and parts, and, finally, the actual fixing of the equipment, we have a rough estimate of… eight years."

The room was silent for a long moment.

"Eight fucking years?" the General said, shock and disbelief obvious.

"Yes, General. And that's an optimistic number. Some believe that the timeframe would actually take... well, General, frankly, many of my colleagues have already expressed to me their fears that there will be no coming back."

"What, Dr. Szalinsky, is your opinion on the matter?" the President asked.

Even with the interference fuzzing through the screen, Ed could make out the sorrow in Dr. Szalinsky's body language.

"Madame President, I believe that it will be generations before we come back, and that's if. For the immediate future, you will still have a few relics of our old life that will still be operable, and these will last for a while; however, as food and water become more difficult to get, the time and effort used to keep those pieces of machinery working will just not be feasible. Within days and weeks, people will be starving. There will be weather-related deaths; people who are unable to get needed medical supplies; refrigeration will be a memory. It won't take long for people to begin to do whatever it takes to survive.

"Because everyone will be so focused on just surviving, on finding the most basic of calorie sources, the idea of gathering enough people to build the parts we need before civilization breaks is asinine. We will cross a point of no return sooner than many of my colleagues believe. I hate to be a doomsayer, but a complete and irrevocable societal collapse, before we are able to bring the grid back online, is nearly guaranteed in my eyes. With that collapse, we are not coming back. I'm sorry, Madame President."

"Why is it that Air Force One works? Our motorcade?" Corinne asked.

"There were precautions put in place on many government assets that would protect against an EMP. Not everything, but some of the more important assets. Anything and everything else that relies on computers and electricity, I assure you, is dead. Air conditioning systems, refrigeration, the banking system, almost every piece of modern medical equipment. None of it will work.

"The luxuries of technology that we have all grown accustomed to will cease to exist, *have* ceased to exist. With the way society has lived over the past several generations, the ability to survive without those luxuries is going to be one put to the test very soon.

"We believe the residents of Phoenix, Las Vegas, Los Angeles, and San Diego will see water shortages within two weeks, and it may even be as quickly as a few days. The situations will be made all the direr due to the intense heat the people of those cities will have to endure, especially Vegas and Phoenix as both cities had recent weather reports predicting near one-hundred-degree temperatures over the coming weeks. Unless the people leave those cities, we believe it is inevitable at least half of their populations will be dead within the month."

"My God," the General said.

"There has never been a time for mankind where prayer was needed more, General," Dr. Szalinsky said. "And I'm not even religious, but mankind could use all the help it can get. Are there any other questions?"

"You said that NASA knew about this two days ago. Why wasn't anyone notified?" The General had a definite tone of anger.

"They were," Dr. Szalinsky responded. "NASA reached out to the President as soon as they got the reports, but they never heard back from him."

The room sat silent for a moment before the General turned to Corinne with a look of pure accusation. "That's something you'd have known about then, Corinne. You'd have seen that come across his desk. Why wasn't anything done?"

"We never got that message. With the Convention, many messages were lost or delayed in making their way to the President."

"Great! Well as long as the President's precious convention was given the proper attention!"

"We never got the message, General. I'm sorry. Believe me, I am sorry. We never got it." She looked so defeated, the General didn't pursue it any further.

"Excuse me," Ed spoke up cautiously after a long, quiet moment. He'd tried to remain quiet, to just keep snapping away at the camera, but he figured this may be his only chance to know. Corinne was giving him a deathly glare.

"Yes?" Dr. Szalinsky said, obviously unsure as to who Ed was.

"Have you heard anything about Australia?"

"Our contacts in Japan mentioned that they connected to an Australian ship. One of their crew had connected with his wife in Sydney, and that city, at least, is dark. We don't know about the rest of the country, but, based on the surrounding areas we do know about, we suspect Australia's situation to be similar to ours."

It was strange. Ed had absolutely no ties left to Australia, but he felt a sudden wash of sadness. It was unexplainable to him, but it was an instant longing to get back to a place he now knew he'd probably never see again.

"Thank you," Ed said cordially before slipping behind his camera once again.

"Well, if there are no other quest—"

The screen was taken over by interference, and Dr. Szalinsky disappeared behind a sea of black-and-white shapes. The room's lights dimmed, and a red light began flashing.

"This is Captain Wilson. Please take your seats immediately." The captain's voice was stern and strong, a dash of worry thrown on top for good measure. There were breaks of interference cutting through the overhead, too, his words coming in more garbled.

"We are making an emerg—landing—Sky Harbor International Airport. Please take your seats and prepare for rapid descent."

And with that, the Captain's voice cut out. Hurriedly, but in a surprisingly cool-headed fashion, the room emptied. Before Ed could get fully strapped back into his seat, though, the plane's nose tilted sharply down, throwing him forward. Using the chair in front of him to keep pushed back, Ed managed to get the buckle clasped. He clenched his eyes tightly, his ears popping constantly as the plane lost altitude.

The pressure in the gut as the plane leveled out was nauseating, and as the brakes were thrown on in full, Ed felt like he was going to go flying out of his seat. The relief he felt as the plane came to a stop on the solid ground was so complete that he let out a huge breath of air he'd inadvertently been holding. With the sudden release of old air and the addition of new, Ed's stomach erupted. He just barely managed to find a puke bag before he lost his dinner.

The passengers remained reasonably calm, beginning to mull around the now-darkened cabin, but when the pilots were seen moving to the cabin door, releasing it, and sliding down the emergency exit slide, people couldn't keep it together. Many followed the pilots, leaving the plane behind. Ed couldn't think of a reason to leave the comfort and relative safety of Air Force One, though. Why would they leave, especially the pilots?

When he found Corinne, her defeat was clear, skin seeming to droop off her bones.

"The plane is dead. Air Force One is dead," she told Ed.

"What? What do you mean?"

"I mean exactly that. It's dead. It won't work again. We're grounded."

Ed couldn't believe his ears. The most fortified airplane on the planet was dead? Just like that?

"It's beyond my understanding, but something to do with constant exposure. The pilots didn't really stop to explain it."

"But why did they leave?" Ed asked, still unable to fully comprehend.

"Who knows? Maybe they deduced what's going on. We do have... a facade of a plan. We are going to walk to NORAD. You're welcome to come with us, but if you'd like to go your own way, then I thank you, and just request your roll of film."

"The film is ruined," Ed said immediately. The thought hadn't even registered in his mind before he spoke it, but he wasn't going to give up his film because of three shots. No. It didn't matter that he may never get it developed; it was his last role that documented the way of life the world would probably never see again. He was not giving that up.

"Excuse me?" Corinne replied, not bothering to hide her doubt.

"When the plane leveled out, my camera hit the armrest and popped open. It exposed the roll. I've already thrown it out. I reckon it's still in the trash can."

She eyed him disbelievingly.

"Whatever. It doesn't matter. We'll never make it to NORAD. Most of the people on this plane have never even been camping. The invitation to come is still available, but if I had the choice, I wouldn't come."

It was an honest assessment that Ed had not been expecting. It was so honest, in fact, that he found it hard to believe, like it was some sort of reverse psychology. The expression on Corinne's face and her droopy skin, eyes glazed over from hopelessness, told Ed it wasn't reverse psychology.

"Thank you," Ed said graciously. "I thank you for bringing me. Good luck."

With that, Ed turned and walked out into the cabin of the plane again, and as the door behind him closed, a single gunshot rang out from within. Even though he flinched, Ed didn't open the door to check what had happened. He knew. Instead, he passed the people now running toward the room and Corinne's body, making his way to the opened cabin door. Taking firm hold of his camera and bag, Ed leaped from the plane, onto the yellow emergency shoot, and slid to the solid pavement.

Glancing one more time at the plane, Ed turned to the skyline in front of him and started walking toward it. The signs at the terminal indicated the city was Phoenix. That would explain the heat.

Moving away from the airport, Ed knew he needed to find shelter. That was going to be his first point of order, but he also needed to work up a plan for what his steps would be after. As he searched for a place he felt would be a good spot to hunker down in, Ed began to toss around what his ultimate goal would be. One side of him was urging him to put aside his human instincts and just document the downfall that was about to occur; the other side of him was urging him to find supplies and/or get the hell out of the city.

As he approached a hotel high-rise in the downtown area, Ed made the decision to gather supplies enough for two weeks and stay in the city for one. After that, he'd head for somewhere else. Where, he didn't know yet, but he wouldn't stay in the city longer than a week. When he entered the hotel, there were a number of people standing at the desk and arguing with a young woman behind it.

"I'm sorry," the clerk was trying to tell everyone. "I'm sorry, but without power, I can't take any new guests."

The crowd didn't seem to like this news, but

when the clerk pulled out a gun from under the counter, the people hurriedly left. Ed, however, stayed in the lobby. The clerk noticed and turned the gun on him.

"Like I said," the clerk said over the barrel, "We are closed. Kindly leave."

"I'm sorry, ma'am, but I can't do that. I do understand that you aren't really able to check anyone in. However, I'd like to make a trade."

"This is a Hampton Inn, sir. We don't barter and trade."

"Hampton Inn won't exist soon, and I reckon you will be bartering and trading in not too short of time."

This caught the woman off-guard. "What do you mean?" she asked, her fortitude with the weapon waning slightly.

"That would be part of what I have to trade," Ed said. "I've got information. I work—well, worked—for the BBC. I was at the DNC earlier tonight. Trust me, what I have to tell you could save you and your family's lives." Ed handed her his press credential.

After eyeing it over, she handed it back, lowering her gun in the process.

"What do you want for this information?" she asked suspiciously.

"Just a room. That's all. I just want a room for one week." The clerk thought it over for a while before agreeing.

Several minutes later, Ed left the shocked and

silently crying clerk in the lobby, heading for his room. He made his way up the stairs to the third floor. He unlocked his door using a regular key as the card system was down, and just moments later, Ed was asleep.

Over the next few days, Ed traveled further and further out from the hotel, gathering spare supplies and snapping photos of the things he was seeing. He'd tried to use his information to trade with a grocer for some supplies, but the grocer had turned him down. As Ed turned and walked away, he felt a respect for the man that was willing to risk all for what he'd built. He felt a sadness more, though, that came with knowing the man would soon have no say in the matter.

On his fifth day of walking the streets, Ed passed by the same grocery store. The same owner was outside, armed with a shotgun and arguing with a growing group of people.

Slowly, Ed crossed the street, camera raised toward the scene. He snapped a few photos as the first brick was thrown at a window. People were getting desperate with thirst and hunger. Hundred-degree temperatures and no air conditioning were beginning to cause catastrophic impacts on people. Judging by the smell on his hotel floor, several people had already died. He was not surprised to see the bricks now being thrown; he was just surprised it took so long.

The shop owner fired his gun into the crowd

of people. It knocked a man to the ground, but it just made the crowd ten times more violent. A perfectly placed brick smashed the shop owner's face. He collapsed back into the crowd, and Ed was certain the man was dead.

The crowd immediately turned to the store and broke out the rest of the windows, flooding in like a river breaking a dam. Ed followed the crowd for a while, snapping a photo of the dead shop owner as he passed him by. A moment he wasn't entirely proud of.

Inside, the worst kind of chaos. Ed snapped photos of the people surrounding him, reverting to their wild nature, but he knew he had to join in. He needed supplies, and that store still had some. If he was going to live, he had to loot.

After loading up a cart with enough supplies to last him a month, Ed looked around. The store was now host to dozens and dozens of people, more flooding in by the moment. Ed wanted more stuff, but he knew that if he took more time, the people would see empty shelves and come after people like him, those with full carts. It was time to go.

Scurrying through the crowd and out of the shop, Ed pushed his cart as fast as he could the mile and a half back to the hotel. He breathed a sigh of relief when he reached his room without another incident.

Supplies stashed, Ed locked his door and listened out of his window as the sounds from the first of many gun battles bounced through the streets. He stayed in the room for the next several days, rationing his food and waiting for the gunshots to slow down. When they did, he was going to take what he could and head toward the mountains. On the fifteenth day in a world without lights, though, the gun battles were still popping off, and things went south.

Ed was awoken in the predawn hours by the sound of the door to the neighboring room being smashed in. Voices were carrying through the walls.

"Is it full?" One voice called.

"Yeah," another responded. "Drinks and food!"

"Good! Grab it, and let's move on to the next!" The first voice said.

There was a knocking on Ed's door. Ed didn't answer. Another set of knocks was followed by the first voice.

"Anyone in this room? Room service?"

"Oi, mate. It's occupied," Ed called through the door. There was some rustling outside, and he could hear the two people whispering at one another.

"We're just coming around," the second voice said, "checking on the mini-bars! The hotel manager sent us to make sure everyone has what they need!"

"Yeah, nah, I'm good, brew," Ed replied.

The voices were replaced by a single shot,

which obliterated the handle to the room's door. Ed startled back in his chair, instinctively protecting, of all things, his camera.

The pair, two middle-aged men that were in desperate need of a shower, shave, and diet, walked into the room and stopped short. They could not take their eyes off the two packets of unopened bottled water and the stacks of canned food.

Without reasoning or explanation, the older and larger of the two walked toward Ed.

"Take want ya, brew! No reason to chuck a wobbly!" The man punched Ed hard.

Again and again, the men took turns whaling on Ed. They beat him until he was left in just a pile of blood, nose beaten to a pulp, eyes swelling. He lost consciousness as the thieves began to push the shopping cart out of his room, laughing as they did.

When Ed came to, his face had dried, and his room was empty. All of his supplies were gone, though they did leave his camera and gear. After gauging his situation, Ed resolutely decided that it was time to leave the city.

Limping, Ed spent the next day dodging random gunfire erupting from intersections and buildings all around. By midafternoon, he'd made it a short distance, but his leg could carry him no further. Looking from building to building, he found a bank that would be a good option for the night.

Adjusting the sleeping bag he'd found under an overpass, Ed limped across the street and up the stairs to the third floor. Once curled up in the corner of the first office, Ed closed his eyes, trying to put the pain out of his mind and drift to sleep.

Suddenly, there was a noise in the hall that called Ed back. He opened his eyes but didn't dare move as the shape of a person walked down the hall. Ed couldn't see from his perspective what the person was doing, but it sounded like they were closing random doors. Going through the rooms, maybe?

A few moments later, the figure, a man that looked to be mid-thirties, entered the room and began getting comfortable.

As Ed watched on from his hiding place, the man didn't seem to be of any danger. In fact, Ed had a warmth begin to spread across him. With the warmth, an overwhelming calmness filled him when looking at the man, so he spoke.

"Oi, you stayin' here? Really? All these rooms, and you choose mine?" Ed said to the startled Sean.

10
Sunday, August 24th

After I told Ed my own story, the night began to fill with sporadic gunfights that ranged from several miles away to just around the corner. I laid there for hours, staring up at the popcorn ceiling, trying to ignore the gunshots and focusing on Ed's story. What Ed had told me confirmed every one of my worst nightmares. It was the absolute worst possible of possibilities.

I had almost gotten all of my stuff ready to go in the morning before Ed woke up. I was hoping to make it out while he still slept. It wasn't that I found him unpleasant, but traveling alone would be faster.

"Oi, where you off to?" Ed asked, rubbing his eyes.

"I have to get moving," I replied. "I've still got a long way to go and trying to go anywhere at midday is going to be impossible."

"Give me a tick, and I'll come with you," Ed said, throwing back his sleeping bag, his leg apparently feeling much better.

"What?" I asked. "You'll come with me?"

"For sure," he said. "If you don't mind, anyway."

"Why would you want to come with me, Ed? I'm going west; you're going north. Trust me, you want to stay out of the desert as much as possible. Go north, Ed. Go to the mountains."

He stood and began rolling up his sleeping bag, saying, "I thought about it last night. You know, in between the gun battles that were scaring the shit out of me. I'm a photographer. My job is to document things, and the story you told me last night is worth documenting."

"Wouldn't what's happening here be better to document?" I asked. "Snapping photos of me just walking and walking? That doesn't sound too exciting."

"It's the story that goes with the picture, mate," Ed replied. "Plus, I reckon you'd be an easy target for people if you travel alone. Having two people may be safer."

I had no clue if it was a good idea. He could have just been luring me into a trap. He could have been a crazy person just waiting to murder me with an ax he'd hidden in a different room. He could have been awful, but he'd had every chance to kill or rob me while I slept through the night, and he didn't. Yes, traveling alone may be quicker, but he made a good point. Traveling in numbers was sure to be safer than traveling solo.

"Alright," I said. "Let's get going. I'd like to be

outside of the downtown area by nightfall."

"We can do that," he replied. His sleeping bag had two straps, which he put over his shoulders. He shouldered his camera and its bag and was ready to go.

I took my backpack off. I couldn't believe what I was about to do, but I felt that warmth flow through me again, like it was telling me this was the right thing to do. Placing my bag on the ground, I pulled out the handgun and holster inside. I held it out to Ed.

"Don't make me regret giving this to you."

"I won't," he said, taking it and putting the holster on his waistband.

I pulled out the AR, zipped my bag back, and we walked into the hall. We'd only reached the landing at the top of the first floor when we heard terrified voices.

The doors to the bank slammed open, and a family came running inside. They kept low, crouching below the window frames. Sliding to what they hoped was safety, they all ducked behind the counter as Ed and I watched cautiously from the stairs, our position hidden by the railing.

The family was young. The mother and father both looked like they were in their early thirties at the oldest, not much younger than me. Their kids were also young. The boy, looking confused at what was happening, was no older than three, and the girl, muddy face stricken with lines of dried tears, was no older than five.

The family kept low, but the father chanced a glance over the counter. As he did, the door to the bank swung open again, and a man that I recognized as Frank walked into the lobby. Behind him, a stream of eight other men walked in. I recognized some; others, I didn't.

My view was partially blocked by a wooden railing post, so as Frank walked into the room, I lost sight of him. When he came back into view, his eyes were locked on the customer side of the counter, right at the section the family was hiding behind. He looked at his followers and pointed.

Several of the men moved to the end of the counter. They were just a dozen feet away from Ed and me, but they were so focused on the family that they didn't have the tiniest of clues they were being watched.

The family saw the men. The daughter began screaming, while the mother tried to hold both of her children closely. The father, showcasing a bravery that I found incredibly admirable, stood, and moved in front of his family, offering any protection he could. He was not much protection.

The first man to reach the family dodged a limp-wristed punch from the father, who had evidently never been in a physical altercation in his life. The man answered with his own punch; one that instantly shattered the father's nose and sent him careening to the ground. The man then reached down and grabbed the screaming mother. Ripping the boy from her arms, the man threw him to one of his friends. The boy didn't make a sound, though his face was filled with terror.

The man then ripped the daughter from her mother's arms. The daughter, being slightly older, fought back. She was kicking and screaming against the man, spitting in his face. The mother tried her best to free her daughter, too, but a kick to her stomach sent her to the ground next to her bloodied husband.

The two men now carrying the children moved over to Frank and held the kids up.

"Good," Frank said. "Take them outside and tie them up. Don't hurt them! The meat won't be as good bruised."

"We have to do something," Ed whispered from beside me, watching on in abject horror.

"What can we do?" I asked. "We're outnumbered and outgunned. We'd be dead in half a minute. If that. We just have to sit here and be quiet. This isn't our battle to fight."

Ed nodded reluctantly.

I hated myself for those words. I had advocated for sitting there and letting that innocent family go through what they were about to, but I was beginning to grow callous to the feelings of guilt from turning my back on those in need. Charlie, Kim, Annie. Now, I could add this family to the list of people I'd let die for my own survival.

The mother and father were lifted to their feet by the remaining men and were dragged into the main lobby, being thrown recklessly at Frank's feet.

Looking the mother up and down, he said, "My, oh, my. What a peach. How old are you, beautiful? 30? 31?"

He waited for a response, but the mother just cried silently.

Turning to the husband, Frank asked, "How did some little pussy-ass faggot like you get a sexy piece of meat like her? You worth a lot of money or something? Big dick? Nah, that ain't it. Must be the money."

"I'm not going to listen to this," Ed said softly, his skin turning a soft shade of green. He stayed crouched as he turned up the stairs and began slowly making his way back to the third floor.

I took one last look at the family. They were just feet away, but, no matter what I did, nothing would stop what was coming. My arms and legs went limp for a moment, head hanging low. The ever-growing hole in my gut continued to grow through the quick prayer I uttered for the family, and that growth hadn't changed a few minutes later as I took a seat next to Ed in the office we'd slept in.

We couldn't hear a sound, and though I was utterly thankful for that, the mind's imagination can be far, far worse than reality. Mine was working overtime, running through scenarios ranging from just bad to flat-out inhuman. None of them were pleasant. I'd gone through three and a half decades without realizing the horrors that the mind can imagine. I wish I'd never have found out. Luckily, the burn from the vodka gave me something else to focus on.

After the first drink, my helplessness finally began to fade, and my imagination got less graphic. The remorse that took its place, however, was excruciating. It wasn't just the remorse from leaving the family; it was all of it. My hands shook at the memory of Charlie begging me to save him; my brow turned damp with sweat as the sound of the rock against Kim's skull crashed through my mind; my muscles twitched sporadically at the image of Annie, so similar to Clementine, sitting as nothing but a hunched-over silhouette in the desert night as I abandoned her. My stomach was twisting, my heart fluttering in an uncomfortable manner. I wanted to scream, to beg for forgiveness for my own mistakes, for the lives I turned my back on.

The restraint to keep from letting that scream out wasn't easy, so in hopes of gaining some control, I poured another drink and downed it quickly. Feeling the burn, I couldn't help but feel thankful for the remorse; I was glad I wasn't as calloused to it as I had thought.

The sound of an agonizing scream tore

through the silent, heavy air, rescuing us from our thoughts.

"That motherfuckin' cunt bit my dick off! She bit my fucking dick off! Holy—" The man was silenced as a gunshot rang out.

The mother screamed as another gunshot went off. A moment later, she was silenced by a third, and final, gunshot.

After waiting several minutes and hearing no other sound or movement, Ed and I began slowly making our way back to the staircase. We both were trying to mentally prepare for what we were to see. Which one of our horrible scenarios would be the one that greeted us? Neither of us wanted to find out, but we had to.

Just in front of the counter, right where he had been before, the young father lay broken and bloody-faced, a single bullet hole penetrating his forehead. His face was as streaked with tears as his daughter's had been. His eyes were wide open, his gaze staring directly at his wife.

The mother was a mess. I pitied her so completely for what she had apparently suffered in those thirty minutes. She was completely naked, her wrists bruised and scraped. Her stomach was wet with a mixture of God only knows what, and blood came from the area of ground her butt was lying on. Like her husband, she, too, had been killed with a single bullet to the head.

Around the mother's mouth, there was a

drying flow of blood. It wasn't hers, though. Instead, the blood led to a penis on the ground before continuing to the corpse of a third man. His pants were around his ankles, and his pubic area was completely doused in blood. He was lying on his back with his own single bullet wound to the head.

When we made it onto the street, I was taken aback by the silence of the city. It had actually seemed to be more active at night, despite the fact that being inside a building with the daytime temperatures was insufferable. People must have figured that any movement by day was too easily seen, so they stayed cooped up in the sweltering homes. That was better than the alternative, that people weren't on the streets because they were dead and decaying in their homes instead.

We kept close to the buildings, protecting at least one side of ourselves. We watched for any movement in the structures parallel to us, but the world was still.

Street after street, the quiet weighed down the air. It hit at us from every side, indicating no one around, but all the while giving us a sense that there was always someone watching. Perhaps, they were residents of the occasional apartments we passed; perhaps, they were travelers like ourselves, hiding in an office until nightfall; or, perhaps, they were deciding if we had anything worthwhile, if we were worth the risk of attacking.

As we crossed an overpass of I-10, a building to my right caught my attention. Across the stainless-steel building front were the words: 'Phoenix Public Library.' An idea came across my mind, and I took off as fast as I could toward the building's entrance. I could hear Ed snap a few photos as he followed behind me without asking a single question. The doors to the library were shut but unlocked. Slowly, I pushed a door open and took a cautious step inside.

The lobby was massive and modern. It was an architectural work of art that felt like an oven. There was a central row of elevators, their framing made of metal and glass, stretching up all five floors. We took the stairs, stopping on each floor for a look around.

"Sean," Ed whispered from behind me as we left the second floor for the third. "What are you doin', mate?"

"Remember how I told you I was going to have to sail to Hawaii?" Ed nodded. "Remember how I told you that I have no idea how to sail?" He nodded again. "Figured a book on the subject could be useful." Ed nodded a third time.

The third floor was the one. We ran toward a section on education and self-learning. Moving up and down the aisles, we eyed each title, hoping to find something. Finally, I found a line of three books. They seemed to be part of a series as they were each titled *How to Sail: A Beginners*

Guide to Ocean Sailing Part 1, *How to Sail: A Beginners Guide to Ocean Sailing Part 2*, and *How to Sail: A Beginners Guide to Ocean Sailing Part 3*. Unfortunately, they were massive, and there was no way I'd be able to carry them all.

I made a quick decision, grabbing the first two and shoving them into my backpack. It was hard to zip it closed, but I managed, and we were soon heading out of the library. We were stopped short, though, as the entrance came visible to us. Seemingly waiting for us in the doorway was a group of five people.

The group was filthy and mangy. They looked like they hadn't eaten in a few days, and times were desperate. They each carried weapons. One of the people, she appeared to have once been a businesswoman in her mid-50s, held a machete in one hand and a small revolver in the other. One of the two men in the group, an older man that looked close to Jack's age, was carrying what looked to be a double-barrel, sawed-off shotgun.

I gripped my AR and looked at Ed as he pulled out his pistol, his hand shaking violently. Those doors were the only way out that we knew of, and with the group blocking them, we knew we'd have to fight our way out. As we reached the last step and moved into the lobby, preparing ourselves for our potentially imminent demise, the group turned and ran out of the building.

We were frozen in confusion.

"Why'd they run off?" I asked.

"I don't know," Ed responded. "But let's not question a good thing!"

He began walking toward the doors, but I didn't move, a wariness filling me. It just seemed too strange that they'd run off. We were fairly even in terms of our weaponry, and I was sure that the group was hungry enough to lash out. But they didn't.

As he reached the midway point to the doors, Ed looked back and motioned for me to come on. Putting the confusion out of my head with a shake, I joined him, and we walked back into the parking lot, still no trace of the people we'd thought we'd have to fight.

Passing each car, we made sure that no one was using them for cover, waiting for us to pass by before popping out behind us. There was no one in the parking lot, though. Reaching the road, we were feeling pretty good about the outlook for the rest of the day, but as we reorientated ourselves and began walking toward the cross street we needed, we saw movement a mile or so in front of us. Through the cars dotting the roads, we could see a group of people talking to another group. The second group was in a truck I recognized as the one that had blocked the exit on the freeway when I first got to Phoenix. The group doing the talking, though harder to make out, was undoubtedly the people from the library.

"We have to get out of here," I said to Ed,

a dash of adrenaline being induced into my system.

"Are those the baddies from the library?" Ed asked, squinting ahead of us.

"Yeah," I responded. "And the people they're talking to? Those are the men from the bank."

"How do you know?" Ed asked, an obviously worried tone coming through.

"That truck belonged to them. I'd seen them on the freeway when I first got into town. Can't imagine too many fifties-style Chevy trucks in that powder blue around."

The truck started moving, quickly leaving the group from the library behind.

"Run!" I yelled, turning and running back down the street.

We sprinted as fast as we could, our heads pounding from the overwhelming heat, chests burning from the stifling air heaving in and out of our lungs, making us feel like we'd crossed into the seventh circle of Hell. Even with the powerful desire to survive pushing us forward, we had no chance against the truck. It was absolutely gaining on us. We did have an advantage of maneuverability through the stalled-out cars, but we were still too slow.

We were also running back into the downtown area, back the way we'd come. Block after block, we ran in the wrong direction. Coming to an intersection, Ed took a left and started running back east.

"Ed," I called, "we need to go the other way!"

"Look ahead," Ed called back.

I did. In front of us, there was a massive building that took up several blocks' worth of real estate.

"That building," Ed continued, "is the Chase Field. No idea who played there, but it's a big-ass stadium. Even if they see us go in, there'll be plenty of places for us to hide."

Ed was right. It was brilliant, so without any more words, I followed after him. We hopped a series of metal fences, smashed in a glass door, and ran into the stadium that had once belonged to the Arizona Diamondbacks.

. . .

I heard only a single footstep before the person slammed into me with all of their mass, tackling me. My AR slid across the ground, my breath violently forced from my chest, and my vision went blurry from the sudden jolt. Slamming into the concrete, my shoulder felt like it was going to shatter, and I was surprised my collarbone didn't snap. The person who tackled me had their entire weight keeping me to the ground, and they were easily north of two hundred pounds.

I tried to turn my head to look at Ed, but the

person on my back shifted their weight, resting their knee on the back of my neck. I felt the circular barrel of a rifle pressing into my skin, just next to the foreign knee. I couldn't see him, but I could hear Ed.

"Oi," he was saying. "Get off my fuckin' neck, mate! You're cutting off my circulation!"

"What are you doing here?" The man on Ed's back asked. I couldn't see him, but he sounded disciplined and precise. He also sounded on edge, like he was almost itching for a fight. I noticed that he didn't seem to ask who we were, just why we were there.

"We were being chased," I said, chest struggling to move up and down under the man's weight.

"Chased?"

"Yeah," Ed responded. "We were coming out of the library, but there were people there. They ran off and were talking to another group of people we'd seen... we'd seen..."

"Earlier this morning, we'd seen them murder a husband and wife and kidnap the kids. They started chasing after us. We figured this would be a good place to hide! We can leave! Just let us go!"

The next several moments passed in silent agony, slowing to a point that time itself seemed to completely stop, a grain of sand floating still at the conjunction of an hourglass. The man could pull the trigger on the gun at any moment, and I would not even feel the barrel warm up before I was dead; I would be dead before I had a chance to even blink. We had no idea who these people were. Were they people like Jack and Gladys, or were they people like the so-called 'men' from the bank? They were either good, or I would never know the answer to that question.

The weight lifted off of my back as the man stood, a pair of military boots resting right in front of my face.

"Stand up," the man said. Ed and I did so without needing a second command.

The men that had tackled us were National Guardsmen. They could have just been dressed the part, but, based on the past several minutes, I knew I was looking at two legitimate National Guardsmen that looked fresh-faced and straight from training. They were each carrying their military-issue weapons whose makes and models I had no idea of.

"Follow me," Ed's soldier said, walking through a final security checkpoint.

Ed turned and followed after him. As I went to do the same, the soldier next to me stopped me.

"Backpack," he said simply, motioning for me to give it over. I did so without question, then followed after Ed and Ed's Guardsmen. My Guardsman brought up the back.

Once passed that last silent security checkpoint from the previous world, we found ourselves on the stadium's interior perimeter pathway, which was lined with concession booths, the ones that had once undoubtedly been charging ten bucks a beer. Now lifeless, those booths were a sad reminder of the ease of life that would not be known again for generations. My attention was drawn, however, to the most unexpected of sights.

The field was visible down a walkway. We were just behind the third baseline. I'd expected it to be dark and vacant. It was anything but. Instead, not just the third baseline but the entire field was filled with people. Old, young, male, female. Everyone of every kind was crowded into the playing grounds.

Tents and bunks filled most of the space, starting from the outer walls and spaced five feet apart. Row after row, they packed the ground. They stopped in a circle around second base, giving it a radius of nearly forty-five feet. In the center of the circle, there was a large table with several massive pots whose steam was stretching high. Behind the table, on the outfield side, there were two fire pits burning. One seemed to be cooking an animal of some kind as it roasted on a spit. The other had a large pot baking on top with what I assumed was some sort of stew.

"What is this place?" I asked.

"It's a shelter," the soldier behind me said. "It's supposed to be, anyway. A few of us on reserve met up with some Red Cross members the night after the incident. We decided that this would be a good place to offer what help we could."

After walking near completely around the stadium, the two soldiers ushered Ed and me into a room with a sign on the door saying 'Security.'

It was a confusing setting. All around the walls, there were screens of all shapes and sizes, the remnants of a society that had grasped and conquered technology. The fluorescent lights that had once brightened the space were as dead as every other light, so the room was, instead, lit by candles. The flicking flames made it feel dungeon-like, a perfect symbol of the new medieval times ahead.

We walked by a pair of guards in front of a desk that had once served as the contact point with guests. Walking down the hall beyond, we rounded a corner and found ourselves in a darkened office, which was also lit with candles. Behind a desk, struggling to write under a wisp of flame, sat a man in what I would refer to as a desk uniform. I wasn't military, so I had no idea the ranks, but it was clear, even in the candlelight, that this was the man in charge.

"Sir," Ed's soldier said, presenting Ed and me before standing at attention. "Phillips and I caught these two breaking in on the south side of the stadium."

"They said they were being chased, sir," my

soldier added.

The man behind the desk finally stopped trying to write, looking up at us. He seemed to be struggling just as hard to see us as he was struggling to write.

"I can't see shit," he said. "Cut through the mess and tell me who you are. What are you doing here?"

I relayed my story first, giving them all the main points. Ed told his after mine, and his had a much stronger reaction.

"Are you telling me that the President is dead?" the commander asked, sitting forward in his seat, voice forceful and full of accusation.

"Yes, sir," Ed said strongly. "I reckon I even have photos of the swearing-in process."

The commander looked from one of the Guardsmen to the other before nodding. The two saluted and exited the room without another word. Instantly, the tension faded.

"We know he's dead," the commander said, sitting back in his seat. "One of the first people to help set this up was on Air Force One, as well. Said most everyone was going to try to get to NORAD but that a few went their own way."

"Yeah, that's right," Ed responded. He quickly corrected himself, though. "Yes, sir."

"Your story checks," the General said after a long moment. "You two are welcome to stay here through the night, but we don't have enough supplies to care for more than the people we already have. You have to leave in the morning. Get on with your trip."

"Thank you," I said, not even bothering to think on the offer. Shelter for the night that also happened to be what was possibly the safest place in the city? Yes, please.

"Your stuff should be out by the door. Better hurry up. They're almost done serving lunch. Stray dog. Yum." He picked his pen back up and began struggling to write once again.

Ed and I looked at one another, turning and walking out of the room, through the hall, and out into the concession area, looking down onto the best of humanity trying to hold it together through the worst it had ever faced.

Stepping out of the stands and onto the field was almost like stepping into the history books. It felt like I was stepping into images of New York's Great Depression-era Hooverville. The only difference was the clothing being slightly more modern, but under that amount of dirt and grime, it was pretty hard to tell.

Most of the people were laying in, or around, their tents. It wasn't as hot as I'd expected it to be, and the tents provided a veneer of privacy. Their faces were draped with defeat, expressions indicating that their fight had left them long ago. The more tents we walked by, the more dejected faces that stared up at me, the more I realized this was far worse than Hooverville could have ever been.

When the Great Depression hit, it hit a society that still had a strong sense of how to survive when times got hard. There was still a toughness that underlined society, where working so hard that callouses became a permanent fixture on your hands was a point of pride. People knew how to dust themselves off after they had been kicked while down.

The people I was looking out on were of a different make. Society had made things so easy for us. We didn't have to struggle in the ways that our grandparents and great-grandparents had to. Not everyone in society fell victim to its comforts, but the vast majority had. We had fallen prey to the ease of delivery that could bring us any kind of food within the hour; we had fallen prey to the interconnectivity of the smartphone; we had fallen prey to the comforts of indoor living. We had lost our ability to take a hard hit, dust ourselves off, and keep moving, though we'd assured ourselves that wasn't the case. Over and over again, after every horrible event that we faced, we'd told ourselves that we could get back up and be better for it. It was a lie, and the faces all around me told me so.

It was more silent than a building that full should have been. Murmurs and some coughs rang out, accompanied by a couple of guitars being played over on the opposite side of the field, somewhere near first base. The people, however, had no reason to talk. They had nothing that they felt was worth saying. They had no strength to talk. If you've given up on hope, why would talking even be necessary? Even the kids we passed sat in silence, the innocence seeming to be gone.

I couldn't help but think how that made sense. Those who had that sort of innocence, sort of like Annie, would either have to lose it or they themselves would be lost. These kids had lost their childhood. They had been so cruelly given a taste of a world of luxury. One day, though, the children suffering in that stadium would be the elders, sitting around a campfire, telling stories about how we once could talk face-to-face with someone on the other side of the globe as if they were right in front of us; telling the youth of tomorrow stories about the wonderful vehicles that could take a person from one side of the country to the other in a matter of days or hours; telling stories about how we were once able to touch the stars; telling stories of the world that we'd so easily taken for granted. They would be the artists painting a picture of our fantastical and wondrous world that, by then, would be but legend.

The smell was not helping their fortitude, either. It couldn't have been. That many people stuck in a single room together without the ability to take a shower would have been unbearable after forty-eight hours, but it had been over two weeks. It was a smell worse than any animal I'd ever smelled. It was absolute destitution and squalor.

It was evident that whatever this place had been the previous week, it was losing its grasp. The ability for these people to stay fed or supplied with water was not going to hold out much longer, and I could only imagine the horror that would probably occur when those gave way. Many of the faces I was looking at, dejected as they may have been, would soon turn ravenous, struck by a primal desire to survive. Others, I knew, would take the path of Annie, all the way to a similar, bitter conclusion.

As we reached the clearing at the center of the field, we stopped at the back of a line that led to the serving table. Slowly, we marched ahead until a person wearing a filthy Red Cross shirt plopped an oozing stew into a metal bowl and handed it to me.

"Dog?" I asked as a chunk of meat floated to the top of the broth.

The Red Cross worker looked at me with eyes that were as desolate as the desert, the rest of her face equally as vacant. She had been beaten down like everyone else, maybe even more so. With the urge and call to help people also comes an increase in stress and more complete destruction of the soul when things go bad.

I didn't press my question, deciding I was better off not knowing. I moved along and sat in a vacant spot of grass nearby. Ed sat next to me, and we ate in silence, trying to ignore the smell. As I finished my stew and placed the empty bowl on the ground next to me, I reached into my backpack, pulling out the bible.

"I'm gonna grab some photos," Ed said a few moments later, standing.

"Sounds good," I said. "I'll be here."

"Good on ya," Ed replied, turning and walking into the crowd.

Laying back onto the grass, resting my head on my backpack, I opened the Bible and began to read.

Later, just as the words on the page were beginning to get fuzzy from pure exhaustion, Ed came hurrying up to me. He had a goofy grin on his face that was completely out of place considering our surroundings. He was the happiest person for miles.

"Good news, mate. We got a ride," Ed said, holding up a game-day brochure.

"What is it?" I asked, taking the booklet.

"Flip it over."

I couldn't believe my eyes. Printed on the back, in big, beautiful colors, was an advertisement for a classic car museum, 'Grand Opening' in big, red letters across the top. There were several cars in the picture, and each was from a time before computer chips took over.

"I think we may have found our next stop," I

said, a grin just as goofy as Ed's crossing my face.

We pulled out the map of the area and found our path. It would be a short walk, but it was through an area of town that had been densely populated. It was going to be risky, but the reward was worth it.

I knew I was too excited for a natural sleep, so I popped a sleeping pill, once again, courtesy of Gladys, and slept a dreamless slumber.

11

Monday, August 25th

The sleeping pills made me groggy when I woke up the following morning. Granted, it may have also been because, despite having taken the sleeping pills, I still only slept about four hours. Either way, as realization set in that we could be just a day or two from the coast, my grogginess was obliterated by anticipation.

By the time we were all packed up and ready to go, the rest of the people in the stadium were just beginning to stir. We slowly made our way through the tents, but just before we got to the stairs leading up to the stands, something in my peripheral made me stop.

There was a man that was kneeling. It was fairly obvious he was praying, one of the few who apparently still had hope. I watched him for a moment before he stood, did the Catholic cross movements, and turned toward us. He was a priest, or had been, at least. Though filthy, his black shirt and white collar were obvious. Even among the muck that wreaked of decay, that man's faith was holding strong.

It hit me once again. Like the times before, I could feel the warmth start to wash through me, starting at my chest. It encased me as I watched the priest walk back to a tent on the outer line. He saw me and nodded in politeness.

I pulled off my backpack and pulled out the Bible. Looking over it, I took in all the crinkled water damage, its scuffs and marks reminders of a life unimagined for it. I didn't fully understand, but it felt like the warmth was pushing me toward the priest, urging me to give that book a much more proper home.

I walked over to the priest, and he straightened as I did.

"Hello," I said politely, trying to put him at ease. I put my hand out, saying, "My name's Sean."

"Father Carrol," the priest responded, shaking my hand.

"Nice to meet you, Father. This may be weird, but I want you to have this." I held out the Bible to him.

Father Carrol stared down at the book for a long moment. He seemed a little confused at first, but when he looked up at me, there were tears in his eyes. In awe, Father Carrol took the Bible from me.

"Thank you, my son. I had lost mine," Father

Carrol said. "No idea what happened to it. When time came to leave my home, I couldn't find it. Now that things are so dangerous out there, this is probably where I'll die. Getting out of this stadium just isn't going to happen for me. I'd never be able to go get it. Thought I'd never get another chance to read the Word again, but our God is a wonderful one."

He hugged me with pure gratitude.

As I bid Father Carrol goodbye, the warmth washed from me like a tide rolling out. In its stead was an overwhelming sense of peace. I had done the right thing. I don't know for what purpose, but it felt like I had just delivered that Bible back to its rightful home.

. . .

The sun still hadn't broken over the distant mountains to hit the valley city, but the sky was already a bright vibrant blue, and the heat was growing. Hopping over the turnstiles and walking cautiously toward the street, I kept my AR raised, my glances scanning the buildings and streets.

Looking down the street in front of us, three men came into view. They were all National Guardsmen; it was clear from their clothes and demeanor. They were one-hundred percent soldiers. Two of them seemed to each be carrying something in their arms. As we got closer, it was clear that they were holding children.

The Guardsman not carrying a child stepped forward and lifted his gun at us when we were just a few dozen feet away.

"Who are you?" he yelled to us, our hands going up in the air to show we weren't a threat.

"We just left the shelter," I called back. "We were taken in for—" I stopped. My eyes had to be lying to me. That was the only explanation I had. The two children were each missing an arm, fresh and bloody bandages covering their stumps, but they were the kids from the bank. "Where did you find those kids?"

"Doesn't concern you," he responded. "Shelter isn't taking anyone in!"

"They weren't going to let us stay," Ed replied. "We were being chased, and they allowed us to stay for the night as long as we left today!"

"It was Phillips and someone else who got us," I said, remembering the soldier's name and hoping that would help with our credibility. It seemed to work as the Guardsman lowered his weapon, and the group walked up to us.

"Where did you get them?" I asked again as they reached us.

"Couple blocks up and to the left."

"Was there a group of guys there?"

"There was," the Guardsman holding the girl said. The little girl was clearly in shock. "Their bodies may still be there."

"Why do you ask?" the first Guardsman said.

"We... we saw what happened to their parents," Ed said. "We thought these little ones were gone for sure. The baddies said they were going to eat them. Glad you got them out before that happened."

"Well," the Guardsman holding the boy said, "before too much of it happened, anyway." With that, the Guardsmen passed us and ran to the stadium, hopping the turnstile and moving inside.

Our walk toward the museum was silent. There were no gunshots or fights that were echoing through the buildings, and any people that may have been around stayed silent and hidden. I had a feeling the silence was an indicator of the worst: The heat and lack of water were, indeed, becoming, or had already become, fatal for many of the residents still in the city. We stayed aware and ready the entire two miles to the museum, but the trip was mercifully uneventful.

When we reached the museum, the glass doors were locked, but a well-placed rock made them open. We carefully walked through the shattered doors and inside. The massive warehouse-like space was completely empty. It had the look of a museum, but there weren't even light fixtures installed yet.

Pulling out the brochure, I finally noticed the

opening date at the bottom. It wasn't supposed to have been open for another two weeks. I was fairly certain that its opening day would have been the day before our visit had things not turned to shit.

All morning, our spirits had been high, believing that we'd soon be riding in an enclosed vehicle, a solid roof providing protection from the baking sun and what would possibly be one of our last experiences with air conditioning. We had spent our whole two-mile journey believing that we'd spent our last night in the city. Instead, it looked like we really were going to have to make the journey by foot.

I turned to leave, but Ed was nowhere to be found.

"Ed," I called out softly.

"Down here, mate," Ed's voice came from a darkened space on the other side of one of the room's only doors. "It's hard to tell, but I think I found something."

Sprinting over, I passed through the door frame, not noticing the stairs until the last minute and nearly taking a horrible fall. I was able to stop myself, though, and I walked down the rest of the stairs cautiously.

Ed was at the bottom, facing out into what had once served as a parking garage. There, along the far wall, were the clear silhouettes of several classic cars, backlit by a gated-up entrance to the garage. I wanted to collapse to my knees and thank our lucky stars or God or whatever cosmic force put those cars there.

"I'll see if I can find the keys," I said instead, turning and taking the stairs two at a time, my confidence nearly fully restored.

Back in the upstairs room, I sprinted to the other side of the space, which took almost half a minute the space was that vast. I passed through the only other door in the room, and into the hallway beyond.

I searched each and every office that hallway housed, and, after half an hour, I finally found the keys locked away in a case. Whoever decided a glass case would be secure hadn't been the most intelligent of people, but it sure as hell made them my favorite person. I smashed it open with ease, grabbed every single key, and ran back to the lower garage.

There were several amazing cars to choose from, but we had to make our decision rationally. We went car by car, reading the gas gauges. The one that had the most gas was the one we took. It was a 1969 VW Bus that was fully restored to original condition. The only thing that wasn't original was the paint job, which showcased a scene from Woodstock.

It was a bigger vehicle than we would have liked, but it would serve a double purpose. Even if the roads were completely vacant, we wouldn't get to Marina Del Rey until at least the next day, so the van would provide us a great place to sleep overnight.

Ed hopped into a classic Ford truck that was parked there, waiting to be admired, backing it up to the exit. He parked it and walked around to the rear of the truck. Ed tied its tow rope around the gate and got back into the vehicle, flooring it. The gate didn't stand a chance, yanking free without a struggle. A few moments later, I was pulling the VW bus out of the garage, Ed in the passenger seat, and our destination of California that much more of a reality.

. . .

As I had expected, we didn't make it all the way to the coast that day. Instead, we made it about halfway, pulling off near Joshua Tree National Park. We hadn't encountered any issues along the way, other than some congestion of stalled vehicles. We also saw not a single other living person or running vehicle, but we did pass by several corpses Ed and I both tried to ignore. It was hard to do that, though, when each one was being picked at by buzzards. It was two hundred miles of ruin and death.

We decided to try to occupy ourselves with one of the sailing books. Ed would read, and I'd listen, trying to take note of anything important. It didn't go well. After fifteen minutes of it, I had retained nothing, and Ed was puking out of the window from motion sickness. It was definitely disappointing as it would have been a lot of time well-spent, and by the time we pulled off for the day, it was too dark to read.

Stopped at what was once called the Cottonwood Campground, just off I-10, Ed and I laid out in the back of the van, wrapped up in our sleeping bags.

"I think we deserved this," Ed said randomly.

"Why?" I asked, rolling over to face him. "Why would we deserve something like this?"

"We aren't a good people, mate," he said somberly. "We like to think we are, but we aren't. Yeah, we may have a good side, but so many people do so many awful things to one another. We rob, rape, and steal without a second thought. Every single day, people murder one another."

"I'm not arguing for murder," I said, "but animals kill other animals all the time."

"Yeah, for food or mating, but not because of ego or something stupid like that. Lions don't kill other lions because they're depressed. Chimps don't murder other chimps because they just like killing. Dolphins don't kill other dolphins and wear their skin around. All in all, we are not a good species."

"Male lions kill baby male lions for *ego*. They don't want future threats to their reign over a pride. That's pretty messed up, too, don't you think?"

"It is. No doubt. Animals do some fucked things. I was too young to remember, but I've read stories about rival monkey gangs during the COVID stuff fifteen years ago. They were apparently taking over the streets and fighting one another while people were locked indoors. Shit happens in the natural world, too. I know. But it's the difference in cognitive ability that makes it worse. We know what it means when someone dies. Animals don't really get it in the same way that we do. Knowing what our actions actually mean sets us apart from the others. When there are gang fights, and someone kills a person, they know what that death means. If a monkey in the streets kills another monkey, brew, they don't grasp it in the same way. Their actions are based on nature, and, too often, our actions are just evil."

"But it all comes down to the same thing. In nature, we fear the competitor. We have our territory, just like monkeys, and when territories aren't abided by, violence occurs. It all comes down to the removal of so-called threats."

"Still, it's the ability to know what it all means. We can empathize and imagine what it would be like for someone to be tortured, and people fantasize about doing it anyway. We can understand the finality of death, and we know the impacts it causes far beyond the immediate, yet we still do it. We want to remove the person, animals want to remove the threat. We are evil."

"There is so much good, though," I said.

"But does the good we've done outweigh the negative and ugly? The evil? I don't think so. We prey on one another like a virus. We take advantage of one another and commit atrocities so far out of the natural order of things. We go far beyond those monkeys in the streets. When we got to a certain point, we crossed the line from natural violence, and we went far beyond. Is a species that's capable, and with a history, of killing millions and millions of one another worth living? Especially if our continued existence means throwing the entire natural order of things out of whack?

"Whether it be nature just working itself out, or some 'roo fucker in the sky smiting us, I reckon we had this coming."

"But without the bad, there could be no good," I proposed.

"Fuck nah," he said. "That's just something good men tell themselves when they sit by and do nothing about evil deeds, brew. We don't need someone to murder other people to be grateful when someone opens the door for us. We don't need to massacre one another in order for us to be charitable. Good does not need evil in order to exist. I do not need a Hitler in order to be grateful for Dr. Martin Luther King, Jr, mate."

"But without the racism the country had been through to that point, would we have even had a need for Martin Luther King, Jr? Men like him are ordinary men; they're just like us. Except, they rise to the occasions of need which are presented to them! Arguably, many of the greatest historical figures came about because they were the good to rise against an evil of their time."

"Do you think someone who had the leadership prowess, intelligence, passion, all those great things that King had, would live a life of obscurity without an evil force? I don't think so. Someone as good as King would find a way to do good, no matter their circumstance. Whether he would have become a politician, a professor, or stayed a pastor, he would have found a way to still have a positive impact on the lives of many.

"Whether you want to believe it or not, Sean, our species was heading towards something like this for a long time. Centuries of bloodshed. Centuries of axes, swords, arrows, and bullets decimating the flesh of brothers. Generations of children turned into child brides and raped at young ages. Slavery in general! My ancestors, the aboriginal people, mate, we got royally fucked. When people can do the things that were done to my people, to people of all different backgrounds throughout the ages, are they worth keeping around? Throw on top of that the fact that we have a tendency to have short memories. We are a fucked species, Sean." Ed stopped for a moment, looking at me with an expression that was slightly apologetic. "We're also a highly emotional species."

"No worries, mate," I said in a slightly joking tone, poorly impersonating his accent. I wanted to break the mood. We already had a really stressful time ahead; we didn't need to add to it. "I can see what you mean, though," I added.

"You got one of those sleeping pills?" Ed asked. "My mind'll be racing all night otherwise."

We each took one.

"I won't argue many of your points," I said, rolling onto my back, and closing my eyes. "Our species has done a lot of horrible things to one another. *I've* done horrible things. I think we all have, but we did *not* deserve this. I won't concede that point.

"For every bit of hate that we put out, we put out a greater amount of love."

Ed tried to hide his scoff in a cough, but it ended up coming out as a choked snort.

"Laugh if you want, but what's the opposite of hate? You talked so much about the hate that we're filled with, the evil, but you neglected to consider the love we put out. See, the thing about love you have to realize is that it doesn't happen on the scale that hate can. It just doesn't really happen that way, but that is precisely what makes it amazing. The everyday love exchanged between two ordinary people. It can be the love of a wife or husband, son or daughter; or it can also be the offering of a hand up to someone in need, even just a happy meal to a homeless person on the street corner.

"We exude it. When communities are hit with disaster, people from all over the world will show up as volunteers to help. A few years back, we were hit by a bad hurricane, and a lot of Orlando ended up flooding. Within a day, there were people from all over the country there, taking their boats from rooftop to rooftop. They didn't do it for money or recognition or power. They did it because they cared. It was a complete act of love and selflessness.

"I get where you're coming from, Ed, but I choose to see the light." And with that, I was asleep.

12
Tuesday, August 26th

I wasn't sure what I'd expected to see when we got to Los Angeles, but it certainly was not what we were greeted by. The city was nearly gone. What had once been a sprawling metropolis with several skylines dotting the landscape was nothing but a smoldering ruin. It was far, far beyond the damage that Phoenix had encountered. The city in front of us looked like it had been hit by a nuclear bomb.

We stayed on I-10 most of the way, but on every single overpass, we would look out of the van's windows, trying to catch a glimpse of the side roads below. Almost every time, we saw nothing but the charred out remains of a city that had been frozen in time. It was strange. It almost looked as if volcanic ash had come over everything. L.A. looked like Pompeii. However, there was much more of the surrounding that was charred, not just ash.

Every so often, a street we saw had been

spared the annihilation, but, even on those streets, there was never a sound. The city was empty of people. Our little bus's engine puttering along was the only noise for miles. We were the only souls in the entirety of what was once the second-largest city in the U.S.

It was like driving through some sort of post-apocalyptic movie; I am Legend, but instead of a cute dog, my companion was a photographic Aussie who thought human beings sucked. It was a decent trade-off. At least Ed and I could have actual back-and-forth conversations. And, of course, no zombie-like creatures.

Still, the Los Angeles we were driving through was one that no director in history would have dared put to screen in a serious manner. It would never have been believable. The critics would have laughed and called it 'utter fantastical in the worst way!' There was no doubt in my mind, though, that what we were seeing was real, and, as we approached the downtown of Los Angeles proper, we discovered why the city had suffered so.

The smell of gas started as no more than a hint, tickling my nose like the first exposure to a scented candle. It ebbed and flowed over the following twenty minutes, growing at times, dissipating at others. It never fully went away, an ever-present fuse waiting for another spark.

As we passed through the massive intersection of I-10 and the 405, there was a loud rattle that shook the roads, stalled cars wobbling back and forth on their paralyzed frames. No more than two miles to the southwest, we watched as several blocks exploded. The fireball was erupting into the sky as if the explosion had been set off in a line, one bomb after the other.

"Oi, fuck me," Ed said in awe. "We got to get to the coast now, mate. Last thing we need is a spark in the engine to set us off, too."

"What's sparking the fires, though? Can't be electrical sparks."

"Metal on metal, maybe?" Ed responded. "Doesn't really matter. Something's setting them off. One goes off near us, I reckon we're dead no matter what the cause is."

He was right, again, so we went as fast as we could, ever wary that we could be there one second and be nothing but human barbeque the next. I tried driving fast, but there were too many cars. We had to take it slow, and the closer we got to the coast, the more cars were stalled. At exit five, we had to stop. The road was too congested for the van to make it.

"Freeway or side roads?" I asked.

"I'd say walk the freeway. We aren't far, now. And down there, who knows what we'll find. Cannibals; gas explosions; rapers. Any, and/or all, and none of them sound too appealing."

I agreed, so we grabbed our stuff and said goodbye to the van. It had been a wonderful treat getting to experience A/C again, though there wasn't any music to listen to. It had been a better vehicle than we'd expected. We'd thought that its tank would need to be filled, but it was apparently enlarged; we'd thought that its maneuverability would have been an issue, but its little bit of extra height made up for it, and sleeping under its roof was rather pleasant. We turned on it and began our walk to the coast.

We kept an eye out for any possible movement, any possible threat that may have been waiting in a car for us to pass. There was no one. The city seemed to be truly empty.

"Where is everyone?" I asked. "Why aren't there people? Phoenix still had people, and it was so much more unbearable than here temperature-wise. That heat…"

"If you'd watched your city explode and managed to survive, would you stick around? Especially when the smell of gas is still lingering around like this? Not sure about you, mate, but I'm not here to fuck spiders. I'd be gone in a tick."

"Not here to fuck spiders?" I asked, laughing.

"Yeah, it's an Aussie saying. Basically, it means 'obviously.'"

"Obviously," I joked.

When the first echoes of the distant waves crashing reached my ears, I wanted to cry for joy. I wanted to just drop down to my knees and thank whatever was up there for helping me. I wasn't sure if their deservedness for overall praise was actually there, but if something was watching over and protecting me, I was going to thank them profusely for doing a damn good job so far.

The trip wasn't even halfway done, though. The land portion was finished, and, even though it'd been a long and horribly dangerous journey, what was to come was still more dangerous. I had no idea what I was doing on the water. I had no idea about sailing or navigating. I was about to embark on what was nearly guaranteed to be suicide.

The smell of the saltwater hitting my nose was another blessing that caused my adrenaline and excitement to increase. I was experiencing an anticipation that eclipsed almost any other similar emotion I'd ever had. In fact, the only times I'd ever felt more anticipation and excitement were before each of my children were born. That was unlike anything else, but knowing how close we were to the water was a close second. Not even the anticipation before my wedding could equal the feeling the smell of the salty ocean on the air gave me. I wanted to skip.

When we made it to the marina, several dry docks had evidently fallen victim to the gas explosions. None had more than a foot or two of wall still standing, remains of boats scattered about, impossible to tell how many.

Luckily, our boat, The Gabby, was not in dry dock. Her home was untouched. She was floating right where Jack and Gladys had said she'd be, a beacon of hope in a world where such a thing was in short supply. Knowing I'd made it that far, to the point of looking onto that magnificent vessel, ready to take sail, I felt the familiar warmth spread from my chest, egging me on toward the boat.

I didn't resist.

. . .

"I'm definitely coming with you, and there's nothing you can do to stop me," Ed said as he began to untie the boat from the dock.

"Ed, I really appreciate—"

"Oh, fuck off with your American pleasantries," he said. "I didn't come back to where I started just to be aimless again."

"Mountains, Ed. Head for the mountains."

"With every other fuckwit from the cities? Yeah, nah, I reckon I'm good without taking that course. I may not know a lot about sailing, but this boat's too damn big for one person. Especially when that one person has no idea how to sail. Two dumbasses with no clue are probably going to be better than one in this situation. A second set of hands, mate."

"I can't take on the responsibility. Too many people have died because of me. I can't take the weight of another death, Ed."

Ed smiled and pushed the boat off. As the boat glided out of the dock, he hopped on. At that point, unless he went swimming, it was going to be the two of us.

"I appreciate the feelings, Sean," Ed said, "but I'm a grown-ass man. I make my own decisions. If I wanted someone else to make them for me, I'd have gotten married. I'm coming, and now, there's nothing you can say or do to change it." He smiled. "What's the command, captain?"

I knew I'd lost, so instead of arguing, I looked around the boat, utterly and completely clueless. I was so far over my head that I'd have felt more comfortable translating hieroglyphics. One thing was clear, though, even to someone like myself: The boat was floating steadily toward another row of docks and boats. If we didn't stop our momentum and turn, we'd crash the boat even before getting out of the marina.

"We have to stop and turn!" I said.

"How?" Ed responded.

"I have no idea," I said.

Without any other idea coming to mind, I looked to the sky.

"What do I do? What…" I pleaded. "What can I do? Please…"

My chest warmed familiarly, pushing me toward the cabin. Following the urge, I ran down the three stairs and into the galley area. I moved to the bench seats encircling the dining table and lifted on the cushions. My body felt like an avatar. I was being moved by some remote player pushing the joystick and x-button. Underneath the bench, there was a storage compartment with lifejackets, a flare gun, an inflatable life-raft, and several oars. I grabbed two of the four oars and ran back up to the deck, tossing one to Ed.

"An oar? We're going to stop this thing with fucking oars?"

"We have to!" I called, leaning over the edge of the boat and thrusting the oar's flattened end into the water. It was a tough stretch, nearly putting me on one leg. Ed followed suit, a shake of his head barely perceptible in my peripheral.

The plan began to work fairly quickly, but our rate of speed wasn't slowing quickly enough, and we were still on a collision course with the other dock. I reacted instinctually, throwing my oar to the deck and firmly grasping a taut line connected from the mast to the railing. Using that as my lifeline, I stepped over the boat's edge, holding one foot out and far extending over the water. Ed saw what I was doing and ran over to help.

As we approached the dock, we absorbed the initial impact with our legs and began to push. I pushed harder than I ever had before, trying to angle the boat out to sea, rather than back into the marina, at the same time as absorbing the impact. We weren't able to stop the boat completely, but we stopped it enough so that the impact did no damage to the hull.

We used the impact to our advantage. With surprisingly quick thinking, Ed hopped off the boat and onto the nearest dock. He put every ounce of strength he could into angling the boat, a guttural scream being forced out from somewhere within. Miraculously, the boat did begin to turn. It wasn't much, but it was enough that, with a hard push, Ed had us floating forward and away from another collision. He jumped back onto the Gabby, and we both ran to our oars.

Leaning again, both on the right side of the boat, or starboard side as I'd later learn, we held our oars still against the flow of water, trying to turn the boat more, preferring to be overly cautious than to regret the inverse later. It was an incredibly pathetic effort, and, in fact, our oars were doing almost nothing to help, but the current was working to our benefit. Finally, the last dock glided past us at a relatively safe distance.

"Thank you," I said, looking up again at the sky that was beginning a shift to the orange of evening.

"Why didn't we just use this?" Ed said, heaving and pointing toward the boat's wheel.

I had no idea why we didn't think of it, so I chose to ignore him, plopping to the ground and catching my own breath instead.

As tired and worn out as my body felt, laying

on the deck, breaths heavy, I had never felt more accomplished in my life. I had been through so much already, the universe seeming to love throwing roadblocks in my way. Yet, every time that had happened, I'd managed to come out on the winning end. Never in my life could I say that was the case—at least, not consistently the case. Obviously, I'd had managed to come out victorious with some things. I was about to be a Vice President, for Christ's sake, but there was always something that would come and knock me down. Yet, when the victories mattered so much more, with the roadblocks being life or death, I had been victorious.

I pulled back my thinking. Yeah, I'd been victorious. To that point, but we were only halfway through the trip. I didn't need to get cocky and make a mistake.

.   .   .

We didn't go far out onto the water, staying within about fifty yards of the dock and anchoring for the night. It was going to be dark in a relatively quick fashion, and, seeing as how neither of us had any idea how to set the sails, we thought that waiting for morning would be a safe bet. We also wanted to take full stock of the supplies on board before losing easy access to land. Ed complained we didn't do that before leaving, but after being reminded he was the one who cast us off before we had a plan, he didn't say much more about it.

When we began to take stock, our spirits continued to rise. We had miraculously steered the boat, and we were lucky enough that it was fully stocked with non-perishable food. The cabinets of the galley were filled to the brim with canned goods and MREs. It was nearly a month's supply for one person.

Ed began to count the canned items while I looked around for water, of which the owner of the boat had seen fit to stow away several cases. This boat was a gift that kept on giving.

The sleeping quarters were rather surprising. From the surface, I wouldn't have thought the boat had the room, but there was one large queen-sized bed coming out in the center of the back wall. In each of the room's corners, there were cabinets stretching from floor to ceiling, bracing two bunk beds which were steadied against both port and starboard walls. Not too shabby.

Along the back wall, over the bed, there was a portrait of an elderly couple. They were embracing tightly with some tropical island behind them, and their grins were bright. They couldn't have looked happier.

As I lay in the queen bed that night, Ed in

one of the bunks, I stared up at the couple's image, wondering what must have happened to them. Had they managed to survive, or were they among the countless who hadn't? Were they trying to get to the boat? What if they got there and the boat was gone? Questions that I shouldn't have been asking.

Then, as I imagined a life for those two complete strangers, I was hit like a ton of bricks. I could do the same with Ed. I had no idea who he really was.

I had been traveling with Ed for days, putting my life in his hands many times, and yet I didn't have the slightest clue who he really was. I knew he was a photographer from Australia, but that's not really him. Who may have a picture of him hanging on the wall, like the couple above me? Who might he have been missing?

"Ed, tell me about yourself."

"I already told you about myself, Sean. I'm a photo—"

"No," I interrupted, "I mean, do you have a family? Are you missing anyone? Who are you, not what do you do?"

Ed sat up in his bunk and looked over at me. "You want to know my life story?"

"Why not? We're probably going to die on this trip, so might as well know what led you to this point."

"Alright," he said, laying back, staring out a porthole lining the wall next to him. "First off, we aren't dying on this trip. I reckon we're going to get to Hawaii and find your family safe and sound.

"Secondly, I guess I'll start at the beginning, then. I'm not actually from Brisbane. I just said it because you Yanks really aren't good with geography. That part, I wasn't really joking. Brisbane's the nearest big city you may know, and I did end up there briefly, but, originally, my family was part of a community of Australian Natives several hundred miles inland. We were set up on that far eastern side of Queensland.

"We had a good existence there. We were far away from big cities which, even at that time, were still pretty racist towards us natives. We didn't have to worry about encountering that. We had everything we needed.

"I was the oldest of three. My little brother was two years younger than I was. His name was Jiemba. My parents named him that because the laughing star was bright the morning he was born."

"What's the laughing star?" I asked.

"It's Venus, the planet. It was incredibly bright that morning, so they gave my brother its name. My sister, Jedda, was five years younger than me. She was born with a wild head of hair, and as soon as I saw it, I told my mom she looked like a djida, or wild goose. I loved those two. We had great childhoods."

"Why do you have such… a bland name?"

"Why do I have a white name, you mean, when my siblings have more native names? Simple: I chose mine. My parents named me Waru, but when I decided to become a photographer, I thought that having a white name may have its advantages. Even if just on paper. Getting a meeting with some top execs with a name like Ed would be much easier than with a name like Waru."

"Should I call you Waru, then?"

"Nah, mate, you're good. Ed is far more representative of who I am today than Waru is. The name Ed stands for every bit of hard work, blood, sweat, and tears I put into life to get the success I had. I am Ed; Ed is my name."

"'Ed' it is then," I said, smiling.

"'Ed' it is. Where was I? Yeah, at thirteen, it was time for me to go on walkabout."

"Walkabout?"

"Yeah, it's a rite of passage almost every native child has to go through. Every one of my people did, anyway. So, with only a small knife, I walked out of my village on my thirteenth birthday and into the bush. Walkabout's very spiritual, mate. Even to this day, many in Australia don't really understand it. They don't see the power of the bush like we do. There's something special in that land, mate, something that the cities and technology drained from the Euros.

"I went into that desert a boy, and I was to

find out every inch of myself, from the strength of my will to the strength of my bone and muscle. I tested my faith in myself, and not only did I become a man in body, but my spirit became a man.

"See, on walkabout, it isn't just about trying to survive. It's about connecting, connecting to the life force that drives everything. It's about connecting with our ancestors and discovering where we come from. Not because we read it in a book somewhere, but because we opened our spirits and spoke with our ancestors directly.

"After about a month, I found myself ready. When I got home, there was nothing but horror. They had been dead a while, my family that is. My parents. My brother. My sister. They were all dead, and there wasn't much left that the scavengers and rot hadn't taken. What was left, even the maggots had left to whither. I don't know what happened to them. I had no way of finding out, and where we were, no one would have seen anything.

"So, I grabbed a few things and began walking. Eventually, I ended up in Brisbane and was taken in by some Catholic orphanage. One day, I was outside, laying on a bench with my head over the edge, looking at the world upside down. One of the nuns saw this, and, instead of reprimanding me, which I reckon many of the others would have done, the next day, she brought me a camera and a book on how they worked. She said to use it to continue looking at the world differently than others, so I did.

"It became my life after. From fourteen until I was seventeen, I stayed at that orphanage, photographing anything and everything. Those photos are the ones that got me the job working for National Geographic. My first assignment with them was the Indonesian Uprising.

"When I went to Indonesia, I... I wasn't prepared for just how bad it was. The news back home in Oz, they weren't showing us the streets. They weren't showing us the villages. It was a sugarcoated, highly falsified view of the tragedy there. Within about ten minutes of leaving the airfield, we passed through a village. I'll never forget what I saw there. It was so bad that I couldn't even put it to film. Every villager was dead, probably a hundred and fifty or so. They were littering the ground, and each one's head was lying next to the body, instead of attached to it. The villagers had been butchered. When I asked the U.N. Peacekeeper there what had happened, he just said, 'The same thing that's been happening the past four months.'

"I was only in Indonesia for a total of two weeks. In those two weeks, over eighty-thousand Indonesians were murdered." Ed paused for a long while, mind off in some far-off memory. I let him wander. After about a minute, he started again.

"When I submitted my photographs, my

editor came to me and asked me if they were real. It being my first assignment, the editor wasn't expecting anything that powerful, I guess. Didn't help that all he was seeing on the news were shots from territory far from the fighting. When he finally got verification on them, he came to me crying and gave me a long hug. He thanked me. He said that my photos had opened his eyes and that those images would open the world's eyes.

"The next day, the photos were printed along with an article some writer made out of a journal I'd kept while there. I got an award for them, and when I received it, the man giving it to me said my photos helped end the war, saving countless lives. Didn't matter to me, honestly. I may have helped end it, but it still happened.

"It took me a year or so to get over the realization of how horrible we are to one another. First, my family; then, all those lost in Indonesia. I'd seen my fair share of death and pain. Now, this." Ed paused for a long while; I said nothing. Then, "So, that about covers my life, I reckon. What do you say, brew?"

It took me a while to say anything at all. Then, "My daughter, Clem, actually told me about you and your photography when it hit the stands. She thought the humanity you captured was amazing. That coming from a then twelve-year-old. I really only remember because she actually wrote a short story about a woman in one of the shots. She made up a whole back story for her. Maybe one day, if we really do make it to Hawaii, she can tell it to you."

"I'd like that," Ed said genuinely. "Do you know which picture it was?"

"I don't know a name or anything," I said. "I can describe it, though. It was one of the black and white shots. It was of a wooden doorframe that looked old and somewhat rotted. The room behind the frame was pretty much blacked out and, sitting at the base of the doorframe, was an elderly woman. She looked like she was probably ninety years old. A man lying on the ground next to her was dead. His head was laying in her lap, and it was cocked to the side a bit. The man's throat looked like it had been slit. But the thing that hit about the photo was the woman's face. It was filthy, so you could see where the tears had dried. She didn't look sad in the photo, though. She just looked… blank. She looked empty, almost."

"I know that photo. You let your twelve-year-old see that photo, brew? How's your mind?"

"I didn't let her. I was pretty pissed off when she told me she saw it, but kids could do more on their phones than I ever could on a computer. She ended up seeing it on some website that was supposed to be educational. Didn't fall under the parental restrictions I set. I kind of understood, though. I'd done the same thing with the picture from Vietnam. The one with the General about to execute the man in the streets."

"That's a great photo. Powerful stuff. And, fair dinkum, you're right. Can't control everything they see, I reckon. Well, the picture you're talking about was in a small village on one of the southern islands that were revolting. We were about two hours behind a crew of government soldiers going from village to village, executing the men and boys. We were in that village for all of five minutes. I have no idea who she was, so I called that photo 'Pain of the Unknown.'"

"You're an amazing photographer, Ed. I hadn't realized that you were *that* Ed Megari. I can't wait to see the ones you've been taking recently. Hope you got my good side," I couldn't resist.

"You have a good side? Why didn't you tell me, brew?" he joked back.

"Do you have any kids?"

"At my age? Nah, thank God. I've been too focused on the career. I mean, I'm only twenty-four, mate. At eighteen, I was photographing war zones. No time for a family of my own. Never even got close. Was always more comfortable just relying on myself, never needing anyone else, and not having anyone really need me. I never had any second thoughts about it, and, looking at the world now, I'm definitely glad I didn't have any." He stopped and looked at me.

"It's alright," I said, preempting him. "No

offense taken. I wouldn't have not had my kids, even knowing what I know now, but I don't blame you for being glad you don't have any."

He nodded.

"Are you going to try to get to Australia?" I asked.

"No reason to go back, I reckon. I'm going wherever the wind takes me," he paused for a second, then, "literally and figuratively."

We laughed for a moment before falling back into silence.

"I'm glad you came with me, Ed," I said finally.

"Of course, mate."

13
Wednesday, August 27th

We were relying heavily on the pictures in *How to Sail: A Beginners Guide to Ocean Sailing Part 1* as we spent the next morning sailing in circles just off the coast. We went back and forth, one steering while the other would try to mimic the actions demonstrated in the illustrations. It wasn't pretty, and we quickly discovered why the big horizontal beam was called a 'boom.'

The thud the boom made against his head was horrible, and it had sent him flying overboard. Luckily, especially since he didn't have on a life vest, he'd kept his consciousness and didn't drown. The cut that Ed had gotten across his forehead wasn't deep, but the swelling on it made it look much worse than it actually was. Soon after, he was able to keep powering on.

By sundown, we may not have been the most seaworthy of people, but we had gotten the hang of turning and adjusting the sails to match the new direction. We'd learned a few new knots that were necessary for the rigging, and we'd learned how to set and retrieve the sails. There was a lot to be desired, sure, but we'd gained a base of knowledge that hadn't been there before.

"What do you reckon, brew?" an exhausted-looking Ed said to me as we paused our work to watch the last of the sun sink below the Pacific. "Tomorrow, we hit the open?"

"Yeah," I responded, my voice softer than I'd meant it to be. One day of practice, one day on a boat, ever, and we were about to try to cross half of the Pacific-fucking-Ocean. "Ready or not…" I mused.

"…here we come," Ed finished.

. . .

Thursday, August 28th – Wednesday, September 3rd

It was an amazing feeling, that cool, morning breeze as the boat cut through the first vestiges of the open ocean. Neither of us had slept, but neither of us felt a bit tired, either. We were high on the endorphins the unknown journey ahead was stewing within us. Our adrenal glands were working overtime.

It didn't take long for the wind to carry us to a point where land was slipping beyond the early-morning horizon. Ed and I watched the smoldering coast slide to invisibility, the last of the life-nurturing land we would see until Hawaii. From that point on, if things went bad, we couldn't just walk or drive away. We didn't have dry land to fall back on. We had thirty-something feet of boat deck, then a darkened abyss that would swallow us, taking us down to the unknowns of its darkness.

Things weren't going badly, though. In fact, the first several days of the journey were remarkably smooth and restful. It was hard work keeping the sails and direction, yeah, but the in-between was full of sitting back and relaxing as we continued making our way through the sailing books. It was not what I had expected.

Despite the relaxation Ed and I were able to enjoy, we never lost touch with the reality of our situation. It wasn't easy, with no reminders around that the world had gone to shit, but whenever I would start to feel that loss fading out, I would think to my family, and my burning would return.

Coming onto the deck the morning of the fourth day, I could see that we were finally facing our first real hardship on the water, and it looked like it was going to be a serious one.

"Been kicking up now for the past half hour," Ed said as he eyed the stormy horizon in front of us. "Looks like we might be right fucked, mate."

The darkened, swirling clouds in front of us lead me to believe Ed may have been right. The guttural, roaring thunder that emanated from the dark underbelly of the storm made it seem even more likely. We were about to be fully tested, our grace period finally at an end.

With a sudden lurch, the boat was hit by an invisible wall of wind blasting out from the storm. The sails flipped direction so suddenly that the boom almost claimed me as a second victim. The sudden pop the sails made as they fully inflated did not instill any confidence in their strength, either, their threads undoubtedly being tested to the extreme.

"We've got to take those sails down," Ed said as he struggled to keep the boat's direction somewhat steady. From the look on his face and straining arms, it wasn't easy.

"Let's just try to sail around it," I responded.

"It's coming up on us too quickly, and I'm not going to be able to hold us steady! And, brew, what if lightning hits the masts?"

I agreed, not sure if it was the right thing to do or not, but it did make some sense to my novice mind. I didn't know if they were flammable or not, but one of the last things we needed was for our sails to get lit on fire by lightning.

It was a struggle to pull in the sails as the wind began to shift. It may have been easy for someone who knew what the hell they were doing, but for Ed and me, it was frustrating as shit. Eventually, we finally got the mainsail lowered, and I was able to loosen the rope for the jib, bringing it in, too.

With the sails finally down, we each strapped on life vests, watching the growing storm move closer. As it did, we began to realize the complete error in our ways. Without the sails, and with no working motor, the boat had no power to move anywhere but where the sea wanted it to.

We couldn't turn the boat; we couldn't guide the boat. We were fucked. When the full force of that storm hit us, we were going to be thrashed around like a child's toy in a wave pool. If we had a chance of surviving that trip, we had just eliminated it. There was no way we were going to survive that. For what would not be the last time that night, I thought my death was imminent.

The waves matched the wind as the two began to intensify. The boat's movements were quickly going from a lull to a full-speed spin-cycle. Waves had doubled in size, and they rolled underneath us, the bow of the boat rising and dropping several feet. I caught air and slammed back into the deck, but that was just the beginning.

With every passing minute, the wind tore by us faster and faster, a whistle almost audible as it blew through the rigging. The gusts would hit without warning, adding what felt like an additional twenty miles per hour to the blast.

The lightning had seemed to stay fairly far away from us, even as the storm had grown closer. However, that changed in an instant, as a bolt of that super-heated plasma came scorching from above, blasting the darkening surrounding with a burningly blinding light. It hit the water so close to us that we could almost see a ripple form at the impact zone.

The thunder that followed was deafening. It was louder than almost anything I'd ever heard before -- I think the only thing that topped it was the sound of the airplane hitting the ground. The thunder was so loud that its vibrations cracked two porthole windows that led into the galley.

Ed and I crouched instinctively. I nearly lost my balance as our handicapped vessel was tossed from one side to another. I caught myself, though, and regained my balance. Ed did the same, moving to the helm. He grabbed a strap attached to the boat's frame and clasped it to his belt.

"Go downstairs, Sean," he yelled to me over the growing torrent of mother nature.

"I'm staying here," I called back defiantly.

"Look, mate, I reckon we got one strap, and if this shit gets worse, waves'll be crashing over us in no time! You'd get swept off the deck! Get downstairs, brew!"

His thinking made sense, so I decided to follow his suggestion. Well, command, really. I stopped and turned back to him.

"What are you going to do? You'll be useless up here!"

"Maybe if I can at least turn the rudder a certain direction, I can aim us!" He must have seen the look on my face. "It's worth a shot, brew."

A wave hit the bow of the boat, turning the hull, water careening over the weathered wood and toward us. The wave had barely broken onto the boat, but its force nearly knocked me off my feet. I had a tight hold of the handrail leading downstairs, though, and was able to stay afoot.

"Get downstairs before it gets worse, Sean!"

I did. It felt like I was running, like I was hiding. Because I was. Ed was right; I'd just be a walking dead man if I were to go back up on deck. Who was I kidding, though? I was already a dead man. Down below, or up on deck, it didn't matter. I was a dead man. We were both dead men.

I was flung back and forth, the movements made all the worse by the fact that there was no warning. I couldn't even see a foot in front of me. With the storm blocking out the light so completely, the entire interior of the boat was an absolute void of sloshing darkness. It sent my equilibrium wheeling. It was terrifying and sickening in a way that my landlubber-self had never experienced.

The whistle of the wind was worse below deck than it was above. Finding the tiniest of gaps to cut through, the velocity it traveled with forced the air in. It was high-pitched and screechy, sounding like it belonged in a Stanley Kubrick movie, rather than a setting I found my real-world self surrounded by. It was a breathtaking chaos that I couldn't see.

However, lightning was filling the sky more and more frequently. With each blast of light, I caught a terrible glimpse of what was around me. It was mother nature's strobe light, torturing me and making me pay for my sins. With each of those bolts sent from hell, the thunder followed along closer and closer, the sound of The Four Horsemen coming to carry me away.

The water at my feet was growing ever deeper by the moment, water streaming in from the waves crashing above. Trying to close the companionway door to the upper deck, my muscles felt like they were going to tear apart from my bones, but no matter how hard I tried, the door wouldn't budge, stuck on something I could neither see nor eradicate. I was beginning to panic when an intensely bright purple filled the cabin, turning night into day. It was gone in a blink, but the thunder that followed vibrated my soul.

A scream from above deck carried on the wind and down to me. I listened for a second, straining to hear through the madness, but I heard nothing. It didn't feel right.

Taking a deep breath, I slid the companionway door fully open and trounced up the stairs. I was immediately pushed back by the wind as my head popped up above the deck. It was easily hitting highway speeds, and the gusts were seeming to hit those which would have gotten a driver a hefty fine. I caught my footing and pushed forward, taking a firm grip of the handrail and walking out onto the deck.

I wasn't sure exactly what I had expected, but the fact the pitch black of below-deck carried outside took me by surprise. We were floating in an infinite blackness that was momentarily penetrated by flashes of purple and torrents of white caps just before the waves broke onto the boat. It was oddly gravity-defying. There is no other way to describe that feeling of stepping up and out into complete darkness with that amount of wind and water and forces blowing and pushing you left and right. It was gravity-defying.

I could almost feel my feet rising off the deck, floating, not thrown, slowly being lifted out of myself and into a vast limbo of nothingness. Then, my feet did rise.

The boat came careening down the far side of a wave, and I slammed back down against the deck. Looking around, I could barely make out the shape of a weary and beaten Ed. He was hunched over and fighting to keep to his feet, his hand raised against his face to block the wind that impacted with a thousand stings.

"Ed!" I tried to call to him, but my voice was being pushed in the opposite direction. "Ed! Are you alright?"

Somehow, he heard me and turned. I couldn't make out much, but I could see him give me an 'A-Okay' hand sign, framed by a whitecap crashing behind him.

Even in that darkness, the whites of Ed's eyes became visible as his body seemed to tense up. He wasn't looking at me; he was looking behind me.

I used the frame of the companionway to brace myself against the wind, turning to see what Ed had evidently seen. I made my turn just in time to register that a wave larger than the Gabby was crashing in on us.

There was no time to react, not even to dive instinctively into the darkness below deck. The water hit with such force that the frame of the boat rippled like a liquid. The wave ripped over the deck, taking with it anything that wasn't tied down, including me.

It ripped me from my feet, and I slammed forward, smashing my face on something that was hidden by the water. Whatever it was, it split my lip, causing blood to pour out into the ocean. That wasn't my concern, though. My concern was that I was being swept off the deck, and though my arms were flailing about, trying to grab hold of anything they could, nothing caught my grasp. I slipped under the wired railing of the boat, trying to grab it. Again, I failed and fell.

After the impact with the water, for just an instant, all was calm. There was no sound, there was no wind, and there was still no light. I really was floating, weightless, held out above an expanse of an unexplored world. My body didn't feel like mine; I didn't feel like me. It was like that body, that floating, weightless body, belonged to someone else, someone far away that lived a far different life than me. That body didn't belong to me, and it never had.

I gasped for air as I breached the surface, coming back to the realization that I really was the one that was fucked. I tried looking around, but there was nothing to see. It was just darkness dotted with white caps and purple flashes. Nothing changed.

I was able to make out the shape of the Gabby as lightning lit the scene. It was a decent distance from me, and it seemed to be righting itself from a side position. It must have rolled when the wave hit, but it was coming upright. It was also moving away from me. We were both being pushed and pulled by the same tides and currents, but, in those conditions, there was no order to any of it.

Second by second, the Gabby grew fainter, turning into a ghost of the night, just a wisp of something you aren't quite sure you see. Then, I was certain I didn't see it. The Gabby was gone. I was alone, floating in that violent, crashing hell, just waiting to be swallowed and consumed by the dark.

I accepted my fate. I had given everything I had to try to get to my family. It was out of my hands. There was nothing else that I could do but lie back and let myself be taken by the vicious, angry ocean of which I was so deserving.

I wanted to see my family again. More than anything, I wanted to see my family and hug them and tell them I loved them. I wanted to kiss my wife and tell her how she had always made me a better person. I wanted to tell her that she had truly been everything I could have ever wanted in a partner and lover. She was my world, and I so badly wanted to tell her that I loved her with every inch of my being.

I wanted to hug my daughters and be by their sides as they entered the world as strong, powerful women that took the best of their mother and me. I wanted to be there as they conquered the world. I wanted so badly to be there by Clem's side when she published her first book. I wanted so badly to be there as Lily cured cancer. I wanted to be there when Hannah walked down the aisle. But I wouldn't be. No matter how badly I wanted to see those things, I wouldn't.

Just like Charlie was going to miss out on any life his children would have, just like he would never be able to hug and kiss his wife again, so shall I go. There was no other option at that point, and I wasn't going to fight it. Like Annie, I was going to accept my fate.

I clumsily removed my life vest and let my body be thrown around by the waves, no longer trying to keep my head above the water. In one set of rolls I was being tossed through, I felt a solid mass hit my foot. I didn't hit it, it hit me. It didn't feel like it was propelled into me by the water, either. It felt as if it was under its own authority.

When the tumbling stopped, I broke the surface and took in a bit of air. I was prepared to let myself drown in that darkness, but I was not prepared to be torn apart by a shark.

I felt the bump again. It was most certainly an animal, there was no doubting. It was massive, too, the part that bumped me feeling like it alone was several feet. Whatever it was, it felt like it was teasing me. It was playing with its dinner.

As a bolt of lightning flashed behind an oncoming wave, it lit through the water, exposing the silhouette of one of nature's greatest hunters. I had no idea what kind it was, but it was most certainly a shark, which was seemingly circling me.

I prepared myself for the pain I was about to experience. I tried to prepare for what it would feel like when the shark's razor teeth clamped down on me and ripped at my body. As the waves continued to pummel me, though, the shark never attacked. I kept waiting and expecting, but there was never any attack.

Once I felt the shark had left for good, my survival instinct had been rejuvenated. I began trying to spot my life vest, but it was impossible in the dark. It could have been a few feet away, but I would never have seen it unless I was looking right at it when lightning hit. By then, it also must have been thirty minutes since I took it off, and, with those currents and waves, it could have been anywhere. Miraculously, though, the Gabby's lifebuoy crashed right into me with a breaking wave.

I wasn't able to grab it, and the wave carried it past me. Putting the last of my energy to use, I began swimming in its direction, getting caught and propelled by a wave in the process. That wave's force carried me the last of the way, and I swam face-first into it. I never held something as firmly as I held that buoy.

The waves were punishing, seemingly unstoppable for hours. They crashed and beat on me and the buoy, wearing out my arms to a point that holding onto the circular life preserver was no longer possible. Trying out a new position, I tried to sit on it, and though the buoy sank quite a bit, it managed to work. I had to reposition after every wave, but it was worth it.

When the first beams of light shone between the horizon and the lightening clouds of the weakening storm, I nearly broke down. I had expected that I'd seen the sun for the last time, and though I was getting to see it again, it became obvious that I was still alone. I was floating in the biggest ocean in the world, with most boats grounded, and my boat God knows where. Even if I kept the life vest on, too, nothing would have been different. I survived the night, but my fate had not changed; it had just been prolonged.

By nightfall, the waves were calm, and the sky was clear. I rose and lowered slowly with each passing wave, but nothing was registering with me. My mind had shut off. There were no thoughts coming or going; I was a floating zombie. My mind and body were seemingly dead.

Several times through the night, I'd fallen asleep, head tilting back into the water. I was startled awake each time, coughing and hacking as I spit seawater out of my mouth. My natural need for sleep was causing me to undergo a form of water torture. It did help to reinvigorate my mind for a few minutes each time, but, as I reestablished my situation, my mind just clicked off again.

It happened a total of six times that night, and by the second morning, I was contemplating giving myself to the ocean once again. The day was going to really suck ass without any water, and suffering through another night of nearly drowning myself was not a pleasant thought.

Why should I fight anymore? I'd survived some crazy shit, but surviving on a lifebuoy in the middle of the Pacific Ocean under "normal" circumstances would be damn near impossible, so in the current circumstance of most boats being grounded, it was impossible. No one was going to find me, and no one was going to come looking for me. Ed may try, but he knew as little about sailing as I did and would never find me. No one was coming—

As I stared off toward the still-dark western horizon, the first light of morning seemed to be hitting something shiny in the distance. It broke me from my self-loathing and pity, forcing my mind to come back to life with curiosity and hope.

I squinted, trying to force my eyes to better focus on whatever it was in the distance. It didn't help, but, as time went on, it became obvious that it was moving with the water. It had to be a ship. And as time continued to go on, I began to realize that it was the Gabby. Somehow, someway, the motherfucking Gabby was sailing straight in my direction.

I didn't start yelling and screaming right away, but when I did, I gave it everything. I was not going to let any chance exist that Ed may not see me.

"Ed, you son of a bitch!" I screamed. "Ed! Over here!"

Only once the Gabby had pulled alongside

me, and I had collapsed on her deck, staring up at a pleasantly shocked Ed, did I allow myself to believe my rescue was real, that I was safe.

I was safe.

14

Wednesday, September 3rd – Sunday, September 14th

I couldn't move. I just didn't have the strength left. Trying to survive the storm took almost everything out of me, and what was left was taken while floating over the next two days. I just closed my eyes and didn't even try to move.

When I was able to stand, Ed helped usher me downstairs. I would have killed for a clean, salt-free shower with full blasting water pressure, but that simply wasn't going to happen. I made do, though, by lining a plastic strainer with tinfoil. Once secured to the strainer, I poked a few small holes into the foil. Then, I held it over my head with one hand and poured a bottle of water into it with other. It was pretty ridiculous, but it worked surprisingly well. The two cereal bars that followed were as equally satisfying.

"Why did you come back for me?" I asked Ed when I had finished the food and water.

"When I got out of the storm," Ed said after a long while, "I could have kept going to Hawaii, right? Well, what do you reckon I'd have done when I got there? Just tell your family that you drowned at sea, and I didn't even try to go back for you? Yeah, nah, I couldn't do that. I had to at least try to find you."

I didn't respond, but it was evident from Ed's expression that I didn't need to. He could see my gratefulness. Ed never ceased to surprise me.

"There is a problem, mate," Ed said after another long moment. "The thing is, that storm, it may have knocked us off course, so we can still head the general west-southwest direction, but, if our angle is off, we could miss the entire island chain. We'd never even know it until it was far too late."

"So, we're essentially sailing blind?" I asked.

"That's about right, brew," he said. "I do have some potential bright spots within this, though."

"Please, by all means, give me something good."

"The second sailing book you grabbed has a map in it. It shows all of the main currents of the Pacific, and we may be able to use this to make sure we end up somewhere close to Hawaii. Hold on," Ed added as he moved into the back cabin, returning a moment later with the water-logged book. Placing it onto the table in front of me and, opening about halfway into the pages, Ed continued, "Right here is the California Current.

It looks like, if we can find, and stay, on the northern side of it, it'll curve northward and take us straight to Hawaii."

As I stared at the illustration in front of me, I couldn't help but shake my head. Ed was right. The picture clearly showed a current wrapping around to the center of the ocean and curving north to the islands.

"One of these days," I said, "our luck is going to run out."

"Until that day, brew, I'm not questioning it!"

. . .

We were able to put together enough pieces to be confident in the guess that the storm had pushed us north. With the direction of the waves, and the angle of the sun before and after, it seemed to make the most sense, so we spent the next couple of days sailing south-southwest, trying to find something to indicate we'd found the California Current.

It was subtle at first, barely registering on the wavy surface. As we approached, though, we were able to clearly make out a small, yet distinct, line in the water. It seemed that it was two sections coming right up alongside one another but failing to mix. If we'd not been looking for it, we would have easily missed it.

It gave us a heading; it gave us a course; it

gave me hope. I was that much closer to finding my wife and daughters, and with everything I'd survived so far, when we turned into the flow of the current, I'd be lying if I said a strange sense of invincibility didn't creep up in me. It was kind of a nice change.

"It's weird," I said as Ed and I sat for our dinner, eating on deck and enjoying the stars. "Movies and books and everything else I'd been exposed to before had made it seem like survival instincts were... either you had them, or you didn't. They didn't come and go."

"What do you mean?"

"It was always made to seem that when someone was in a bad situation, their survival instincts would kick on and stay on through whatever was happening. It was like it was there and it never waned. If you didn't have it, you never would. Through this... through this entire hell we've been through, that hasn't been me; that hasn't my survival instincts. Even with my family to drive me, to keep me alive, one minute, I have the fiercest fight possible trying to come out, but the very next minute, I'm removing my life vest and letting the ocean take me. It isn't like we were told."

"That's human nature, mate," Ed said, a comforting firmness in his tone. "We can think and deduce possibilities and outcomes, and we can grasp what a situation really means to us. Like I said before, we know better than any other animal what it means to die. Our survival instinct is not just instinct, brew, it's our power of deduction and knowledge. Everyone has moments where the truth is overpowering, where the instinct to survive is overtaken by the power of knowledge, by knowing exactly what is happening. The real test, Sean, is how you fight back. Do you let your survival instincts, your drive to see your family again, come alive, or do you let the knowledge of a desperate circumstance consume you? So far, you're coming out ahead. Your survival instincts are working just fine.

"I mean, do you really think I'm all 'Hey fuckers, throw everything at me, and I'll just shit rainbows'? Yeah, nah, mate. I'm constantly fighting with myself to keep going. The world was bad enough before, when we had all those wonderful luxuries, but look at what it is now? Like, really, why would anyone want to fight to live in a world like this? Why would anyone fight to survive in a world where little children are eaten? That thought crosses my mind every minute of every god-forsaken day, and I don't have the fluffy view of humanity that you do. Also unlike you, I don't have a family to keep me fighting. It's really just me.

"It was a meme once, but it's fitting: The struggle is real. The struggle to stay positive; the struggle to want to live, to want to fight to live, but that's just the world we live in now. And just like before, there will be days where we wish the sun had never come up. Those will be hard days, harder than we could have imagined, but there will also be days, brew, where we wish the sun would never set. Those are the days that keep me fighting, and you know why?" I shook my head. "Because, like how you said love doesn't need to be big to be special, just one of those days is worth a hundred of the other."

. . .

We spent the next week traveling with the California Current. We were graced by calm waters and steady winds, so we used the time to continue growing our sailing abilities. We went through each page of the first book, being much more thorough in our attention to detail than we had been before the storm, and we each took turns practicing tasks and maneuvers on our own. We wanted to make sure that if something happened, both of us had the ability to keep going without the other.

We also began testing out our fishing chops with a couple of rods that had been hidden away. It went surprisingly well, with each of us catching a fish within ten minutes of our first cast. It was nice to know we could have some sort of fresh protein that night, instead of another night of cereal bars.

We also spent that time trying to position ourselves in the proper area of the current. Turning the boat, we sailed in one direction, perpendicular to the current, for as long as we could. When we got to the edge, we took note, turned the boat, and sailed across the current again and to the other end.

This maneuver gave us a rough estimate of the width of the current. From there, we knew we needed to be in the upper half of the flow. Using that information, we turned the boat and began sailing toward a spot we hoped would take us to where we needed to go.

One thing we hadn't counted on, though, was that, due to the current initially going further south than we'd planned, our supplies did not look as if they would last the full trip. By the time we reached the point where the current turned north, our supplies were down to a quarter of where they should have been at that point in the journey. We began rationing immediately, while also putting more of an emphasis on catching fish and any freshwater we could.

Two days after our turn northward, our luck took another painful hit. As our supplies were dwindling to borderline-dangerous levels, the means of our movement came to a complete stop. It started around midday, and by the time the sun was setting, the wind was gone. With it, the current had also seemed to completely disappear underneath us.

Hour after hour, we sat there, our hands essentially tied behind our backs. There was nothing we could do. We were stuck in a dead zone, a Bermuda Triangle that had taken away our mobility.

Without a breeze, the temperature also began to skyrocket. Instead of the oven that was Phoenix, the sweltering heat on the ocean made it so that we were living in a sauna, humidity so fierce that we were breathing more water than we were air. It weighed down our lungs and made our feelings of helplessness even worse. Not even the shade from the limp sails provided relief, and downstairs was murderous, the air stagnant and boiling. It was desolate and terrifying, watching the sunset into night with no hint of a change in weather.

The beauty of the night sky did make it a little easier to endure our circumstances. The desert sky had been astonishing, but being out there on the water, the sky's beauty was on an otherworldly level. The flat water served as a mirror for the infinite space above, making it feel like our ship was sailing right through the heart of the galaxy. It would have been an amazing thing to share with Lily and a telescope. I couldn't help but imagine, staring up at the twinkling Milky Way, that she would have had a smile on her face that would have lasted for weeks, no matter what she was going through.

I couldn't tell if I was finally beginning to hallucinate from the sun and lack of food and water, but as the stars all around twinkled through the darkness, they seemed suddenly connected, each a tiny neuron firing a signal to another. The universe had become a living, breathing entity all around us, and we watched in awe, not caring if it was a hallucination.

At just before dawn, my senses tingled. My eyes opened, revealing I had fallen asleep on deck. I knew something had woken me up, but, looking around, I couldn't quite figure out what it was. Getting to my feet, I was beginning to grow confused. What had woken me up? I felt something. I knew I did, but Ed was still passed out beside me, and there was nothing around, not even a bird.

Then, I felt it again.

"Ed," I cried. "Wake up!" As I shook him, the breath of wind brushed my hair ever so slightly. "Wind! I felt a little wind!"

Ed startled awake at this, and we prepared ourselves for the wind to start up. We were ready. Waiting and ready. By midday, it was obvious, though, that tease of wind was just that: A tease.

The day inched on, the sun creeping across the sky at a pace that even a snail could have surpassed, and with the sun creeping higher, the temperatures soared. By afternoon, the heat and humidity were becoming demoralizing. They were relentlessly beating at us, hurting physically and mentally. Several times throughout the afternoon, I lost my grip on what was in front of us, swearing up and down I'd seen land. There never was any land. By nightfall, the temperature began to fall, and I was able to regain control.

"I'm going to sleep inside tonight," Ed said to me as he left the bow, several hours into the night. "Back's killing me from sleeping out here last night. Bed's not much better, but I'll take it."

We said our goodnights, and he went back downstairs. I didn't follow. I wanted to stay on the deck a little longer. It was a shitty situation, but it was still the most beautiful natural sight I'd ever seen.

Like the night before, I watched as the stars making up the galaxy twinkled, once again creating that flickering breath above. There were tinges of blue and dark purple throughout that seemed painted by the hand of Bob Ross himself, and, like the night before, the dimensions of unbounded space and time stretched out their reign to the mirror world we floated on.

There were so many stars that I could not make out any particular constellation. It was a shroud of a billion burning balls of gas blocking out the familiarity of Orion and the Dippers. The number above was so vast that the light produced was greater than a dozen full moons. It was Beethoven. It was van Gogh. It was perfection.

In a vastness as grand as that floating below me and soaring high above, it was hard not to question my importance, especially when I was struggling to stay strong. In a space as overwhelming as my surroundings, in a disaster like the one we were living, how could something as completely minuscule as myself have any real meaning? In a universe that held billions of galaxies even more insanely massive than the one currently on full display, how can something I do matter in the scheme of things?

There's no way that anything lowly old Sean Lucas Heevy will ever do, or has ever done, that could cause the greater expanse to realize he'd even existed, even if I talked about myself in the third person. What happened on the other side of the galaxy was going to happen, no matter if I existed or not. Everything that lay out in front of me would one day end, and no matter what I did, there would never be any true, long-lasting meaning.

"One does not need to change the universe in order to have meaning," I heard a voice say. It was soothing. It was obviously male, but it seemed almost as if it had traveled through the ocean to reach me. It also completely startled me.

I scurried around, sliding on the deck and kicking out my feet at whoever had just spoken. There was no one on the deck, though. I was alone with Ed still downstairs. Who the hell had spoken?

"Here," the voice came again, and my head turned almost as if being guided.

It took me a second to register what exactly I was seeing in front of me. It was hard to comprehend. With the strange reflective surface of the ocean, it appeared as if someone were flying beside the boat, but a flying person would have been more believable than what I was beginning to realize it actually was. With a flying person, it could have been some random do-it-yourselfer that had built some sort of crazy-ass jetpack; instead, this person was standing on the water, the mirror-like quality only making it seem as if the person were flying. Walking on the water was way more damning for my sense of sanity. There was no device someone could make that would allow them to walk on water without even causing the slightest hint of a ripple. Whatever I was seeing either wasn't real or wasn't human.

It had to have been just another hallucination. It wasn't real. No one walks on water. Period. Let alone the surface of the Pacific-fucking-Ocean. Unless it wasn't a hallucination.

"Those who have meaning, Sean, need not change the tides," the person said. Despite the incredible amount of light the stars were putting off, the figure remained just a silhouette, both above and below. I couldn't make out a single determining feature. It had to be a hallucination. Had to be.

"Those who have meaning," the figure continued, "need only change *a* world, not *the* world. You, Sean, may not see the meaning in your life. You may look around at the world you find yourself in, and ask, 'What is the reason for this? Where is the purpose?' I cannot tell you that, Sean, but you, and every other person on this planet, have a meaning. You all have a purpose. Some just have a wider reach. That does not make that meaning or purpose greater or lesser than any other."

"Well, what was the purpose of Charlie surviving? What was Charlie's purpose, huh? He survived the plane crash only to be killed the next night by a flood!? What is the purpose in that?" I reacted with a bit of hostility toward the figure, despite still being ridiculously confused.

"I will not explain myself again, so I do hope that you realize the power of my words to come. Charlie had many purposes. First, he introduced a young man and woman to each other. Those two died in a car crash a year after they were married. Because Charlie introduced them, they were celebrating an anniversary with a dinner out. Because it was a celebration, the young man was a bit too inebriated to drive. Because he drove anyway, he ran a red light and hit a van. Because he hit the van, its occupant died.

Because the occupant died, he was unable to carry out his plan of attacking his workplace. If he had not been killed in that car accident with the young couple, thirty-eight people would have died.

"Charlie's second purpose will not be seen for another two hundred and eighty years. At that point, his descendants will be great warlords of what you know as the Smoky Mountains. His direct descendants will eventually be responsible for the coalescing of several dozen tribes into one.

"Charlie's third, and final, purpose was to help you. Before you interrupt, let me explain. Charlie's was the first death you feel you are responsible for. Charlie's was the first death where you had tried to help, but you couldn't do anything to stop it. It was the first in a long line of events that will, and already has begun to, lead you to a realization of control. Charlie's death helped you realize the horrors of what would be coming your way and prepared you for further actions you would need to take.

"Knowing that you and Charlie had many things in common hit your subconscious, telling you that you must never give up and that you must fight at all costs to reach your family. That if you did not do that, you would very likely never make it.

"Each one of you has a purpose, Sean. Continue to have strength, and have faith that you are on the right path."

Before my astounded mind could react, the silhouetted man disappeared into the cacophony of galaxial light. I blinked and seemingly washed away the rest of the night.

In that millisecond of a blink, the universe above and below relinquished its hold on my surroundings, and I found myself below deck. I was curled up in the woolen sheets of the bed, my head pounding. Somehow, I had just gone from above deck to being fully tucked into bed below deck in a literal blink of an eye. Not only that, but the sun also seemed to be coming up.

Through a shattered porthole next to the footboard, I could see the first sliver of sunlight break the horizon. I'd lost what I was certain to have been several hours without the slightest idea as to what had happened.

Had that all been a dream? Was it all just a dream so vivid it blurred my memory to a point that I couldn't remember going to bed? Was I really that exhausted and beaten? Perhaps it was me just getting up from a head injury in the storm. Maybe I'd been in a coma and was only then waking up. Looking out the window, though, the ocean was still motionless. It wasn't a coma, but maybe a dream?

"Morning sunshine," Ed said as he entered the sleeping area from the galley beyond.

"Morning," I responded automatically. "This may sound weird, but what day is it?"

"The fuck you on about, mate?" Ed responded. "How am I supposed to know?" he laughed at the seeming absurdity of my question.

"This is probably going to sound weird," I said.

"I think weird is better than the alternate new reality of bad," Ed said. I chuckled and continued.

"I had a dream that was so real that it's kind of fucked with my reality. I'm not sure what day it is or what's going on."

"You don't remember anything? Fucking 'roo tits, mate. Well," he continued, "I don't know a lot, but I can tell you what I know. Your name is Sean Heevy and you're on your way—"

"No," I stopped him, laughing at Ed's presumption. "I don't have amnesia or anything! I mean that… I remember being on deck with you what I think was last night. You said your back hurt, and you were going to sleep downstairs. At least, I think I remember it. It seems almost unreal, though. Like it's a fake memory."

"That's real, mate," Ed said. "I left you upstairs and came down here. I was asleep a few minutes later. I woke up a few minutes ago, and you were down here, strewn out on the floor. It looked pretty uncomfortable, so I picked you up and put you in the bed. You're heavier than you look, brew!"

"Thanks," I said jokingly. "I'm actually on a diet. Okay, so, then," I stopped, not wanting to speak my clarifications out loud. It already seemed crazy enough; I didn't need to start spouting the fact I thought I'd maybe been in a coma. I thought Ed would laugh it off, but you never know. "Nevermind."

"What was the dream, brew?" he asked curiously. "No way you can ask a question like that and not tell me about the dream!"

My groan was almost audible. I'd really hoped he wouldn't ask anything else. I couldn't blame him, though. I'd have asked more, too.

"Someone, something, seemed to appear to me last night on the water. I couldn't see who it was. It was really just a silhouette. I should have been able to see some features, but I couldn't. It was a male. I could tell by the voice, but the voice was muffled like he was talking through one of those tin-can walkie-talkies. Remember those? He sounded like he was talking through one of those but underwater. It was weird.

"He was telling me about… about how we all have meaning, even if we can't see it. He told me to have faith and that everything would be okay. I don't know what the fuck that means, because right now, I don't have much faith in anything but you. But after that, I blinked and woke up in bed. It was literally a single blink. I closed my eyes, and when they reopened a split-second later, I was tucked into bed."

"This may be a good time to tell you," Ed said, a hesitancy to his voice. "The day after the storm, I'd thought you'd died, fair dinkum. I just collapsed onto the deck and held my head low. If you died, what the fuck was I going to do? Well, as I knelt there, broken, defeated, lost… I heard something.

"At first," he continued, his face in a contortion of confused memory, "I thought it was the wind, but it wasn't. I couldn't even convince myself that it was. I didn't move, I just crouched there and listened.

"'Have faith,' I heard the voice say," Ed continued. "Have faith? I'm not a religious man; I have no faith. But it said again, 'Have faith. You have made the right choices. Trust yourself. Find Sean.'

"It sounded like rubbish to me. Even though I was determined to try to find you, I never really thought I'd actually accomplish it. At most, I figured I'd find you floating, face down, life vest keeping you on the surface.

"When I first heard you calling out, I couldn't help but wonder about that fuckin' voice. Yeah, nah, it could have been a hallucination. For sure, but it sure as hell didn't feel like one. It was what I'd expected to experience while on Walkabout. Like I'd told you, walkabout was about many things, one of which was connecting with your ancestors, with their spirits, with their beings. At least, that's what I'd been led to expect when I headed out into the vast open wilds of Oz.

"I never found them. For me, I came back because I was bored. I hadn't felt a single connection to any spirit or ancestor. I'd found a good watering hole with decent wildlife to hunt, and I was living fine, but I was thirteen and bored, so I went home. The feeling from that voice was what I'd expected on Walkabout."

"Did it feel like God?" I asked bluntly.

"God? I don't know. I reckon God doesn't come down like that. He doesn't speak to people like that. Not anymore. That's Biblical times kind of stuff. He doesn't do that in the twenty-first century!"

"Maybe he does, and we had just gotten too busy looking down at our screens to notice."

There was no follow-up as we both felt the slightest movement beneath our feet. Exchanging glances, we turned and hurried onto the deck, hoping our senses hadn't lied to us. The sea was still just as flat as it had been, but off in the distance, there was a clear line of movement heading across the surface. We stood and watched as that line grew closer and closer, splitting the water into two entirely different oceans, just as we had seen when coming upon the current.

When it hit, it was instant ignition. Our sails popped out to their full breadth, pulling tight against the suddenly powerful winds that had come out of the horizon.

With the winds, came the current, carrying us, once again, in the direction of the tropical paradise of Hawaii.

We slept in eight-hour shifts for the next several days, each still working our way through the second sailing book. Through it all, we each still battled moments of confusion, reality blurring with visions of things not really there. Each time, our determination and fight won out, clearing our minds to the tasks at hand.

As our eighteenth day on the boat came to a close, Ed and I sat on deck to watch the sunset, tiny rations of cereal bars serving as our dinner, when something on the northern horizon caught my eye. It didn't look flat. The horizon rarely did look flat, since you could see distant waves on it, but this was different. This wasn't just a ripple in the water. This was something solid and still; something shining bright in the setting sun; something massive that had to have been reaching high into the sky.

"Is that…" Ed began.

"Hawaii!"

15

Monday, September 15th

I wanted to make our way onto shore that night, but Ed had managed to convince me otherwise. We had no idea which island in the chain we were looking at, and we had no idea what we would run into when we landed. Onshore, there could be a vast wasteland full of people who had starved or been shot.

It was the right decision, I knew, but I'd been through so much to get that far, I didn't want to wait any longer. My family was just right there. Just a few miles from me, my girls and my wife were there, hopefully eating dinner and drinking clean water. That was what I told myself, anyway.

I took the darkness of the island that night as a good sign. The darkness meant it wasn't burning like the cities we'd seen already. It didn't mean anything else, but, for me, knowing it wasn't a smoldering pile of ash was extremely reassuring. Then again, that part of the island may have always been uninhabited, far from the cities.

With the anticipation of what the next day could bring, I was restless all night long. Thoughts ran through my head of all the possibilities. Since the night of the confrontation at Jack and Gladys's, I'd been able to keep at bay the most horrible of thoughts about what condition my family may have been in, but with the islands so close, I couldn't continue to keep the horrible thoughts at bay. I imagined what it would be like if we were to land the next day, only to discover my entire family had died. I couldn't imagine what I'd do if that was the case, but I knew that it was a very real possibility.

If they were alive, how would they look? Would they be mirror images of me at Jack and Gladys's, eyes sunken in with greyed shadows that would likely never disappear, cheeks protruding to add to the gaunt appearances? Would they be injured? Would they be starved? Would they be healthy? Would they even be there?

By what felt like three in the morning, I began to control myself a bit, repeating the words, 'Do not waste energy worrying about things you cannot control,' the phrase being repeated so many times that it began working like the counting of sheep, lulling me to sleep for a short time.

I didn't want to sleep, though. So little was my urge to sleep that my body woke itself up not long after, just as the first tinges of blue and orange began appearing on the eastern horizon. Instantly, I was out of the bed and hurrying above deck, and before Ed even woke up, I had the anchor up, and our jib was pulled taut with wind.

By the time Ed had made it onto the deck, I was rounding an outlet of the island. He had a map of Hawaii in hand, and as he opened it, he studied the coastline.

"See that glowing up there?" Ed asked as he pointed to a soft orangish glow we were coming up on. "That's not fire, brew. That's lava. Looks like this is the Big Island."

"What's that mean?"

"Basically, it's the first island in the chain. We've got a bit further to go."

A bit further was a bit more than a bit, taking another day before the shape of Oahu's Diamondhead broke the horizon. With it, the city of Honolulu came into view. It had not been spared the fate suffered by Phoenix and L.A. It, too, was a shattered, smoldering memory of a once-great metropolis, this one destined to become the next Atlantis.

I tried to remain positive as we put the city behind us. It was made a bit easier as we passed Pearl Harbor, and the military base seemed to be fully intact and not on fire. It was a good sign that a place that held military weaponry seemed to have remained stable.

Within the hour, we were passing Waimea. After a second hour, we rounded a patch of reef, coming face to face with the Ahupua'a 'O Kahana State Park and the resort we'd traveled so far to reach. Having the only permit to build in the state park, the resort sat alone. The thought of that site had kept me going, though never fully believing I would even get close to making it. But it was real; it was really in front of me. I was not hallucinating.

I struggled to keep my excitement down as I took in the building and its surroundings. The resort was just a couple of years old, and it looked as clean as ever. There were no broken windows, the grass—what little there was—was still trimmed down, and the vegetation was not overgrown. From our angle, it was hard to see, but it looked like a part of land had actually been cultivated.

Everything looked normal except there seemed to be no movement as I turned the boat, steering toward the docks jetting out into the water. There were no people walking the land or swimming in the pool overlooking the beach. No one was swimming in the waves. The resort seemed to be completely vacant.

As we grew nearer, two small boats appeared from behind us, gaining on us. Each of the boats seemed to be carrying three men, two of the men in each were working the oars, while the third in each had pistols held at the ready.

We lowered our jib to slow ourselves down and show we meant no harm. This was probably a dumb thing to do. We had no idea if they were from the resort or just men that had gone back to their wild roots like those in Phoenix. We slowed down, anyway. They were going to catch us no matter what, and we were already close enough to try to swim for it if needed.

"What are you doing here?" yelled one of the men as the boats came up alongside us on both sides.

"I'm looking for my family," I said, not wanting to waste any more time. I was not going to beat around the bush. "I'm looking for a woman and three girls. Their names are Ellie, Clementine, Lily, and Hannah. I'm Ellie's husband. I'm the girls' father. They were staying here, and I've come to find them. I've got a picture of them if you let me get it." I pulled the photo from my wallet and held it up to him. "Hannah is the youngest. Lily is the one in the middle. Clementine is the oldest. Ellie's the one with me in the back. Are they here?"

"Drop anchor, grab your stuff, and come with us."

"Are they alive?" I pleaded, desperate for any word on how my family was.

"Everything will be explained to you when you're onshore."

Deciding that pressing the issue and pissing

these armed men off was not a proper course of action, I didn't ask again. Instead, I moved to the rail and began my struggle to transition to the smaller boat. Even with the help of the men on it, I still nearly fell into the ocean. Ed was coming from below with his camera in hand and its bag around his shoulder as I clumsily made it onto one of the small boats.

When we made it to shore a short time later, another small group of men exited the resort and met us on the beach. They all looked to be native Hawaiians, much like the men on the boat, and they were all dressed in uniforms with the name of the resort on them. They were the employees.

The men from the boat relayed our story, and the two groups parted ways without issue, leaving us with the resort employees.

"Follow us," one of the younger workers said, and we did.

Inside, the resort looked as if nothing had changed. It was clean and organized; nothing was broken. It was as if we'd entered a time machine and come out just before the world went to shit. The only thing that was missing from the picture was the guests. That made me worry a bit, but there was no sign of a struggle, so I continued to keep my emotions in check. We passed through the lobby, our escorts still not saying anything, my palms growing sweatier and sweatier.

"Seems a bit odd," Ed whispered sideways to

me. "Where is everyone?"

His question was answered almost immediately as we were led to a set of glass doors at the far end of the lobby. There, on the other side, was a central courtyard the rest of the resort was built around. In the middle, the land was being farmed by the guests. There didn't appear to be any forced compliance, either. Each guest's face that we could make out had a smile, and they were all seeming to converse and laugh with one another.

The massive fire pit at the center of the courtyard looked to be serving as a gathering spot, a group of men standing around it like a Sunday afternoon barbeque, the only things missing were the bottles of beer in hand. The two pigs being spit-roasted over the flame were beginning to crispen, the color darkening and their smell wafting through the air. They smelled delicious, but my focus was elsewhere.

My eyes moved over every one of the people as we opened the door and stepped through. To our immediate right, only visible once through the doors, was a group of kids running and playing. My muscles seized, and I could feel a delirious mixture of chemicals releasing into my body as I tried to find the faces of my girls.

I heard her before I saw her. Hannah's laugh was infectious, coming from deep in her gut. She had a jolly, old fat man's laugh in the body of a six-year-old. I would have recognized that laugh anywhere.

When her black, curly hair came bouncing around a blossoming pineapple bush, I couldn't stop myself.

"Hannah!" I screamed, my legs moving as fast as they could, tears exploding free. "Hannah!"

I watched as she stopped, realized that she recognized the voice calling for her, and turned.

"Daddy!" she cried as she immediately began running toward me.

"Dad? Dad!" I heard another familiar voice say. Clementine appeared from my left, from within the group of people tending the crops.

I was overwhelmed as Hannah and I crashed into each other, arms wrapping tightly around one another, tears soaking each other's shirts. I never wanted to let go. I had finally found my family, and I was never letting go again.

Clem arrived a few seconds later, and our embrace grew larger, emotions more wildly out of control. Home was finally right in front of me, but it wasn't complete.

"Where's your mom? Lily?" I asked through tears of pure joy.

"Lily wanted to show her some sort of bush she'd found. They should be back for lunch anytime. Dad, how in the hell are you here? We'd thought you were dead!"

"I almost was," I said, wiping away those tears. "I'll tell you all about it when we find your mom and sister. I bet you have a story to tell, too."

I kissed my girls' foreheads and took their hands in mine. I let them lead me the short distance across the courtyard, through a hotel corridor, and out the other side. We didn't need to go far before Lily's voice came through the foliage. She was excited, evidently talking about something she'd learned.

We turned a corner, and there they were. They had their backs to us, but they were unmistakable. My wife. My Lily. We were all there.

"Mommy!" Hannah said.

"Hannah," Ellie started before she had even turned around, "I told you to stay..." She stopped dead, and we locked eyes.

We took each other in, and I could see that she was unsure if I was real. There was a confused, stunned look there, like her brain had momentarily reset.

"Sean..." she said as she realized that I was real. Her face contorted, instant relief of all the stress, worry, and pain she'd inevitably built up over the time we were separated. The not knowing was bad for me; I couldn't even imagine how bad it had been for her, having the girls and being in a strange place, knowing that I was on a plane when everything had happened. I could only assume she had come to terms with me having died.

We ran toward one another, and when we embraced, it was like it was the first time. It was that first kiss, that kiss when you realize you found the love of your life. It was an embrace that makes you feel like you're complete. It was the sensation of touch that made two souls into one, and she and I were once again whole.

When my daughters each ran over, wrapping themselves into us, we were all sobbing with the emotion of something happy in a world of horror. In that moment, there wasn't air, there wasn't space, there wasn't even Earth; there was just my family and me. We were all together, something none of us really thought would ever happen again.

"Dad," Lily said, the first to pull from the hug, "Who's the guy with the camera?"

I turned my head, my face a slobbery mess, and saw that Ed had been standing a good distance away, not wanting to intrude, but still trying to get the shot. His face looked as bad as I'm sure mine did. By then, he had as much invested in this as I did.

"That, sweetheart, is your daddy's friend, Ed," I responded, a smile across my face. "He helped me get to you. I wouldn't be alive today if not for him."

It was Clementine that first went to Ed.

"Thank you," she said to him. Still crying, she embraced him tightly.

Little Hannah followed suit, running over to

Ed, and wrapping her arms around him.

"Thank you for bringing me my daddy," she said.

Ed and I exchanged looks, his painted in a genuine, overwhelming humbleness.

"Lunch should be starting soon. What do you all say we get some food?" Ellie asked, cheerful and optimistic.

. . .

The spit-roasted pig was as delicious as it looked, and after we'd eaten, we must have been the most well-fed people in the state. I actually felt like I would need to untie Jack's swim trunks, which, yes, I was still unfortunately wearing. It felt like I had just had the most magnificent Thanksgiving dinner and was now ready to collapse on the sofa and watch TV until I passed out.

It may not have actually been Thanksgiving, but that feast was absolutely a 'thanks'-giving feast for me. I had more to be thankful for at that moment than I'd ever had before. It was contentment of the best kind.

It didn't last long, though, as a man came up to us and introduced himself.

"Aloha," he said. "My name is Likeke, and I'm the resort manager. I understand that you are tired from your travels and reunion, but I must intrude. I would like to speak with you alone for a little while. I would like to discuss the situation in the world outside. You know better than any of us here what is going on."

I looked at Ellie, who responded, "Go, Sean. Likeke is a good man. We'll be here."

I'd expected to be led into some office somewhere, but Likeke, instead, led me to the front drive area. It was a large, covered strip of concrete that would have inevitably once been filled with excited tourists and sweating valets, airport shuttles and taxis coming and going every few minutes.

Just outside the awning, he sat on a concrete rail that once protected a fountain, and I took a seat next to him.

"You are the only one here," he said, "that has seen the outside world. No one here has seen anything off of this island. We have no news from the mainland about what's going on in the world. Tell me. What does the world look like now?"

I told him. I told him the good and the bad, sparing no details. I told him of the rapists and cannibals; I told him of the make-shift Red Cross shelter in Chase Stadium. I told him of the President's pacemaker failing, and his subsequent death and the probable collapse of the government. I told him of holdouts like Jack and Gladys, and I told him the worst of the worst:

This was not a short-term event.

"It's that bad?"

"Yeah," I said. "It may even be worse. We were doing all we could to keep moving. We didn't stick around to find out how bad it really was."

"That certainly isn't the news I wanted to hear. We'd heard stories similar to yours from those coming out of Honolulu. We'd hoped the mainland wasn't the same."

"It is. We saw Honolulu coming in, and it lines up pretty well with what we saw in L.A. and Phoenix."

He sat in silence for a long moment, eyes staring into a palm frond that was blowing in the breeze.

"Well, you and your companion are welcome to stay with us. We seem to have found a good balance here, and I don't think two extra mouths will make much difference."

"Thank you, Likeke. I really do appreciate it."

"Of course," he responded with a warm, yet sad, smile. "Now, go back to your family and enjoy your night."

16
September – March

It happened virtually overnight. That resort became home. My family and I, Ed included, felt all our stresses disappear. In fact, that simple existence led us to be happier than we'd ever been.

We were no longer spending our days away from each other, taking part in tasks that just felt pointless. We weren't sitting in front of screens, harboring and nurturing relationships with avatars, instead of people. We weren't focused on the opinions of screennames or bosses that felt better than us because they had their own parking spots.

We were together, spending every moment by each other's sides. We were putting our energy into activities that bore literal fruits. We were putting our minds toward knowledge that we could actively use to better ourselves and those around us. We had never been as isolated, yet we had never been as close.

Ed and I were shocked at how well things at the resort were run, too. Though things were never forced, there was a routine that everyone was taking part in. The kids still had classes, taught by three tourists that had been teachers in their previous lives. The adults, other than the teachers, each took one two-hour shift a day, and each day, their shift would be made up of a different task. One day, a person could be helping with the crops, and the next, they had housekeeping duties. It all worked.

I discovered a passion for farming that I had never even imagined possible for myself. There was just something about getting my fingers dirty, putting forward all the energy and effort, and getting to watch something grow into existence. In a way, it was like fatherhood. You plant a seed and water it, nurture it until it begins to sprout, but that's when the real work begins. You have to protect it, feed it, and, in many ways, love it like you would a child. You put blood, sweat, and tears into it, and the plant grows. I found myself really looking forward to those days.

With such short shifts, it left each person a great amount of time to do as they pleased. There was a lot of lounging about, not doing anything, as one might expect, but there was also a flourishing of creativity, art, and, of all things, philosophy.

One of the guests, a German with the highly

original name of Hans, had taken several old TV sets, busted out the screens, removed the wiring, and replaced it all with soil and plants. An elderly Japanese woman named Ms. Wong had begun to use old linens from unused rooms to sew new articles of clothing. She even made me a pair of pants out of a set of window curtains so that I finally had something else besides the uncomfortably short swim trunks.

Every night, as everyone gathered in the courtyard for dinner, conversations would often turn to reminiscing, people speaking fondly of the times they once enjoyed. Though they spoke fondly of those times, the sense of loss grew fainter and fainter every night. Once the kids all began heading to bed, the adults when invariably turn to the bigger questions, the questions our minds had once been too busy to even try to ponder.

Religion and meaning were always a hot topic. Back and forth, the conversation was always a good debate on what the recent events meant for God and religion, what they meant for the purpose of life and the society that so many generations had worked so hard to build. There was never an answer, and most people seemed okay with that.

I never shared with them my experience on the boat, my visitation, shall we say. I never told them about the message of meaning my probable hallucination had imparted on me. I enjoyed sitting back, my wife in my arms, just listening to them going back and forth, enjoying life. If there was ever a perfect society, that was it.

Local fishermen would come by every few days to trade. They would bring the resort several large fish, and we would give them some of our fruit and veggies. It was a mutually beneficial arrangement that helped top off our well-rounded diet.

Relationships began forming amongst those of us at the resort, as well, both platonic and romantic. Ellie had struck up a close friendship with a woman named Dianna from Kentucky. Before I'd even arrived on the island, they were each other's strength. Ellie had depended on Dianna to help with the girls while I was gone. Dianna had helped comfort Hannah when she cried over missing me; she helped Lily catalog the different butterfly species she was spotting around the resort; she even helped Clem find notepads and paper for writing new stories.

There were several dozen young people, single and under thirty, too, so romance was ever-present. Sometimes, it was heated and aided by alcohol. Other times, the feelings seemed genuine.

"Hey, dad? Um… I have a question," Clem said to me one afternoon as she and I were tending to some veggies that were just about ready for picking.

"Okay," I responded. "I probably have an

answer."

"You like Ed, right?" There was a hesitancy in her voice. "I mean, I know, of course, you like Ed. If you didn't, why would you have sailed with him? Stupid question."

She was flustered, and I knew why. In the eight weeks since Ed and I had arrived, I'd noticed the two of them exchanging looks.

"Clem," I said, trying to put a bit of reassurance in my voice, "I like Ed. And sweetie, considering what humans have been through recently, I assure you, you won't find a better partner."

There was a sudden shift in her demeanor, almost like Clem had been lifted slightly, a weight having dissipated. A smile crossed her face that was nothing but pure, giddy young love.

"He really is a great photographer," she said. "He told me you told him about the story I wrote about his picture. He said, since I don't have the story anymore, I should try to write a new one. He keeps talking to me about my writing. You know, like pushing me to start up again. I can't imagine…"

As she talked, I listened actively, taking in every word she had to offer me. I had found heaven on Earth. Everything had finally fallen into place, and things were right with the world.

Friday, March 11th, 2037

We were all enjoying the final flavors of our dinner when Likeke approached.

"Sean, can I talk with you for a few minutes?"

There was a worry and tension in his voice that I'd not heard there before. Even when Ed and I first arrived, he never sounded quite like that. He led me into the ballroom we'd been using for medical purposes. Usually quiet, the room typically only having to service minor cuts and scrapes, with the occasional bouts of the flu, it was filled with weak sounds of pain and suffering.

In the far area of the room, Dr. Cheema, an Indian doctor who had been vacationing with his family, was standing over a makeshift gurney. There was a spotlight, once used for shining onto speakers addressing the room, shining down onto the gurney, now serving as a surgical light.

The man being worked on was moaning, his head slowly plopping from left to right. We had no anesthesia, so as I saw what Dr. Cheema was doing, I was surprised the man was even conscious.

The doctor's fingers were moving around, second-knuckle deep, within a massive cut along the man's side. Slowly, Dr. Cheema pulled his fingers out of the cut, a long, jagged piece of metal clasped in between his middle finger and thumb.

"Now, let's talk," Likeke said as he ushered me out of the room.

When we arrived to his office, Likeke sat behind the desk and rubbed at his eyes, pressing hard. He'd worked so hard to get the community to where it was, I could see that whatever happened to that man had Likeke extremely concerned.

"It looks like it's finally happening," he said. "For a while now, I've been worried about Pearl Harbor. So many well-trained soldiers. Killers, really. They must have the same kinds of constraints on supplies that we do, you know, but they also have a lot more people to care for. Figured, one day, they'd no longer be able to care for their people. What would happen then?"

Likeke went silent, and I wasn't sure if he wanted an answer or not. I had no idea what he was talking about, though, so I had no answer to give. I hadn't even thought about Pearl since Ed and I first got to the islands. Staring out of the window, Likeke continued.

"It looks like that day has come. We now know what would happen. Stevie, the young man you saw, was on a trip around the island with his father and brother. They were taking their little sailboat to just kind of keep an eye on things, check-in on the coasts. Didn't get all the details, but something drew them to land just north of the base.

"There was some sort of uprising. From what little Stevie was able to tell us, it sounds like the groups there are heading out in different directions. We believe they each are looking for new places to settle, maybe even just to raid and steal others' supplies.

"Either way, when they get here, and it is 'when,' not 'if,' we won't stand a chance. We don't have the weapons or skills to handle them. This little community we've worked so hard to build and sustain... Well, it... its time is coming to an end. And that, Sean, is where you come in."

"What do you mean?" I was so confused by everything he was telling me. It was so sudden; there had been no recent hints of potential issues.

My mind flashed back to the images of Phoenix and L.A. Living in such a blissfully cut-off and protected place such as that resort for so long, my mind had successfully begun to block out the horrors of what the outside world actually was. It had blocked out those scenes so that, to me, they may as well have never happened, but the horrors were apparently returning.

"Your boat. It's still anchored right offshore,

and we did the math. At its size, you could carry twenty-two people off of this island and back to the mainland."

"You can't be serious? Ed and I barely made it here, and we only did because of sure dumb-fucking-luck. Putting us in charge of twenty other people while we cross the Pacific Ocean is not the smartest of ideas."

"You're right. It's a stupid idea, with a lot of risk, but, Sean, if those twenty-two people stay here, I don't think they will live. You and Ed proved once already that it can be done. Do it again."

"Okay, so, say we take them, and miraculously, we make it back to the mainland in one piece. What next? Where would we go? A band of almost two dozen people isn't going to be easy to hide, let alone supply along the way."

"When you first arrived, you spoke about a couple. They were an elderly couple that I think you said were living in Arizona. They had extended you a welcome to return with your family. Take them there."

"They extended a welcome to my family. Five people. Not two dozen. They had supplies and shelter for that many, yeah, but they had a family of their own."

"You, yourself, said that their family would probably never make it to them."

"And I also said that I would probably never make it here, but I did."

"Sean, I don't want to argue with you. The plain and simple truth is that this place will be overrun. The people still inside may not die when that happens, but what will be left for them after? Chances are that nothing will be, and with that, there goes their hope.

"For those that can take the boat, there will be a chance. Times will get hard, but there will be a hope for survival at the end of it. That is the difference. The outcomes may end up the same, but if people can have hope on the way out, fuck it, give it to them."

"How would you even choose who goes? You know that people will freak out if they know they're being left here to a pretty certain death."

"Lottery. It's the only way. Everyone gets a number. If their number is drawn, they can choose an additional three people."

"What if they have a family of five?"

"Some people chosen may only have one or two others they choose to take. If that is the case, they may give their extra spots to those without enough for their whole family."

I had no response. It was one of the stupidest ideas I'd ever heard. As much as I didn't want to admit it, though, staying behind would probably rank as an even stupider idea.

"Think of your family, Sean. Do you want to give them a fighting chance, or would you rather you all just sit here, just waiting to die?"

When I rejoined my family a few minutes

later, my mind was racing. Likeke wanted to know by morning if they had my buy-in or not. They'd follow through with the plan either way, but if they had my buy-in, since it was my boat, they would let me and Ed go, with each of us able to pick three passengers.

I had my doubts that the military members and their families would cause too much devastation to the resort. I just couldn't see them taking part in the murder of a peaceful community, but I had to admit, it wasn't like it hadn't been done before. It was entirely plausible. So, after talking the plan over with Ellie and Ed, we all came to the conclusion that heading back out to sea, though painfully stupid, was still smarter than staying behind.

Once I gave Likeke my answer, the pieces immediately began moving. Necessary supplies were being packed and stowed securely on the boat, as the residents began spreading rumors as to what was going on.

While this was happening, a list of every person at the resort was gathered, a number being assigned to each name. Without letting the guests know, Likeke held the lottery in secret, pulling a set of six names who, based on their expected number of guests, would fill up the boat, and no one would be leaving a family member behind.

I had mixed feelings about doing it in secret. I understood how it could help keep panic low, but I also felt it was a bit immoral to keep the situation from those it would impact.

"Once you and your passengers are sailing away, I will tell everyone. Not before. I will not risk panic by spreading the news too soon."

With that, Likeke and several of his employees began going to the doors of those lucky enough to have been chosen. Surprisingly, when he returned, they had to draw more names. Not everyone was as eager to leave as he'd expected they'd be. Many had the same thoughts on it that I had originally.

Eventually, they filled the boat's capacity, and we had our passenger list, and, to my great relief, we were still not going to be splitting up any families. Unfortunately, no one on the list had any sailing experience outside of Ed and me. There were three under the age of ten, and three over the age of seventy-five. Many that were chosen to come would be of little help on the water. Three of the people chosen, though, made me a bit more confident. They weren't sailors, but Josh Acon, Kyle Hitchens, and Louis Gonzalez were all stout men that had natural athleticism.

Dinner that night was awkward for me. For the first time, as I looked at the faces around me I now knew and cherished, I did not feel warm. Everyone knew something was happening, that was clear from the activity to and from the boat, but they were all still just rumors for most of them. Their stares and glares were piercing, too.

With it being my boat, they all assumed that I knew what was going on. I couldn't bring myself to make eye contact with any of them. From the looks of the others that would be joining us, they, too, couldn't seem to look anyone in the eye, their faces staring intently at their plates.

To make it just a bit worse, I still hadn't told my daughters, so as I watched Lily and Hannah playing with the friends they'd made there, my chest began to sting.

"Let's get the kids," I told Ellie. "It's time."

With my family sitting on the edge of the bed in front of me a short while later, expectant and worried expressions, my heart was pounding.

"You all know your mother and I love it here, right?"

They nodded.

"You all know that we wouldn't leave if it wasn't important, right?"

"You and mommy are leaving?" Hannah asked worriedly.

"We all are," Ellie responded, picking Hannah up and holding her tight.

"What do you mean, mom?" Clem asked.

"I mean, we're leaving as a family. It isn't safe here anymore."

"There are several groups that are apparently spreading out from Pearl Harbor," I told my daughters. "We don't know the details, but they are coming this way, and they don't seem to be coming in peace. We're leaving on the Gabby, daddy's boat. Us, Ed, and sixteen other people. We're going back to the mainland. Tonight."

"You can't be serious, dad," Clem said.

"I am. I didn't want to go, either. Not originally. What we have here is so good, but it won't last, I promise you that, and I'm not going to just sit here and wait for someone to kill you."

"Dad, we can't just go sailing across the Pacific. Hannah is only five years old!"

"Clementine," I said, pulling her in for a tight hug. "It will be hard, but we will be okay. Trust me, I wouldn't risk it if I didn't think it was the right choice. Ed and I have made it across the ocean once; we can do it again."

A few hours later, the resort sat in complete midnight stillness. There was no movement, with almost everyone asleep. Slowly, though, the grounds began to fill as the evacuees silently strode across the beach and to a dinghy waiting for them. Inside, Likeke sat, oar in hand.

He ferried three at a time to the boat until it was down to the last trip of Ed, Clem, and me. Leaving under the cover of darkness, sneaking as silently as possible, felt more like we were escaping a cult, rather than leaving behind friends. I felt ashamed.

"Do not feel that way," Likeke said, somehow managing to read me in the darkness. "You are doing what needs to be done."

Minutes later, once aboard the Gabby, I watched the dinghy and Likeke fade off into the dark of night, waving a final farewell. I collapsed to my knees. This world had taught me that what needs to be done is rarely the easiest path. Most times, it is the most difficult of paths, and just simply knowing that does piss-all to help.

"You did the right thing," Ellie said as she came up behind me.

"I hope so," I returned. "Where are the girls?"

"They're below deck with Dianna. It's crowded down there, but it'll work."

"Did everyone take the Dramamine?"

"Yeah. Ed just finished passing them out."

"Good." Looking at her, I continued. "This time, at least you're with me."

We kissed.

17

Saturday, March 12th – Sunday, April 4th

The journey across the Pacific was easier than it had any right to be. There were a couple of nights when the waves got a bit choppy, but the weather remained storm-free, and the two dinghies, which held the supplies that wouldn't fit onboard, ran into no problems whatsoever as they were towed behind the Gabby. We had constant, steady wind, and with each passenger reading the sailing books along the way, the further we went, the more hands we had to help.

There were no nights of the mirror sea to share with Lily, but even without that effect, staring at the stars and galaxies with her, watching that smile spread across her face, was even more magical than I'd pretended it would be. Even when I wasn't around, she would spend countless hours just staring up.

Hannah kept herself busy by playing with the two other kids her age onboard. She'd also seemed to really fall in love with fishing. At first, she thought the bait was gross, but she would still ask me every morning if she could fish. So, that became our routine on the water, starting every morning with a cast-off, trying to catch a bit of something to add to our lunch.

Clem spent most of her time with Ed. I'd be lying if I said it didn't make me feel a bit nauseous. Seeing my firstborn falling in love was kind of like getting punched in the gut, while, at the same time, winning the lottery: It hurt, but I was ecstatic about it. I was glad to see that what they'd been through, what they would always be going through, was not impacting how they'd live their lives.

We did have a bout of illness spread through a number of the passengers. It started with the seventy-nine-year-old Hazel Regis and a fever that came on quick. Unfortunately, she wasn't able to recover. After her, seven other passengers turned feverish, myself included. The experience was made even worse by the rolling waves, but we were all able to kick it after several torturous nights filled with cold sweats and body tremors. Even after the fever broke, it took another couple of days to recover.

The day after I started feeling myself again, we found land. Unfortunately, the land we found had once been Mexico. With enough supplies still in tow, we decided that it'd be safer to continue sailing north along the coast, back to the ruin of Los Angeles. Our decision purely came down to language. People were turning back into animals, and if you couldn't even communicate, you were not setting yourself up for survival. Granted, if someone was desperate enough to eat you, it probably didn't matter one tiny bit if they could understand anything you were saying, but there was always a chance.

It was another three days before we passed the coast of what was once San Diego, but we continued our trek northwards. Ed and I knew the route from L.A, and it was as close to a straight shot as we could get. There was the risk we'd get to the city and the gas would still be an issue, but it was a risk we felt was worth taking, and it paid off.

When we grounded the Gabby on the beach alongside the Santa Monica Pier, the smell of gas was completely gone, going the way of the city's population. We immediately sent three of our twenty-something-year-old crew members off to try to find vehicles. It was a tall order, everyone knew it. The likelihood that they'd find a vehicle big enough to carry all of us and our supplies was not strong, but we had to try.

As we waited for them to return, I noticed that the sounds of technology had quickly been replaced by the sound of birds. The chirps, squawks, and songs were coming from all around. Most came from seagulls enjoying the person-fee beach, but there were at least a dozen different species of birds flying around. There were calls of anger, happiness, and hunger, all echoing out from the birds, replacing our own cries of the same kind that once filled the landscape.

Allowing ourselves a bit of relief, we decided that a swim would be a good way to pass the time. The water was too cold for me, but watching my wife and daughters play in the surf was worth every bit of shit I'd been through. They didn't get to enjoy the surf for long, though.

It was only about an hour after the trio had left when the sound of engines first reached our ears, none of us sure what to think. When we saw two old trucks and a school bus come down the windy corner and pull into the parking lot at the base of the pier, we didn't hold back our excitement, throwing caution to the wind and cheering loudly.

We did move quickly, loading up one truck bed with supplies, and covering it with the tarp from one of the dinghies. Within ten minutes of the trio returning with the vehicles, we were packed and loaded.

We soon found ourselves on I-10, and, as we passed exit 5, I glanced out of the window. There were at least half a dozen lanes in between, but we were moving slowly, and the paint job was easy to see. The VW bus that Ed and I had used to get from Phoenix to L.A. sat on the other side of the freeway.

"Ellie," I said. "Girls! Look! You see that car

over there? The one with the crazy paint job?"

"That old hippie wagon?" Clem asked.

"I like the flowers!" Hannah chimed in.

"That's the vehicle Ed and I took from Phoenix to L.A."

Moments later, the bus was invisible through the stalled vehicles.

It was midday when the remnants of L.A. passed below the horizon and we were officially on the open road. It had already been a long day by that time, so, with the tires lulling a humming lullaby, almost everyone fell asleep.

"Do you miss Orlando? Our old life?" Ellie whispered.

"No," I said without hesitation.

Something was jabbing into my back as I leaned against the bus wall, feet outstretched to the other side, but I didn't care because Ellie was curled up on top of me, my arms wrapped around her. Since finding her, I had tried to never take those moments for granted again. I tried to take in every little detail. The smell of her hair; the tickle it gave my nose when it blew with the slightest wind; the weight of her against me; the feeling of her chest moving up and down as she breathed, as she lived. I tried to take every bit of it in.

"I don't either. This life is harder. We have to work harder for anything we want, but this life is also better in so many ways. I don't miss PTO meetings, or having to juggle the girls and work.

I don't miss the phony people or the twenty-four-hour news cycle. Politics? Nope. Don't miss it at all! I do miss Wal-Mart, I won't lie about that."

"Good old Wally World. You know, Wally World is probably the perfect symbol for what our civilization had turned into. The good, the bad, the ugly. Man, that's pathetic!"

We laughed softly, each of us falling to sleep soon after.

Dianna had pulled off the interstate just as the orange of sunset faded to the dark blues of early evening, the two trucks pulling in behind her, our group setting up camp at the familiar Cottonwood Campground.

Teams of four kept watch throughout the night, working in four-hour shifts, but the night was calm and quiet, besides the extraordinary chorus of desert crickets.

We left just as the sun was breaking the horizon the following morning, and within the hour, we were pulling into the parking lot of a long-dead gas station. We weren't going to even bother trying the pumps, but there were enough cars in the parking lot that we figured we could siphon enough to get us most of the rest of the way.

The store itself was empty, long looted of anything edible or drinkable. It wasn't that we needed anything since our supplies were still holding up, but, I won't lie, a chocolate bar or Starburst or Skittles or even a Slim Jim would have been a nice treat. It took about thirty minutes, but we did manage to fill up each tank to the halfway mark.

When we got to the ruins of Phoenix, it was the same as L.A. It was a complete ghost town. No one had stuck around. I was half tempted to have Dianna take a detour by the Chase Stadium so that we could check in on the shelter. There was no point, though. When we left, the shelter was already on its last leg. Seeing what it had become would only tarnish my memory of it. Not to mention how stupidly crazy it would have been.

We meandered slowly over the freeways, at times needing to use the weight of the bus to push stalled vehicles out of the way, but we made it through the city without any major issues. It was another in a recent line of victories no one had been expecting.

Three hours later, we passed our first sign for the Petrified Forest National Park. My body went tingly with excitement, the chemical mixture just making me want to sing and dance for joy.

"How much further you thinking it is?" Dianna called from the front seat.

Pulling out the map and looking it over, I said, "Should be about two hours from here."

"Alright. Well, this beast is going to need another feeding!"

At the next exit, we again pulled into a gas station. As Ed began the siphoning process, I took Hannah and the other two little ones inside to again look for a score of candy. The inside was a disaster, though, with product packaging and fixtures littering the floors.

I committed the biggest sin anyone in a world without lights can make: I let my guard down. I was laughing and joking with the kids, throwing the trash around reminiscent of a food fight. That's why I didn't hear the door to the gas station's office open.

"Daddy!" Hannah yelled from behind me, her fear obvious.

The terror hit me before I even consciously registered her voice. Turning my head, I instinctively pulled out the handgun I had begun to always wear strapped to my waist. As I leveled it, my brain finally registered the scene in front of me.

Hannah was just in front of me and to the left. She was facing the counter, behind which there was an open door. In the door frame was a ragged, bearded man that looked both frail and fit at the same time. His eyes were wild as they darted from Hannah to me to the two other children on my right. The pistol in his hand followed the same path.

I hesitated. I should have just pulled the trigger, but I hesitated.

The man looked back at me, his gun remaining on the two children on my right. There was a moment, an instant, a millisecond, where I knew what he was going to do. I had no fucking idea why he was going to do it, but I knew what his next action would be. I couldn't take my shot. I still had never fired a weapon, and if I missed, it would end in tragedy. Instead, I jumped, turning my back to the man and taking the two little ones into my arms, pulling them to the ground with me as the man opened fire.

He'd fired at least four shots before I heard a second set of gunfire coming from the entrance to the store. After several shots from the entrance, the room went quiet.

The quiet was short-lived, though, as Hannah screamed, starting to run over to me.

"Daddy!"

"No!" I heard Ed yell. "Hannah, sweetie, stay where you are! Joe! Martin! Someone was here! Check around back for others!"

A moment later, I finally began to relinquish my grasp on the two children. They had remained motionless, so I was terrified of what I would see. Luckily, as I looked down, I saw two sets of wide, petrified eyes staring up at me. They were unhurt.

It didn't feel like I had thought it would. Being shot, that is. Maybe it was the adrenaline that had been sent through my veins, but I really didn't feel much at that moment other than a strange numbness, like a portion of my back had been given a general anesthetic.

With vision and sound starting to pass in and

out of fogginess, I watched Ed from my prone position on the floor as he checked behind the counter, gun at the ready, pointed into the office. He turned back into the space, and the room erupted into cries of panic as everyone else came running in.

The children's parents grabbed the kids, their faces a contorted mess that even I could see through my blurry vision. I'm sure they were not calmed by the fact both kids were splattered in blood.

Ellie and Clem came to my side, faces as worried as I'd ever seen them.

"Are you okay, dad?" Clem asked. Before I could answer, Dianna pushed her way in between Ellie and Clem.

"Watch out," she said urgently, first aid kit in her hand.

With our kit being put to full use, Ellie and Dianna wrapped me tight, gauze blocking the hole in my lower back that was oozing more blood than I really felt all that comfortable with losing. The wound had remained almost painless the whole time they'd been treating it, but when they began ushering me to the bus, that changed. As we began trekking through the final stretch of our journey, I felt each pothole, bump, or vibration was going to be the rock to my head.

My vision was continuing to go in and out of focus, my wife's beautiful eyes staring down at me through tears she couldn't keep fighting. My hearing was likewise going in and out of focus, but in moments of clarity, I could hear my girls around me. I even heard Ed comforting Clem. For a moment, I was able to be thankful that he was far better at comforting than I was.

As the bus came to a stop, I tried to glance out of the little window above my resting head. Just outside of it, I could see several arms of a giant saguaro cactus. I conjured enough strength to hold myself up, looking out of the window and down onto a valley below. The valley was covered in saguaro cacti that still looked like they were moving. I knew that landscape, and I knew that small adobe home in the middle of the valley. We had actually made it to Jack and Gladys's.

By the time I was being helped out of the bus, taking a ride on Ed's back, a familiar figure strode up to meet us at the brim of the valley. He held the shotgun that I knew so well, his eyes scanning the faces in front of him. Behind Jack was a near-spitting image of him, just a couple of decades younger. I knew it was his son, Kevin. Somehow, Jack and Gladys's family had made it to them. When Jack registered it was me, he lowered his gun and ran to my side.

"Sean? Is that really you?" he asked, his voice breathy with amazement. I smiled weakly.

"Believe it or not. I'm sorry my family turned out to be bigger than I'd expected."

"It's okay," Jack said. "We've got room. Let's

get you down to the house. Kevin, go get the medical supplies!" Kevin darted back to the house without pause.

I held onto Ed as if letting go meant dying. When we were halfway down into the valley, he slipped on the decline, and the rocks seemed to destroy my muscles on contact. I mercifully passed out.

. . .

Regaining consciousness, I found myself in a familiar setting. It was the room I'd stayed in half a year earlier. It was comforting to know that's where I would die.

I tried to move, but I didn't even have the energy to lift my hand. I tried moving my head from side to side, and it seemed to take more effort than running a mile once had.

"Sweetie!" Ellie said caringly from my side. There was an apparent pain there, too. "Don't move, sweetie."

"Yeah, daddy, you need to rest," Lily said.

I smiled weakly at her, replying, "Okay, baby, I will."

She hugged me, and, despite the shooting pain throughout my body, I felt free. I saw Ed behind her, so when she pulled away, I asked for a moment alone with him.

"How bad is it?" I asked him once everyone

had made their way out of the room.

"It's not good, Sean. Luckily, Jack and Gladys here had penicillin and some other medicine for infection. The nurse, Janice, injected you with some, and she got you stitched up. Problem is, she wasn't able to find the bullet. She isn't sure what you're looking like inside, mate."

"Sounds like my luck finally ran out."

"Not yet, it hasn't. Don't give up on me, brew."

"Watch out for my family, Ed. My girls will need you around, especially Clem. Do right by them."

"I'd never dream of doing anything else."

I smiled softly, knowing I could trust him, knowing my family was safe, and he would help make sure it would stay that way.

It was a heavy silence until, "I'd like to say goodbye to my girls." Ed nodded and went to the door. I stopped him. "Ed, thank you for what you've helped me do. My family wouldn't be here if it weren't for you. Thank you."

"No worries, brew," he said through held-back tears. "What else did I have to do, you reckon?" Sniffing, he exited the room.

A few moments later, my wife and girls were sitting around me again. I'd like to tell you every word I told them. I'd like to share every life lesson that I'd tried to impart to them over the last hours. But I won't. That will remain forever mine and my family's.

When we all had said our parts, I turned to Clem, saying, "Clem, I'd like you to do me a favor."

"Anything, dad."

"I want to tell you everything that I've been through, if for no other reason than to provide clarity to myself. From the very beginning, and I want you to write it all."

"I don't think that's a good idea," Ellie said. "You need to rest."

"I need to get this out," I responded.

Reluctantly, Ellie agreed. Clem grabbed a notepad and pen from her bag and pulled a chair up beside the bed. Hannah crawled into the vacant space on my uninjured side, cuddling me. I held her tightly, knowing that it was a moment that must last. Ellie and Lily crawled onto a loveseat on the other side of the room, holding one another as I began to weave my story, and as time went on, and I got deeper into that story, the room grew more crowded with everyone trying to catch a listen.

Approaching the end of my retelling, my strength was gone. I didn't even have the strength to turn my head. It was getting harder to breathe. My chest just had no energy to move, and, though they were crying out for air, my lungs were growing near incapable of inflating. My stomach was beginning to burn from the inside, but I soon felt that familiar, and pleasant, warmth spread throughout my body, evaporating the pain.

"The warmth," I said to the room, my eyes looking distantly at the ceiling. "I feel it. I can feel... It's... it's pleasant." Turning to look at my wife, Hannah, and Lily, I added, "I love you. I love you." I looked at Clem. "Thank you for writing my story, Clem. I love you." I fought back gags and coughs for air, struggling to talk. "Daddy is proud of you girls. Don't you all forget that. I'm proud of you."

With the room fading around me, the faces of those I held dearest smearing to indistinguishable blurs, I felt Ellie give me one last kiss. The room was almost completely gone when I heard the voice from the ocean.

"Rest easy, Sean. You have had meaning."

"I had meaning," I said to the room full of twenty-one people I'd helped save, and my eyes closed.

I had meaning.

THE END.

Printed in Great Britain
by Amazon